MIDNIGHT SACRIFICE

Also by Melinda Leigh

She Can Run
Midnight Exposure
She Can Tell

MELINDA
LEIGH

MIDNIGHT
SACRIFICE

Montlake
Romance

The characters and events portrayed in this book are fictitious. Any similarity to real persons, living or dead, is coincidental and not intended by the author.

Text copyright © 2013 Melinda Leigh

Published by Montlake Romance
P.O. Box 400818
Las Vegas, NV 89140

Cover design by Jason Blackburn

ISBN-13: 9781611098846
ISBN-10: 161109884X

To Tom, for knowing how to begin this story

CHAPTER ONE

December

Winter in Maine was more than a season. It was the enemy.

The December wind whipped down the alley and smacked Mandy in the face. Her eyes watered. Another gust grabbed the glass door. She held on tight, muscling it closed. To her right, the alley opened into a small parking lot behind the building. Her car would be as cold as a walk-in freezer and wouldn't begin to warm up on the six-block drive home, but at least she'd be out of the wind and off her feet.

Helping her mother run the family's bed-and-breakfast, then waiting tables at the diner had left her arches crying for a hot bath and a soft bed. But if she ever wanted to get out of this town—and she did—the extra shifts were a must. No way could she squeeze tuition payments out of the Black Bear Inn's nonexistent profit margin.

With gloved hands, she pulled her knit hat over her ears and trudged forward. Wind slipped into her coat at the throat. Turning her back to a frigid gust, she made sure her knee-length parka was zipped to her chin and her flannel scarf wound securely around her neck. Being a Maine native did not make her impervious to the temperature.

"Mandy, get in."

She startled and spun around. The diner's owner, Nathan Hall, had pulled his SUV into the alley. He was leaning over the passenger seat. The window was down. She took a half step toward him. She stopped midstride, a prickly sensation sliding along her spine. Under her thick coat, the primitive tingle lifted goose bumps that had nothing to do with the abominable temperature of her hometown.

Something was wrong.

Nathan jumped from the truck, rounded the front of the vehicle, and approached her. He wasn't wearing a hat or gloves. The smell of smoke wafted from him, and his eyes gleamed with a weird fervor. He stepped into the light cast by the fixture over the door. What were those dark stains on his pants and shoes? Blood. As he got closer, its raw, meaty scent thickened the air.

He reached for her arm. Instinct kicked in, and Mandy stepped back. He caught her wrist. "I love you. Just get in the truck."

"No." Mandy stared at him. Fear pulsed into her throat. "What's wrong with you, Nathan?"

Instead of answering, he tightened his grip and tugged on her arm. Mandy resisted. He pulled harder, dragging her toward his SUV. Her purse dropped from her arm and hit the ground with a *thunk*.

"Let me go!" She planted her feet on the pavement and leaned back. "Nathan, what are you doing?"

His silence fueled the panic gathering in her belly. "I said let go of me!"

He let go and raised his hand. The slap knocked her to her butt. She pressed a glove to her burning cheek. Nathan glared down at her, rage and madness transforming his handsome face into an ugly mask, as if someone else had taken over his body. "Shut up and get in the truck."

Her friend Jed barreled out of the diner. He grabbed Nathan by the jacket. "Don't you touch her!"

Nathan moved. Silver glinted in the streetlight. Jed doubled over. His mouth went slack. He looked at Mandy and gasped, "Run."

But she couldn't leave him. Nathan turned toward her, a knife clutched in one hand. Blood dripped from the tip. Jed's blood.

The scream burst from her throat. She crawled toward Jed, who was sinking to the ground. Just before she reached him, Nathan leaned down. His fingers clamped around her wrist again. He yanked hard. Mandy resisted, sinking her butt toward the icy pavement.

If she went with him, she would not be coming back.

"Get in the truck now." He pocketed the knife, lifted his free hand, and cracked her across the face again. Her cheek stung. Tears streamed down her face as he hauled her toward his vehicle. Terror scrambled in her belly. She was too small, too light. Her feet skittered along the icy asphalt as he dragged her closer. She tried to scream again, but panic clamped down on her vocal chords.

A dark figure flew in front of Mandy and tackled Nathan. She fell backward. Her savior and Nathan tumbled into a snowbank. Nathan landed on top. He leaped to his feet and ran to his truck. Turning, Nathan pointed at her. "You're mine."

With one eye on the retreating Nathan, Mandy crawled to Jed's side. *Oh my God.* There was so much blood. It was welling out of Jed's stomach, through the hands he'd clenched there, and into the dirty snow piled against the building. Jed stared up at Mandy, his brown eyes glazed with fear and pain. His hands fell away from his belly. His eyelids closed, and he went limp.

"No," she whispered. She pressed her hands to Jed's wound. The blood kept coming. Her rescuer scrambled to his feet and poised to give chase. Nathan's car door slammed, and the truck took off down the alley.

"Help him, please."

3

The man was on his knees beside her in a second, gently nudging her aside. She moved her hands, and he fumbled to open Jed's jacket with one hand. The other he held out at an awkward angle. Had he hurt his arm tackling Nathan? Mandy unwound her flannel scarf, folded it up, and handed it to him. He pressed it over the wound and leaned on it with one hand and a forearm.

Shivering, Mandy glanced sideways. The stranger was lean and dark. He looked at her, and she drew back. His eyes were turquoise, clear as the Arctic Sea, and they were filled with nearly as much shock as Jed's. In the subfreezing temps, sweat beaded on the stranger's forehead.

"You have 911 service here?" His voice shook, but he worked through his obvious distress.

"Yes."

"Call them. If you don't have a phone, mine's in my jacket pocket. Right side."

Her purse had fallen somewhere. Mandy reached into his pocket and dug out his phone. Wet hands slipped on the cell.

"How far's the hospital?" he asked.

"Forty minutes."

The stranger frowned. His hands trembled as he worked to stanch the flow of blood. "He doesn't have forty minutes. Tell them you need a medevac."

Mandy made the call.

"What's your name?" He swallowed hard. His eyes were too wide, his breathing rough and raspy.

"Mandy."

"Please keep talking to me, Mandy," the stranger said.

Mandy watched him fight for control. His determination and strength kick-started her brain. "Who are you?"

"Danny. Danny Sullivan." He shifted his position. "He's still bleeding a lot."

Think. She knew basic first aid, but Jed's injury went beyond any of her scout or wilderness training. Her gaze fell on the snowbank. Numbness and desperation temporarily suppressed her shock. "Snow. We'll pack him in snow. Lowering his body temperature should help."

Danny nodded. "It's worth a shot."

She tried not to look at the red smears in the snow as she scooped it with her hands to pack around Jed's torso.

Jed moaned. His legs twitched. Mandy grabbed more snow.

He had to live. He just had to.

CHAPTER TWO

Four months later

A steady April rain shower pattered on the windshield. Water dripped off the visor onto Danny's thigh. He wiped the seam between the convertible top and the windshield frame with a paper napkin. His restored 1970 Dodge Challenger wasn't the most practical vehicle, but she was Danny's good luck charm, and considering the purpose of this trip, he needed all the good vibes he could get.

Long shot didn't begin to describe his chances of accomplishing his goal.

Switching lanes, Danny stepped on the gas. The car responded with a surge of speed, the throaty roar of the powerful V-8 an audible middle finger to the powder-blue Prius humming along in the slow lane.

He'd restored her in high school, and like a valiant charger, she'd carried him safely through his youth. The days of perceived immortality. Illegal drag races on Front Street. Skipping school to cruise to the Jersey Shore. Hot summer days with the top down and the sun beating on his head. A decade later, the black bucket seat was molded to his ass, and a glance in the back filled him with wistful memories of fumbling hands, steamed windows, and teenage girls rebelling against their parents with the neighborhood troublemaker.

Ah, those were the days.

The days before he'd learned exactly what a well-placed IED could do to the bodies of a dozen men. Or what horrible deeds two psychos would attempt in the middle of the Maine wilderness. At twenty-nine, Danny's head was filled with more than enough violence for a lifetime.

A green exit sign flashed in his peripheral vision. He rested his left wrist on the wood-grain steering wheel and ignored the twitching of his fingers. Thanks to an Iraqi insurgent, that hand no longer worked as it should. With his right, he checked the map resting on the passenger seat. This was it. He exited onto a country highway lined on both sides by a forest vast and thick enough to conceal the most horrific of crimes.

Four months before, while on a photographic assignment in this small, isolated town, his sister had been kidnapped by a pair of psychotic killers. One killer had died. The other, Nathan Hall, had slipped away and was still on the loose. According to the last phone call from the lead detective, the police had all but given up their manhunt. Dammit. His sister deserved a future untainted by the fear that the escaped crazy ass was going to come after her. Danny was going to do his best to get it for her, even if his chances of succeeding were less than winning the Mega Millions.

Even if being back in Maine sent his gut into a free fall.

Danny turned up the radio volume. "Paradise City" blasted over the speakers, but his attempt to drown out his worries with thoughts of green grass and pretty girls was unsuccessful.

On the surface this trip was all about giving his family peace, but there was another reason he was here, one that was much more selfish.

Danny cruised past a green sign announcing that the town of Huntsville, Maine, was two miles ahead. Queasiness rolled through his gut. Back in December, he'd come here to rescue his sister but ended up saving another of Nathan Hall's victims instead. That night had been a turning point in Danny's new civilian life. For the first time since his medical discharge from the army, he'd functioned under pressure. His combat first aid training had overridden his post-traumatic stress. He'd contained the guy's guts and his own panic until the medevac had arrived.

Go him.

He rounded a bend and descended into a valley. The small town of Huntsville spread out in front of him like a travel brochure photo. Buildings were sturdy, practical, and showed the beatings of harsh New England winters. Colonial Yankee colors dominated the scene. Lots of barn red and pale yellow. Mountains on the horizon framed the picture. But for Danny, the country charm was tainted by memory. A vision stormed into his head. A haze of blood and fear, a dying man, and the most beautiful woman he'd ever seen right in the middle of it all. The woman whose voice and trust had helped him beat back the darkness. The woman who belonged to another man.

Mandy Brown.

The selfish reason he was here.

The business section of town was only a few blocks long. His car turned off Main Street as if on autopilot. A minute later, Danny pulled up to the curb and looked up at the large three-story house. The Black Bear Inn, owned by Mandy's family, stood tall behind a sloping lawn of pale spring grass. The white clapboards looked tired, as if winter had been particularly rough to weather.

Was she inside?

Though he hadn't seen her since that night, her soothing, steadying voice was etched in his mind. He'd mentally replayed it through four months of therapy, exercise, and balanced meals. Was she as beautiful as he remembered, or had his imagination exaggerated her perfection?

As the car idled, nerves hummed in Danny's belly. He could go inside and find out what she knew about the status of the investigation. Right. As if that were the reason he'd headed straight for the inn. Or he could drive out to the house and get settled.

Danny turned in to the driveway. He hadn't driven eight hundred miles—not to mention blown the family's savings on an expensive psychiatrist—to wimp out now. Time to man up. He parked in the small lot behind the inn, shut off the engine, and looked up at the house. A bay window on the back porch gave him a view of the inn's kitchen—and the woman inside.

In his chest, his heart fist-bumped his rib cage.

Nope, his imagination hadn't exaggerated one bit. She was as perfect as he remembered. Wholesome, beautiful, sweet. Everything he wasn't. Her dark hair was pulled back into a long ponytail away from a face that was as deceptively delicate as her slight frame. He'd seen her wrestle her fears and help save her boyfriend's life. Mandy was far tougher than she appeared.

But how would she react to seeing him again?

Only one way to find out. Danny opened the door, and Huntsville greeted him with a damp cold that suggested winter wasn't quite finished with him yet.

A lifetime of doing the right thing could be completely obliterated by one lapse in judgment. One mistake.

Granted, it had been a doozy.

Mandy added flour to the stainless steel bowl. Inside the heavy-duty mixer, a dough hook spun the mixture into a soft ball. She shut off the machine, and the kitchen fell quiet. Listening to the sound of rain tapping on the back porch roof, she turned the lump out onto her marble board. Practiced hands kneaded the dough until it was soft and elastic. She set it aside to rise.

On to the muffins. She preheated the oven then pulled a stainless steel bowl from the cabinet and measured ingredients without any need to consult a recipe. Heat from the oven banished the dreary chill. The kitchen was her favorite room in the rattling old bed-and-breakfast, which had been owned by her family for three generations. With commercial appliances and plenty of space, the dated country oak and gold Formica could be overlooked. It would never be the swank urban restaurant she'd dreamed of running, but it would have to do.

Mandy wasn't going anywhere. She was barely twenty-seven, and her dreams were dead.

Gently stirring the batter, she glanced out the window. Raindrops plunked into puddles in the lot behind the inn. The entire area needed grading and a fresh layer of stone. Winter had been tough on the Black Bear Inn and the Brown family, but things were looking up. Jed was recovering from his terrible stab wound. Her mother was recuperating from a triple bypass operation. And Mandy had almost stopped jumping at every noise, in the daylight anyway.

Nighttime was a whole different story.

Her hand strayed to the .38 nestled behind her right hip. A baggy sweater made the handgun invisible, but its size and weight were a comforting reassurance.

On her way to the freezer for a bag of last season's wild blueberries, she opened the door that led to the family quarters. In the living room, her mother reclined on the sofa. The roots of Mae Brown's dark auburn hair were gray, something she never would have allowed before her heart attack over the winter, and her body was far too still. Holding her breath, Mandy tiptoed closer. Her mother's chest rose and fell. Relief coursed through Mandy. She backed away, nearly lightheaded, and slipped back into the kitchen to finish her breakfast prep. Her mom's recovery had been slow. Mortality had checked into the inn as a permanent guest.

Things were never going to be the same.

She folded the blueberries into the batter and carefully filled the muffin cups. The baking tin went into the hot oven. Mandy set the timer.

An engine rumbled. Likely guests returning. The weather hadn't dissuaded the fishermen, hikers, or kayakers staying at the inn from enjoying their vacations. They were making the most of every day, an attitude Mandy was trying to emulate. She filled the teakettle and set it on the stove, then started a pot of coffee. Even the most die-hard outdoor enthusiasts felt the cold at the end of a rainy spring day.

A car door slammed. She moved to the window. An old convertible was parked at the rear of the lot. Strange. Most of her guests drove SUVs.

The doorbell rang. Mandy deposited a tray of biscotti into the dining room, then ducked into the reception area. She looked through the peephole. A man stood on the front porch with his back to her. Mandy paused. The set of his shoulders was familiar. He was brushing the water droplets from his jacket with one hand. Daylight reflected off hair gleaming and black as a raven.

It couldn't be.

As if he sensed her, he turned. Turquoise eyes focused on the door. Shock swept her brain free of all thoughts but one. It *was* him.

Danny Sullivan.

She smoothed her hair, wiped her hands on her apron, and opened the door.

"Danny." She stared at him. Her mind reeled with memories of that traumatic night, while a different kind of tension gathered in her belly.

"Hi, Mandy."

She moved back. "Please, come in."

The foyer closed in on them as he stepped into the house. She shut the door. He'd filled out a little since December. His face was still lean, his body tall and rangy. But he'd lost the sickly pallor, and the desperate look had been kicked aside by determination. Thick hair, wet from the rain, curled over his collar and was just unkempt enough to be sexy without crossing into sloppy territory. A leather jacket highlighted broad shoulders, and sinfully worn jeans hugged lean hips.

If he'd been handsome then, he was devastating now.

A thrill, hot and delicious as melted chocolate, poured into her belly. She tamped it down. *Relax!* He'd protected her from Nathan, and then Danny had helped her save her best friend, Jed. Some attraction to her rescuer was natural. It wasn't real. It was some kind of hero worship that psychiatrists probably had a clinical term to describe. Everything was just starting to feel as normal as possible under the circumstances. But the heat rushing through her was anything but ordinary.

The oven timer dinged. Mandy blinked. How long had she been staring at him? Warmth flooded her cheeks, and she tugged her gaze back to his face. His eyes were sweeping over her just as intently. When they settled on hers, the look on his face was hotter than her oven.

"Come back to the kitchen with me." She backed away from him. Danny followed her down the hall. By the time she reached the kitchen and retrieved the muffins, she'd composed herself. Somewhat.

"Sit down, please." She gestured to the stools tucked under the center island. Then she retreated to the other side of the counter, putting a large slab of butcher block between them. "Coffee?"

Danny slid onto a seat. "Sure, thanks."

She filled a mug and handed it to him. "Cream or sugar?"

He shook his head. "Black is fine."

One by one, she lifted the steaming muffins to a wire cooling rack, putting the last one on a plate for Danny. "How's your sister?"

"She just got engaged."

"That's great." Mandy choked back her envy. Danny's sister had risked her life to save three young men from death. She deserved happiness. "Have they set a date?"

Danny shook his head. "Jayne wants to, but Reed is too focused on protecting her right now. They bought a house just a couple of blocks from our brother Pat's place. Reed is still fine-tuning the security system. By the time he's done, the president will be able to visit and feel secure."

"What brings you back to Maine?"

He set his coffee on the counter. "We got a call about the case."

Mandy fumbled the plate. It dropped to the floor with a crash. Bits of ceramic flew in every direction. The muffin rolled across the tile.

"I'm sorry." Danny rounded the island. "I shouldn't have blurted it out like that."

"No, it's not your fault." She grabbed a broom from the pantry and swept up the debris. She emptied the dustpan in the trash, the excited flutter in her belly giving way to nausea. She wanted to ask him what happened, but fear silenced her voice like sawdust smothered a fire. On one hand, paranoia was getting old. On the other, there were things no one knew. Things she didn't want anyone to know. And for the sake of her family, things she hadn't told the police...

To cover the slight trembling of her hands, she kept moving. She washed up and gave Danny a new muffin.

"Thanks." He went back to his stool, as if he knew she needed the space, but he didn't touch the coffee or pastry. Instead, he just looked at her with those striking eyes that seemed to see everything she was hiding.

She reached for her risen dough. A quick punch deflated the spongy lump. She floured her marble board and dumped the bowl onto it.

Danny leaned both elbows on the counter. "Has the detective been in touch?"

"He stopped in a few weeks ago." She divided the dough into quarters and reached for her rolling pin. The familiar motions settled her. "There aren't any leads. The case is going nowhere. They think Nathan is probably dead."

"Does it bother you not to know for sure?"

Mandy hesitated. "There's nothing I can do about it. Frankly, I just want to put the whole thing behind me." That, at least, was the truth. She rolled the dough into a rectangle.

"He tried to abduct you. He stabbed your friend. He killed people. Aren't you afraid he'll come back?"

Yes. Mandy's fingers tightened on the wooden handles. The .38 pressed against her back. "It's been four months. If he's still around and interested in me, what's he waiting for?"

He let her question go, but his mouth tightened into a line as flat as the edge of her cleaver. "I'm meeting with Detective Rossi tomorrow."

"Why?" For Mandy, digging into the case would be like poking a hibernating bear with a stick. She'd had more than enough of State Police Detective Rossi, with his sharp eyes and I-don't-miss-anything demeanor.

"My sister doesn't sleep at night. Do you?"

Mandy paused. Exhaustion washed through her. Damn him. Why did he have to rehash everything? She was having enough trouble maintaining her staying-vigilant-but-trying-not-to-think-about-it balancing act. She pounded the dough flat, formed a loaf, and shoved it into a greased pan. "Detective Rossi said we might never know what happened to Nathan. I have to live with that."

"But can you?"

"You make it sound like it's a choice. It's not." She slapped another quarter of dough onto her board and attacked it with the wooden pin. "Do you know how many people have tried to find him? What makes you think you can make a difference?"

"Because for me, this is personal. I have to try."

Mandy stared at her abused bread dough. It was personal for her, too. Her family was just as much at risk, maybe even more so, than Danny's sister, who was now hundreds of miles away.

If he only knew…

But she couldn't tell him anything. Her own family had to come first. She raised her chin. "You don't know the area or any of the locals, and you don't exactly look like you're familiar with the wilderness."

Danny's gaze met hers. His eyes hardened with anger and wounded pride.

"Thanks for your time." Danny straightened. "I'll let you know if Rossi says anything interesting."

He turned away and walked out, leaving a swath of emptiness and vulnerability in his wake. Mandy followed him to the door and flipped the deadbolt with a finality that spanned more than the moment. Three generations of the inn being open and welcoming had come to an end. The *snick* of the lock represented the end of an entire lifetime of feeling safe and secure.

Returning to the kitchen, she finished forming the loaves. She placed the pans in the refrigerator to cold-rise overnight, even though the dough's chances of rising evenly were iffy because she'd beaten the daylights out of it. She paced the kitchen. Emotions that had been worn smooth before his visit were freshly honed. Normally, cooking was therapeutic, the kitchen her sanctuary, but not today. Despite his ruthless determination to dig up all the emotions she'd buried, Danny Sullivan made her feel other things she couldn't afford. A bond had formed when they'd saved Jed's life together. Lying to Danny gave her an ache in the pit of her stomach.

She moved away from the oven.

No, she couldn't help him in any way. The threat she'd received had been clear enough. Mandy already had enough guilt on her conscience to make a psychiatrist salivate like one of Pavlov's dogs.

Thunder boomed in the distance. The rush of falling water drew her to the front parlor window. The rain had increased from drizzle to downpour. Water was pouring off the eaves. A clog in the gutter. Grateful to have something physical to do, Mandy donned her waterproof jacket and jogged out the back door. Rain and damp air cooled her face. She stopped short at the sight of Danny sitting in his old car in the parking lot. A pang of longing zinged through her. She ignored it and jogged across the lawn.

Why couldn't she have met him before December, before the shadow of fear and death cast her life in darkness?

By the time she reached the garage, her sneakers were soaked. The overhead door rattled up on its tracks. Inside, she grabbed work gloves, then hauled the aluminum ladder down from its hook and dragged it across the lawn. Heaving one end up to the side of the house, she wished for the billionth time in her life that she was bigger than the average ten-year-old. At the top she curled her arm into the gutter and rooted for the blockage. Her fingers encountered a blob of slimy muck. She swept it clear, scattering decaying leaves and twigs on the grass below. Something slippery hit her cheek. She wiped it off with a forearm as rain rushed unimpeded through the cleared gutter.

She climbed down just as the mail truck was pulling up to the curb. Raindrops echoed in her nylon hood. She pulled off her gloves and headed down the walk, stopping to pluck a few weeds from between the bricks. Mandy stared down at the street. Large old homes occupied stately lots, their lawns greening with spring rains, early bulbs poking out of the flower beds. For visitors, Huntsville was lovely, quaint, and quintessentially New England. For Mandy, her hometown was a pretty prison. She'd lived in the old inn all her life, and it was likely she'd die in it as well.

The mailbox opened with a creak. She shuffled through the mail on the front porch. Bill, bill, bill, junk, credit card offer. Her fingers paused on the last envelope. Her breath dammed in her lungs.

Her name was neatly typed in the center. No return address. No postmark.

Just like the one she'd found resting on her pillow back in December.

She slid her finger beneath the flap and ripped it open. A photo of her brother, Bill, sitting on the front porch swing, slid out. A red line slashed across his neck. Her hand trembled, blurring the letters stenciled onto Bill's chest in crimson ink.

SECRETS SAVE LIVES. DON'T FORGET IT.

CHAPTER THREE

Danny sat behind the wheel in the parking lot. Through the kitchen window, Mandy finished her bread with jerky movements that belied her natural grace and broadcast her distress. A moment later, she pulled on a jacket and walked out onto the back porch. She flipped a hood over her shining brown ponytail. Halfway down the steps, she saw him. And froze. Her eyes stood out vivid blue against a sky of unrelenting gray, and the sadness welling from them was clear from across the parking area and strip of lawn.

Emptiness filled Danny's chest. He wanted to go to her, to comfort her the way she had soothed him the night of Jed's attack. But she didn't want anything to remind her of what had happened, and that included him. She wanted to move on, but Danny knew firsthand that the ostrich approach to handling trauma didn't work. Hiding the horrors in his own head had come back to bite him on the ass, big-time. Pretending everything was fine didn't make it so. At some point, everyone had to face his personal demon.

Whether it was an explosion that shattered a Humvee and a dozen men or a psychotic killer wielding a knife in an alley on a frigid winter night.

Still, everyone processed things at different speeds. Maybe with some time, she'd be able to talk about the attack. Maybe with some time she'd be able to…

No. Don't even go there.

Rubbing his achy forearm, Danny watched her run across the grass, open the garage door, and wrestle with a ladder that was much too heavy. She dragged it around the far side of the house, out of sight. Her slight, feminine body wasn't cut out for heavy chores. Instinctively, he reached for the car door handle.

A pickup pulled into the lot and parked by the garage. Danny stopped. The thin man who stepped out looked familiar. A sixty-watt lit up in Danny's head. The skinny dude was Jed Garrett, Mandy's boyfriend. Danny had only seen him unconscious, but Jed's face as he lay bleeding out on the snow was imprinted in Danny's mind like everything else from that night. Another man climbed out of the passenger side. He was huge and blond and walked with an awkward, coltish gait. Mandy's brother.

The two men walked in through the back door, marked PRIVATE, without knocking. Obviously, Mandy and Jed were still together. Danny swallowed his disappointment and started the engine. Jed could help Mandy with her task. Danny had upset her enough for one day, and he had no desire to see Mandy and Jed together. Not yet.

Everyone processed things at different speeds.

Danny drove out onto the street and turned toward the main drag. A few blocks down he passed through the main intersection and the empty lot where the municipal building had burned down in December. Cleared of debris, the empty lot was a sad reminder of the town's losses. Next to it, the diner that Nathan owned sat vacant and forlorn on the corner. Someone crossed the adjacent alley, the same alley where Danny had come across Nathan attacking Mandy and Jed. What used to be the hub of town life had been rendered useless by the events of one night.

A quick stop at a convenience store at the edge of town yielded a few breakfast basics. Fifteen minutes and a few turns later, he navigated a narrow opening in the pines and stopped in front of a black wrought iron gate marked by the number twenty-seven in fancy gold script. The driveway disappeared into the woods. Budding spring foliage obscured the view of the house Reed Kimball, the man who had saved his sister, used to live in. Reed had put his house up for sale and moved to Philadelphia to be with Jayne, keeping her far away from the Maine woods that had nearly killed her.

Ignoring the stone call box next to his window, Danny leaned across the seat and grabbed the gate's remote control from the glove compartment. He pressed the button. The black iron barrier swung away from him. The drive curved through the forest and opened up into a small clearing. The cedar and glass home blended with the wilderness around it. Danny sighed. He was city born and bred, but Iraq had dulled his enthusiasm for urban living. Now he didn't feel he truly belonged anywhere. Though he'd attached a truckload of discomfort to the small town of Huntsville, he'd been looking forward to the seclusion and solitude.

A red Nissan was parked out front. Danny parked next to the sedan. Reed's house was supposed to be empty. Considering all that had happened when Danny had been here last, his instincts snapped to full alert.

He went back to the glove box for the Leatherman multi-tool he kept in case of an emergency. Like a Swiss Army knife on steroids, the Leatherman was everything from pliers to a knife, and most importantly, it was a whole lot easier to explain than the switchblade Danny had carried in his misspent youth. Sure, he'd cleaned up his act, but eight years in the army and two tours in Iraq hadn't exactly mellowed him out. He got out of the car and stared at the house. A chill swept over him. The spring thaw had left Maine damp and a whole lot colder than mid-April back home.

The front door was wide-open. A lockbox dangled from the door handle.

The hair on his nape rose. He unfolded the knife blade and stepped over the threshold. Stale air, filled with the slight taint of mold and mildew, rushed at him. His running shoes were silent on the wood floor. In spite of the cold, clammy sweat broke out on his back. "Hello?"

"In here."

Keeping the knife out of sight along his thigh, Danny followed the female voice to a wide, open kitchen. A bank of windows looked out onto the forest. In the center of the huge expanse of black granite and steel, a woman in a skirt, heels, and red wool coat was staring through the glass, watching a young couple having an animated conversation in the rear yard. She was likely in her late forties, but her too-thin face and bleached-blonde spiky hair added a few years.

"Carolyn Fitzgerald, Northfield Realty." She gave him a let-me-sell-you-a-house smile.

Danny exhaled. Overreact much? Maybe his post-traumatic stress wasn't as controlled as he'd thought.

Wrinkles fanned from the corners of mildly predatory eyes as she walked toward him. She held out a bony hand. "Are you interested in the property?"

He folded the knife against his leg and slipped it into his pocket before accepting the handshake. Social niceties made him thankful that the bomb had affected his left hand instead of his right. Small favors. "No. I'm Danny Sullivan. My sister is engaged to the owner, Reed Kimball. I'm looking in on the house."

"Oh." Disappointment flickered across her face, like a cat that just missed a baby rabbit. "Will you be staying here long?"

"Probably a couple of weeks."

"Well, then I'll be sure to call before I bring any more buyers through."

"I'd appreciate that." Danny accepted her business card.

"Not that there are that many." Carolyn's gaze drifted to the window. "It appears as if they're done and that they won't be making an offer." The frown deepened. "Maybe with you here, I'll have better luck selling it. Vacant houses aren't very appealing."

Danny glanced into the yard. The couple was walking toward the front of the property.

He escorted her to the front door. She put the key back in the lockbox and gave the numbers a spin. Danny watched the red sedan pull away. Standing on the stoop, he surveyed the surrounding woods. Beneath the trees, patches of leftover snow were spread on the black earth like reverse Rorschach tests. Tiny buds dotted tree boughs and underbrush. Life starting anew. Though struggling to shake off the grip of winter, things were growing.

Could spring in the country work its magic on him? Could he shake off the cold that had lodged itself in his soul?

He took a deep breath of fresh air. The clean scent of pine flushed the smell of the city from his nose. Birds tweeted. Wind rustled leaves. Danny closed his eyes and gave himself over to the peaceful sounds and smells. Something small scurried through the underbrush. Things were alive all around him. The wilderness was more subtle than the sounds of traffic and people that signaled life at home. For a city dweller, the woods were strangely soothing. But then, northern Maine was the polar opposite of Iraq. Not even the memory of December's tragedy could taint the peace of the forest.

He wasn't sure how long he stood on the front stoop, but by the time he turned to go inside, the house was encased in the shadows of the surrounding woods. Even in a blackout, the city was never this dark. There were always headlights and billboards and other signs of humanity. Next time he went out, he'd be sure to leave on a light or ten to keep the night at bay.

He thought back to Mandy's expression as he'd asked her if she slept. She deliberately hadn't answered him, and the shadows under her eyes suggested long-term sleep deprivation. Danny knew it well. As soon as he'd mentioned the case, she'd gone on evasive maneuvers.

What else was she hiding?

Shaking off the thought, Danny grabbed his bag from his trunk. He pulled the utility knife from his pocket and opened the glove compartment to put it away. His hand stopped halfway there. He put the knife back in his pocket. Better safe than sorry.

He took his stuff inside. All modern glass and hardwood, the house was much nicer digs than the apartment he shared with his older brother, Conor. But the whole minimalist design didn't appeal. Danny liked his houses old and broken-in.

Reed had wanted a totally fresh start with Jayne and was selling the house furnished. At the end of a short hallway, Danny found the master bedroom. He threw a set of old linens on the bed and stowed his shaving kit and a couple of towels in the adjoining bath. His duffel bag went on the dresser.

All unpacked. He was a live-out-of-the-suitcase kind of guy.

The unexpected encounter with the real estate agent had left him edgy. He paced through the house, checking exits and locks and possible escape routes by habit. The laundry-room window was unlocked. Danny secured it. Gotta love one-story dwellings. Every window was a door.

He meandered into the kitchen. Sleek and shiny, with top-of-the-line everything, the room had a commercial, sterile feel. The coldness was exacerbated by the emptiness of the space. Good thing Danny didn't have any intention of cooking. He plugged the fridge in to chill overnight before he bought groceries beyond coffee and cake.

He stared out the window at the thick forest. Four months ago his sister, Jayne, had stopped at Reed's place and gone on to the Black Bear Inn. Soon after, she'd been abducted. Could

Danny flush the crazy ass out of hiding by retracing his sister's movements?

He could only hope.

Danny fingered the knife in his pocket. There was only one way to make sure she was safe. Kill the killer.

"What's wrong?"

Mandy looked up at her brother, Bill, staring at her from the porch. He was holding something behind his back. "Nothing. Just thinking." She shoved the note in the middle of the junk mail.

"You're sure there's nothing wrong?" Bill's eyes were worried.

Mandy put on her happy face and headed up the walk. Bill didn't know much about what had happened in December. He had enough anxiety issues. "Positive. Where's Jed?"

"Inside, putting stuff away." Bill's face lit up. He brought his hidden arm around with dramatic flourish. In his hand was a pot of pansies. Purple-and-white flowers nestled in a round terra-cotta container. "I brought you these."

"Those are beautiful. Thank you."

Bill beamed. "I know you love flowers, especially the kind you can plant, not the kind that die."

"I certainly do." She jogged up onto the wide porch and stood on her toes to give him a quick hug. On the covered porch, she flipped her hood off her head and took the flowers from him. His empty hand trailed down to rest on the elegant head of the yellow lab standing at his side. "Did you have fun with Jed?"

"Oh, yeah." Under a mop of freshly trimmed hair, Bill flashed a lopsided grin. Though six foot four and thirty years old, her brother had the intellectual and emotional maturity of a child.

Jed's dog, Honey, rubbed her head on Bill's leg. "Honey came with us, and after we got our hair cut, we picked up burgers on the way home. I'm going inside to eat mine." He opened the front door and held it for the dog. The edge of a long scar, whitened with age, showed just behind his ear.

As Bill went in, Jed Garrett, Mandy's best friend since first grade, stepped out. Formerly lean and fit from a lifetime of outdoor activity, the hunting guide's new buzz cut emphasized that his face had thinned to the point of gauntness. Several rounds of surgery had debilitated Jed for months. Though mostly healed from the horrific injury, his body hadn't recovered 100 percent. Mandy wondered if he'd ever be the same. More guilt piled onto Mandy's conscience. Jed had suffered a knife wound in her defense.

"Thanks for taking him." There were few people who could manage her brother's anxiety. Jed had been hanging around the family so long, he was like a brother, and he hadn't put down his own handgun since he'd been released from the hospital.

"No problem. He never gets upset if Honey goes along." Jed squinted at the ladder still propped against the house. "What's with the ladder?"

"The gutter was clogged."

"You didn't climb up there by yourself?"

Mandy lifted her chin. "I certainly did. Just because I'm small and female doesn't mean I'm helpless."

"I never said you were. Doesn't mean you have to do everything yourself." Jed scraped a hand through the half inch of hair he had left. "Why are you so stubborn?"

"Why are you so bossy?"

Jed's lips thinned. "Think about this. Your family needs you. God forbid something happens to your mother, you're the only person Bill has in this world."

Mandy's eyes burned. She looked away as pressure built in her chest. He was right. Like it or not, Bill was her responsibility. Forever.

"You should let Bill do more around this place." Jed frowned at her. "He's not helpless either."

An engine rumbled. Jed and Mandy turned in unison to watch Danny's old car turn from the driveway onto the street. The top was up, but the driver was visible.

"Is that who I think it is?" Jed gaped at the car.

"Yes." Mandy turned. "He stopped in a little while ago."

"Were you going to tell me?"

"Of course. Arguing with you distracted me." Mandy crossed her arms over her chest, clutching the mail closer. "I'm surprised you recognized him."

"There are things about that night I'll never forget." Still staring down the street, Jed absently rubbed his belly. "Why is he here?"

"Something is up with the case."

"Like what?" Jed's eyes snapped back. He paled. Since coming home from the hospital, he rarely mentioned the assault or his injury. Did he sleep at night?

"He didn't say anything specific."

"Didn't you ask?"

"I was so shocked to see him, I couldn't think straight."

Jed nodded, as if he understood her reaction. Not prone to excessive conversation, he was quiet in a way that made people underestimate him. But Jed could read people as well as a trail. "Did he say anything?"

"Not really. He wanted to know what I knew. He's meeting with the detective tomorrow."

"The cop said Nathan was probably long gone, maybe even dead." Jed looked out into the rain. "But if anybody could survive the winter out there, it'd be Nathan. I worry about him coming back for you, especially now that the snow's gone and it's easier to move around in the woods."

Mandy worried, too, but Jed didn't need her paranoia on top of his own. "Why would he do that when he could be hundreds of miles from here?"

Jed turned to Mandy. His jaw muscles tightened, and resolve replaced the surprise on his face. "I never liked the way he looked at you. I know you worked for him for a couple of years, but he didn't treat you exactly like an employee. Are you sure you don't want me to move in here, at least temporarily?"

Mandy shuddered, and fear clenched her belly as tightly as she gripped the mail. Jed didn't know, did he? No, Jed would never be able to keep that knowledge to himself. He'd be furious, and she'd never hear the end of it.

She was tempted to let him stay. But Jed went overboard on everything that involved her. If she let him move in, he'd take over. And what if there were more notes? How would she keep them from him? She hugged the mail closer. "It's been four months. If he were going to come after me, why wait that long?"

And why send a second note four months later? She'd kept her mouth shut. Was it a coincidence that Danny and the threat arrived on the same day?

Jed scratched his chin. "I don't know. Crazy folks do crazy shit."

"The inn is in the middle of town. Not the ideal location for a kidnapping," Mandy reasoned, covering the doubt in her mind. Someone put the note in her mailbox. If not Nathan, then who? And why?

"Are you forgetting that a kidnapping took place right on your front lawn in December?"

Mandy patted the gun on her hip. "No one was expecting it then. I won't let my guard down. I'll be fine here. You have your dogs to take care of, Jed."

"You don't think I'd put you before my dogs?"

"I didn't mean that." An ache pulsed in Mandy's temples.

"Never mind. I guess I'll go take care of my dogs." He brushed past her. "I'll put the ladder in the garage on my way out."

Mandy stopped him with a hand on his shoulder. The muscles under her fingers tensed. "I can get that later."

Jed yanked his arm away and glared at her. "Mandy, I'm fine. Stop trying to protect me. I'll never get back to normal if I don't act normal." He stomped down the steps and yelled over his shoulder, "I'm not your brother."

Mandy didn't miss the wince as he lifted the ladder under one arm. Which was all her fault. Everything was her fault. She couldn't do anything right lately.

Jed whistled. Nothing. He opened the door and called, "Honey, come."

With a jingle of dog tags, Honey trotted obediently to the front door. But her head was low and her tail wasn't wagging as they disappeared around the side of the house. Twilight descended on the yard. Lengthening shadows chased Mandy inside. She needed to make dinner for her mother and finish the breakfast prep.

She turned toward the family quarters and her room, acutely aware of the note hidden in the mail. Every rustle of paper amplified her guilt. The Tell-Tale Heart had nothing on her conscience.

With the door safely closed behind her, she lifted her mattress and pulled out a matching envelope. Two pages slid out. On top was a picture of Bill on the front lawn of the inn. A hole had been punched in the center of his chest. Block letters were scrawled across the snowy foot of the page. *If you love him.* The second photo was her and Nathan locked in a passionate embrace in the alley behind the diner. It read: *keep your secrets.*

She stashed both threats back in their envelopes and stuffed them under the mattress. Someone was watching her. It couldn't be Nathan. He certainly hadn't taken the picture of them, and the first note had come the morning after the attack. Huntsville had been crawling with police. There was no way Nathan had sneaked into the inn in broad daylight. But Mandy didn't know of anyone close enough to him to take that kind of risk. Nathan's only family were his uncle and son. Suffering from a progressive and debilitating genetic brain disease, his uncle and coconspirator had killed himself rather than be caught, and Nathan had taken his son with him.

Had the new note been put in the mailbox before or after Danny's visit? Before would mean an awfully big coincidence. If it had been after, then whoever was threatening her was close by. Turmoil gathered behind Mandy's breastbone. The pressure shortened her breaths.

She could call the police. But what would that accomplish? Despite police presence in December, her tormentor had waltzed right into the inn—right into Mandy's bedroom. The police hadn't been able to catch Nathan over the course of an entire winter. The only thing telling them about the note would accomplish was putting her brother in danger. No. She couldn't take any risks with Bill's life. For now, she would do exactly what she was told. She would keep her mouth shut about Nathan. But she'd keep her eyes open around town.

Someone besides Mandy had a secret.

What would Danny learn tomorrow? Had the police uncovered any new leads on the case since last week? She pressed a hand between her breasts, where her heart rapped against her sternum. The detective didn't know as much about Nathan as Mandy did.

She was the one who'd slept with the killer.

CHAPTER FOUR

Mandy blinked sleep-heavy eyelids and stared across the dark bedroom. The sudden surge of blood and the prickling of her senses sharpened her focus. Shadows shifted on the hardwood. Just branches moving outside. Sweating under the heavy comforter, she flung off the covers and padded barefoot across the floor. She undressed, then tossed her flannel pajamas into the hamper and pulled out a pair of cozy yoga pants and an oversize hoodie. The chill swept across her damp skin. She tugged her clothes on.

Crossing to the window, she stopped behind the curtain and peered around it. Outside, the clouds had dissipated, and the sky was dotted with stars. Moonlight flooded the yard. Tree branches and their shadows shifted in the wind at the rear of the property.

Her gaze searched the yard. Anything could hide out there.

Mandy shivered. The tingle on the back of her neck that had woken her drifted down her spine. Eyes. She could feel them on her through the glass. Was someone watching her, or was her imagination working overtime thanks to Danny Sullivan's suggestion? She pulled away from the window. Returning to the bed, she reached between the headboard and the mattress and slid her gun from the holster she'd secured there.

She grabbed a pair of thick socks from her drawer and tugged them on. Treading softly, she emerged from the family quarters and checked the windows and doors on the first floor. All was secure. She put her weapon in the front pocket of her hoodie.

In the kitchen, she bypassed the light switch and stared out into the moonlit yard. The wind kicked up, blowing against the glass. The inn creaked like old bones. Empty and cold, Mandy filled the kettle and set it on the stove with shaky hands. There was no way she was going back to bed tonight. A few more hours of sleep wasn't worth the risk of a return visit from her nightmare.

She scooped loose green tea into a mesh ball and dropped it into a china pot. Steam, fragrant with jasmine, rose as she poured the hot water. Leaving the tea to steep, she closed the blinds, shutting out the memories and the darkness that sparked them.

She needed Danny and his curiosity to stay away. Nathan couldn't be out there. No way. Anger slid over her, warm as a blanket. Despite Nathan's illness, she had no room for pity. Nathan had stabbed her best friend. He'd lied to her, killed two other people, and put her family at risk. If he showed up at the inn, she'd put him down like a rabid animal.

Unless he killed her first.

Sacrifice and survival were inseparable. In order for life to continue, something had to die, and Kevin sincerely hoped a nice fat trout gave itself up for breakfast. That wasn't looking likely, though. In previous years, this section of the Long River had been in no particular rush. The waterway meandered through the Maine forest and spilled out into Lake Walker about a hundred yards downstream. But this week, while not white water, recent storms swelled its banks, and the current was likely stronger than the surface indicated.

He glanced over at his ten-year-old son. Twenty feet away, just far enough that they wouldn't hook each other when casting, Hunter held his fly rod over the riverbank.

"Not too close to the edge, Hunter."

"OK, Dad." Drawing his rod back to cast, Hunter answered without turning away from his task. Under his dark-blue Yankees cap, the boy's freckled face was locked deep in concentration. His tongue poked out between his front teeth. The line flowed back and forth smoothly and sailed out over the water.

Pride swelled in Kevin's chest. Teaching his son to connect with his primitive self on their annual fishing trip always put Kevin in a philosophical mood. Even on a windy morning, it sure beat sitting in his cubicle at the insurance company headquarters in New Jersey. He loved his wife and daughters immensely, but this manly-man time alone with his boy was precious.

Kevin let out a foot of line and whisked his arm back over his shoulder. With a gentle forward movement, he cast the rod toward the river. The fly soared, and he laid the line down on the water with one smooth motion. The bug touched down with a gentle plop.

"Man, you're good at that."

Kevin looked over his shoulder. His brother, Tony, emerged from the woods. He crossed the strip of weeds to the riverbank.

"When you've got it, you've got it." Kevin was *not* telling Tony how many hours he practiced casting in his backyard. Fly-fishing lessons, two hundred dollars. Besting his younger brother? Priceless.

"Morning, Uncle Tony," Hunter said with a happy grin.

"Morning, Little Man," Tony answered, scratching his belly through his sweatshirt. He tucked his hands into the kangaroo pocket of his hoodie and hunched his shoulders against the chill. April nights were still cold this far north, and the wind that had blown the rains away overnight persisted.

After a quick check to make sure Hunter wasn't any closer to the water's edge, Kevin turned his attention back to his line. Keeping the tip of the rod down, he lifted the line from the water.

Tony sipped from a travel mug. "Do you actually like getting up this early?"

"I have four kids. My house is chaos. I haven't slept past six in more years than I want to count." Kevin flipped the line back and cast again. Satisfaction welled as the fly set down like the real thing. Still, the trout were MIA this morning. "You'll see. When's Jenna due? September, right?"

"Yeah. Honeymoon's over, I guess." Tony grimaced. "Is it really going to be that bad?"

Kevin laughed and smiled as Hunter sent another fly out over the water. "Kids are great. They just think sleeping is a waste of time."

"Fish get up early, right, Dad?" Hunter added.

"Right." Kevin played the fly across the river's surface. "And if you hadn't tried to keep up with Paul tossing back the Heineys last night, that gong wouldn't be ringing in your head right now. You'd be enjoying the morning with me and Hunter."

Tony bowed his head in mock shame. "I let Paul lead me astray. It's his fault."

"You're too old to keep up with our baby brother." Kevin laughed. Just twenty-one, Paul was still in spring-break-no-real-job mode. "Is college boy still sleeping?"

"Like a dead man." Tony drained his cup.

"More like a single man."

"No sh—kidding." Tony corrected himself with a glance at Hunter. "I'm getting out of the cold. I'll start breakfast and brew a fresh pot."

"Cool. I'm starving," Hunter said.

Tony grinned. "OK, kid. Coming right up. How does bacon and eggs sound?"

"Awesome." Hunter popped his fly across the water like a champ. He stopped suddenly and gave his uncle a pointed stare. "Do I have to eat fruit?"

"Nope," Uncle Tony answered. "This is Man Week, a vacation from balanced meals, personal hygiene, and all things pink."

"Woo hoo." Hunter pumped a fist in the air and grinned.

Kevin winced. His boy was going to smell like a sewer by the end of the week. But he'd be happy. With three younger sisters, Hunter often complained their house looked like the inside of the Pepto-Bismol bottle. They lived in Barbieland. "Since my superior angling skills have failed to land a trout, bacon and eggs sound great to me, too."

"I'm on it." Laughing, Tony headed back toward the cabin.

The breeze picked up and rustled through nearby trees. Kevin zipped his nylon jacket to his chin. His stomach rumbled. Coffee and bacon would hit the spot. Maybe when the wind died down, they'd land a few fish. They still had five more days of Man Week, but Kevin wanted his son to land a trout. This week was special to the Dougherty men. "Come on, Hunter. Let's get some food."

"Can we try again later?"

"Of course. We have nothing else to do all day." Kevin packed up their stuff. Hunter led the way, heading up the narrow trail that serpentined back to the cabin. A shiver swept over Kevin as they walked into the shadow of the forest. A dozen yards into the woods, an itchy sensation between his shoulder blades pulled his eyes to the path behind him. Empty.

Something splashed in the river. Probably the trout mocking them.

A scraping sound, like metal over rock, lifted the hairs on his arms. He glanced backed again. Nothing. But he moved closer to his son.

They continued up the trail. What was his deal? Sure, upstate Maine was a hell of a lot different than the North Jersey suburbs. That's why they drove all the way up here, to get away from the

horns and the exhaust fumes and the cell phone that buzzed 24/7.
To relax. To bond with his son. Usually, Kevin loved the solitude
of the deep woods, but this morning it didn't feel as empty as
usual.

Or as empty as it should.

Something moved in the underbrush.

Putting a hand on his son's shoulder, he quickened his pace.
What kind of predators lived up here? Bears? Wolves? A figure
stepped out from behind a tree.

"Tony?" Kevin squinted.

The man moved forward, closer to Hunter, out of the tree's
shadow. Not Tony. This guy was tall and wiry. His khakis and jacket
were new, at odds with the scraggly blond hair and beard. His piercing blue eyes had this weird look in them. Fanatical? Or feral.

"Can I help you?" Kevin pulled Hunter behind him. His
spine tingled with inexplicable discomfort. The guy was probably
just a lost fisherman or camper. It happened, especially to guys
not accustomed to the wilderness, like Kevin and his brothers.

He glanced up the trail. The stranger was between them and
the cabin.

"Yes, I think that you can." The stranger pulled something
out of his pocket. Oh, shit. A gun! Kevin blocked Hunter's body
with his own. No, wait. It was black and yellow. What the—?
Something buzzed. Tiny darts flew from the point. Every muscle
in Kevin's body went rigid at once. Paralyzed, he fell over like a
downed tree. Unable to fling a hand out to break his fall, his body
crashed to the hard earth.

"Dad!"

In Kevin's mind he yelled at Hunter to run. But the air
whooshed from his lungs, and his throat refused to obey his
command. His limbs wouldn't respond either. Hunter was no
dummy and took off down the trail, yelling, "Uncle Tony, help!"

But he was no match for the stranger's longer legs. The tall man had the boy around the waist in seconds. One hand clamped over Hunter's mouth, silencing his shrieks.

All Kevin could do was twitch and watch in agony as the stranger hauled his kicking and writhing son toward the water. His soul screamed as they disappeared from sight. The stranger returned in a few seconds. He pulled a sack over Kevin's head and tied his hands together. Blinded and bound, panic rose in his chest. Where was his son? Hands grabbed his ankles, and his helpless body was dragged through the dirt. His torso bounced off rocks and exposed roots. The ground smoothed out, then water lapped at his clothes. He was lifted, and his body landed on something hard. Metal echoed, and the scents of river water and fish flooded his nostrils. A canoe or kayak? He managed a slight roll and came up against a small body. Hunter?

The vessel rocked as his captor pushed off and climbed in.

Kevin moved his feet. The connection between his brain and body seemed to be recovering. Had he been Tased?

A rope encircled his ankles and went tight.

"Hold still unless you want your boy to go for a swim right now." His captor's voice was flat, and the lack of emotion sent a new wave of terror crawling through Kevin's bowels. "The way he's trussed, he'll drown in seconds."

Despair filled him as he obediently stopped moving. Whatever this crazy man's plan was, Kevin and his son were completely helpless.

CHAPTER FIVE

Danny steered onto the ramp and followed the directions into the town of Northton. After passing a Walmart, a few strip centers, and an army/navy surplus store, Danny cruised up to the one-story gray clapboard Maine State Police Barracks. The cop who was handling his sister's case, Detective Rossi, was part of the Major Crimes Unit, a handful of detectives sprinkled over a huge expanse of territory.

The morning sun hit Danny's back as he crossed the parking lot, but inside, the station was chilly and damp. Danny gave his name to the secretary behind the counter. Ignoring the plastic chairs, he paced the dingy linoleum while he waited. The cold and early morning drive time had left his muscles cramped. The fingers of his left hand had gone twitchy again. He shoved it in his jacket pocket.

Police stations always gave him the willies. In his youth, he'd spent some time on the wrong side of the counter.

"Mr. Sullivan."

Danny turned.

Detective Rossi looked the same as he had in December, tall and wiry, with sharp, gray cop eyes that swept over Danny and categorized every inch of him in three seconds. "Come on back."

Trying not to feel like he was fourteen and in trouble, Danny followed the cop to a small, generic conference room.

"Coffee?"

"Sure, thanks." Danny slid into an office chair.

Rossi handed him a Styrofoam cup. "I'm not sure I understand why you're here."

The coffee tasted like acid. "The family was disturbed by your last phone call."

"I can understand that you're upset."

"Upset?" Danny set the cup on the table. "You're closing Jayne's case while one of the men who abducted and tried to kill my sister is still at large. Nathan Hall also kidnapped three boys, including her fiancé's son, and tried to kill them in a ritual human sacrifice. He murdered a college kid and a chief of police. And you've stopped looking for him?"

"I never said we were closing the case, and we'll be looking for Nathan Hall until we find him dead or alive." Rossi leaned back in his chair and scrutinized Danny. The cop's determined calm was sandpaper to Danny's nerves.

He stared back. Anger boiled under the discomfort. He wasn't a juvenile delinquent anymore. He was a man who'd sacrificed for his country, and then come home to even more violence committed against his family. This damned cop owed him some respect. He straightened. Veterans didn't slouch. "My sister deserves an end to this bullshit."

"I agree completely." Rossi sat up, laced his fingers, and rested his forearms on the edge of the table. "But I'll be honest with you. It's been four months since Nathan Hall disappeared. Despite an extensive statewide manhunt, there have been no substantiated sightings of him. None. No activity on any of his financial accounts. No evidence that he's still alive. Unless he had help from someone, we have no idea how he vanished. As far as we can tell, no one in town knew the truth about his disease. The only loose end in the whole case is the unknown girlfriend."

"What girlfriend?"

Rossi drank some coffee and made a sour face as he set it aside. "We did find some evidence, like receipts for flowers and condoms, in his office at the diner that suggested there was a woman in his life, but we haven't been able to identify her. Apparently he kept the affair a secret."

"Why would he do that? He's single."

"But maybe she isn't," the cop said. "We can't find anyone in town who knew about her."

"That's a really small town. Seems odd no one knew."

"No one who's talking anyway. Only one other lead has come in lately."

"What is it?"

The cop stood. "Let's take a walk."

Rossi led him through the building and out the back door. A chain-link fence encircled the rear lot. Heavy-duty chains secured the extra-wide gates. They passed a few rows of police cruisers, then some civilian vehicles. They went into a large garage. Dampness seeped from the concrete floor through the soles of Danny's running shoes. Rossi stopped in front of a rust-spotted SUV with four flat tires and broken windows.

"This is Nathan's SUV. Last week we pulled it out of the Long River about three miles north of Lake Walker. As you can see, it appears as if it's been there all winter."

"I assume he wasn't in it?"

"No. No sign of a body in or around the vehicle, but with the temps of the water in winter, there's no way he survived if he went in with the car."

"The key word there is *if*," Danny pointed out.

Rossi nodded. "True." The cop wasn't prone to bullshit. It was the only thing Danny liked about him. "Evidence techs pretty much came up empty, too."

"How did the SUV get into the river?"

"Looks like it went off in front of a small bridge just before the beginning of the guardrail."

"So maybe an accident. Maybe not."

"Exactly." The detective sighed.

"Do you think he's dead?"

"I don't know." Rossi's frown lines went Grand Canyon. "Officially, the case is still open. But Nathan Hall suffers from a genetic brain disease. The neurologist we consulted said he could live another eighteen months at the most. The condition is degenerative. His ability to function will deteriorate over time. In six months to a year, Nathan won't be a threat to anyone no matter where he is."

That was a long time for his sister to stew. Danny tensed. The ache in his arm intensified. A psycho could do a lot of damage in a year. "But you're not actively looking for him anymore?"

"Nathan is still at the top of our Most Wanted list, and we will investigate any sightings, but unless new evidence comes in, I honestly don't know where we'd look. We combed this state and came up with nothing." Rossi crushed his Styrofoam cup and tossed it into the trash. "If he's still alive, he's probably far, far away."

"But you don't know that."

"No, I don't," Rossi said. "But northern Maine is surrounded on three sides by six hundred miles of Canadian border. It's impossible to secure the entire length of it, even with air patrols and sensors."

"So, you're giving up?" Danny's mood and voice went flat. Damned cops. They always had plenty of time to chase down teenagers, but murderers? Too much effort. "What about the unknown girlfriend?"

"I told you we ran into a wall with her." Rossi walked toward the exit. Danny had no choice but to follow. "This case is a very big deal to us, Mr. Sullivan. Maine has less than twenty-five murders annually, and we close ninety percent of those cases. We will keep it open, but the trail is ice-cold. If I get any more leads, I'll let you know. Can I reach you at home?"

"I'll be in Huntsville for a couple of weeks." Danny gave the cop his cell number.

Rossi pulled a small notebook and pen from his pocket and wrote it down. "You're not going back to Philadelphia?"

"Nope. Not just yet."

Rossi scowled. "The residents of Huntsville have been through hell. They don't need all this dredged up again."

Danny didn't respond. He and Rossi stared at one another for a few seconds.

The door opened. A uniformed officer leaned into the garage. "Excuse me, Detective Rossi. The captain needs to see you."

Rossi held out a hand. "I'm sorry I couldn't help you, Mr. Sullivan. Remember what I said."

"Thanks for trying." *Not.* Reluctantly, Danny returned the handshake. He took his time following Rossi back through the station and into the reception area. A new energy buzzed through the air. People were scurrying around and looking worried. On the way through the building, Danny caught snatches of conversation from three cops huddled around a desk.

"Man, I hate it when people just disappear."

"I'm telling you. Kid fell in the river. Dad went in after him. They both probably drowned. They'll find the bodies downstream."

"Man, that's horrible. But you're probably right. It's still weird, though. All their stuff was at least fifty feet from the water."

They clammed up when Danny passed them. Outside, the air didn't feel as fresh as it had earlier.

The lack of closure was giving his sister nightmares. She should be able to have a normal life. Danny couldn't think of a better wedding present for Jayne and Reed than Nathan's head on a silver platter, metaphorically speaking. Or not.

It's not like Danny had anything else to do. During his stint in the army, his three older siblings had managed Sullivan's Tavern just fine without him. He wasn't really needed at home. Danny started the engine. Buildings and other signs of civilization gave way to pristine forest as he drove back to the interstate. An 18-wheeler in front of his car belched out a dingy gray cloud of exhaust. Danny's imagination was pulled back to the cops' conversation. *I hate it when people just disappear.*

Danny couldn't agree more. Maine wasn't the perfect place it appeared to be. Just like everywhere else, evil lurked, and Danny was determined to find it.

But he'd start with finding Nathan's girlfriend.

Steam rose from the sink. Mandy turned her face away and adjusted the water temperature. Shoving the greasy frying pan under the spray, she added a squirt of dish soap. She glanced at the counter bar, where her mother and brother were finishing breakfast.

"This is really good, Mandy," Bill mumbled around a mouthful of French toast.

"I'm glad you like it." Mandy shut off the water. Leaving the pan to soak for a few minutes, she dried her hands and reached for her jumbo mug of coffee. So far this morning, even a massive caffeine infusion was unable to cut through the cobwebs last night's insomnia had left in her brain.

"You're the best cook in the whole world." He swirled the last few pieces around in peach sauce and shoved them in his mouth. Draining his glass, he carried his dirty dishes to the sink.

"Excuse me." A woman in her midtwenties stood under the arch that led to the dining room.

Bill jumped. The glass hit the bottom of the sink with a clatter. He backed toward the exit as if there were a wild bear in the kitchen instead of a pretty girl. The connecting door slapped shut as he disappeared into the apartment.

"I'm terribly sorry if I disturbed your breakfast." Ashley Trent, a hiker from Boston, was staying in the top-floor suite with two friends.

"It's fine. My brother is a little shy." Mandy smiled. "What can I do for you?"

"I overslept. Could I please still get a cup of coffee?" Ashley's eyes were puffy. Though it was past nine in the morning, she was dressed in a sweatshirt and pink-striped pajama bottoms. Her long brown hair was pulled back into a messy tail. The last two mornings, she and her two friends had been out the door by seven. Hadn't anyone at the inn slept well last night?

"Of course." Mandy set her cup down and headed for the coffeepot. "I thought I saw your friends go out earlier."

"I was tired from the long hike we took yesterday. I told them to go without me. No sense in them missing out on the beautiful day." Ashley squinted at the bright sunlight streaming through the window.

"I'm sorry you're not feeling well. Do you need anything?" Mandy handed her a cup of coffee.

"No, thanks. I'll be fine tomorrow." Ashley sniffed the steam rising from her mug. "This smells fabulous."

"Let me make you some breakfast."

Ashley shook her head, then winced. She pressed three fingers to her temple. "No. I couldn't put you to any trouble. I'm not very hungry. I'm going to take some aspirin and go back to bed."

Mandy pulled down a tray and bustled around the kitchen. "At least let me give you some muffins in case you get hungry later." She added a bottle of water and a banana to the tray.

"Thank you." Ashley took the food and retreated. Her slippers scuffed on the hardwood, leaving Mandy and her mother alone in the big kitchen.

The muffled sounds of lightsabers and speeding spacecraft seeped through the apartment door. Mandy rooted under the sink for a scrubber sponge. "He needs a new movie."

Mae sighed. "Sorry, hon. He's a *Star Wars* junkie. That's not going to change."

"It could be worse, I suppose. At least it's a classic." Mandy scoured the remnants of sausage from the frying pan. "I wish he were more comfortable with strangers, though."

"It's not like we haven't tried."

"True." If a lifetime of living in a bed-and-breakfast hadn't accustomed her brother to strangers, Mandy doubted anything would.

"Those muffins looked good," her mother said wistfully. "I'm getting tired of egg whites."

"I know. I'm sorry." Mandy rinsed her pot. "I have a new whole-grain muffin recipe for tomorrow, and I'll work on a heart-healthy French toast, OK?"

"I'm the one who's sorry." Mae collected her dishes and brought them to the sink. "You've done everything for the past month. I have no right to be grumpy. I am so grateful for everything. I don't know what I'd do without you." Mae rinsed the dishes and put them in the dishwasher. "Every day I thank God

I have you. It's a comfort to me knowing that Bill has you to look after him. I'm not going to be around forever."

"Don't talk like that, Mom." Mandy was not ready for that responsibility.

"I'm just being realistic, Mandy. I'm fifty-eight years old, and I've already had a heart attack."

Mandy's heart clenched. "If you stick to your diet and exercise plan, there's no reason you won't live a long time yet." Her mother's recovery was much slower than anyone expected, including the doctors.

"I sure hope so, but eventually, Bill's going to depend on you permanently. I'm sorry, but there's no getting around it." Mae poured another cup of decaf and sank onto a stool. With a shaky hand, she stirred artificial sweetener into her coffee. Her face was pinched with pain, her eyes sad. "As much as I wish he could be independent, we both know that isn't in the cards."

"I know, Mom." Mandy put a hand on her mother's arm. "I've always known." Though she'd hoped to experience a little of the outside world before the responsibility came crushing down on her.

"You'll never finish school or work in a fancy restaurant."

"I know that, too." Mandy shook her head. There was no sense dreaming about things that could never be. She peered out the window. Sun gleamed on the dew-wet grass. The yard seemed so wholesome and fresh now, unlike last night, when she imagined all sorts of evil hiding in the shadows. She shuddered. Jed's pickup pulled into the lot. "Jed's here again?"

Mae wiped the counter. "He called earlier. He's going to prune the maple tree out back."

"You should have told him not to come," Mandy protested. "Jed isn't completely recovered yet. He needs to rest. That tree doesn't need to be pruned today."

45

"He isn't well enough to hike around in the woods for days on end, but he's well enough to be bored out of his wits," Mae said. "It's good for him to be needed. He's a big help. You could do worse than Jed."

Mandy choked on a mouthful of coffee. "What?"

Mae turned and gave her a level you-heard-me stare. "Jed is a good man. He loves you."

"I love Jed as a friend. I don't love him *that* way."

Her mother pointed at her with the sponge. "Romance is for fools. I wish I had listened to my brain instead of my hormones or my heart. I wouldn't be alone. Your father left as soon as things got tough." Mae lowered her voice. "Bill was a lot of work back then. The therapy and doctor's visits. The bills."

Fear sprinted through Mandy's belly. She dumped the remains of her coffee in the sink. Could she handle Bill all by herself? Jed had been a big help these last few weeks. She barely remembered her father, but her memory of the night he left was clear. At five, she learned all about abandonment. Taking care of Bill alone was a frightening proposition. What if she wasn't as patient as her mother? What if she screwed up and he got hurt? What if something happened to her? Bill would end up homeless or in a state facility, completely vulnerable.

"Jed would never leave you," her mother said.

Mandy shook her head. "It's not enough, Mom."

"It should be. I worry about you. I'd feel much better if I knew you'd be with Jed. He'd take care of you and the inn. He's used to Bill."

"I can't marry Jed." But as she objected, a little voice in her head said *why not?* She reached for the bottle of aspirin in the cabinet.

"I'm so glad I have a good girl like you, but I worry. You shouldn't have to do this all alone."

In front of the garage, Jed got out of his truck and opened the overhead door. Yesterday she'd cleaned leaves out of the gutter, and today Jed arrived to trim her tree. He couldn't control her, so he'd do what he could to make sure she was safe. Maybe her mother was right. Jed would take care of her. Exhaustion pounded in her temples. With three hours of sleep and a whole day of innkeeping ahead of her, being taken care of sounded pretty appealing.

CHAPTER SIX

Boston, February 1975

Scuff, scuff, scuff.

Nathan looked at the ceiling. He didn't need to go upstairs to identify the source of the sound. Above his head, his mother's slippers moved across the hardwood as she paced the length of her bedroom. It's what she did now.

Cross-legged in front of the TV, Nathan tuned out the Fonz and concentrated on the low conversation in the kitchen. He shivered. The redbrick fireplace in the corner sat cold and empty. He pulled the afghan off the sofa and wrapped it around his shoulders.

"I don't know what to do." Despair edged Dad's voice, as always when he talked about Mom these days. She hadn't been the same since Christmas, when she started wandering the house at night instead of sleeping. It was as if the insomnia she'd suffered from for years went berserk.

Scuff, scuff, scuff.

Fear wormed through his stomach.

"Aye. It's verra bad indeed, Robert." Nathan's uncle Aaron, Mom's brother, had just come from Scotland a few months ago. When he talked about Mom, sadness thickened his accent. Tonight it sounded like a foreign language. "Bloody hell. Our mother had the same sickness. Did Gwen ever tell you about that?"

Probably not. Nathan had never met anyone in his mom's family except Uncle Aaron. Mom's parents were dead, and her few remaining relatives still lived in the mountains of her homeland.

"I dinna think so."

"I've taken her to five doctors. The medicine they gave her made her worse." *Dad sniffed and his breath hitched.*

Was he crying? Nathan's stomach cramped. Couldn't be. Dad didn't cry. Dad was tough. Nathan pulled his knees to his aching chest and wrapped both arms around them, but he still felt like he was going to fly apart.

"Doctors canna help her, Robert." *Uncle Aaron's voice rang with certainty.*

Even from the rec room, Nathan's dinner hardened in his stomach.

"The priest is coming tomorrow to talk to her," *Dad said.*

"You must listen to me, Robert. No one can help her. Not your doctors nor your priest. This...sickness. It will get much worse. She will do things..." *The deep voice hushed to a murmur.*

Nathan rose and switched off the TV. Happy Days *disappeared with a blip as the glass screen went blank. He eased to the kitchen, hesitating in the doorway. At the table, his father's blond head rested on his bent arms. Uncle Aaron put his hand on Dad's shoulder and squeezed.*

"But I've been researching something that may work. Something old and powerful." *His uncle's burr deepened.*

Nathan pulled back. Eavesdropping wasn't polite. But Uncle Aaron's blue eyes lit up. He gave Dad's arm a final, comforting pat. Broad arms nearly spanned the small room as Uncle Aaron opened them wide. "Come here, lad."

Nathan slid into the embrace, even though he was too big for hugs. He leaned into his uncle's solid bulk and rested his head against his wide chest. The scent of the beef stew his uncle brought hung in the kitchen, like the kitchen used to smell before Mom got sick.

Like Nathan wanted it to smell again.

He inhaled, trying to bring back the past. A sour odor lingered under the smell of dinner. Something in the icebox must have gone bad. Dad wasn't as good at housekeeping as Mom.

"Robert, I need you."

They turned. His mother stood in the doorway. She twisted her hands together over and over, like she was holding a dishrag that refused to wring dry.

"Gwen." Dad rose and moved to her, pulled her close. Her thick brown hair mingled with Dad's straight blond. Usually, they were perfect complements: the dark and the light.

But tonight everything was just dark.

—————

Nathan wiggled the last two-by-four into place and secured it with a screw. He stepped away and admired his winter's work. After four months of toiling, his masterpiece towered over him, a hollow wooden sculpture composed of three cages stacked on top of one another. The finishing touches lay to one side, ready to be added on the special night.

The bottom section was occupied with the fisherman and the boy, both sprawled in a drugged slumber. The top two cages remained empty. He hoped six sacrifices were enough. The barn roof limited the size of his effigy.

A breeze drifted through the converted barn. He glanced through the open doors. From the meadow beyond, the scent of fresh grass swept over him, obliterating the stale odors of mold and dust. Originally built to house dairy cows, the building had been gutted years ago to store large equipment. The farm's deceased owner had been a fisherman. Nathan had discovered a flat-bottomed boat and trailer under a heavy tarp. He'd made use of the old but working tractor to pull the boat along the mile-long track to the lake. A day on the water did wonders to restore a man's soul. Water was cleansing, almost as purifying as fire. Spotting the fisherman and his son had been a sign. The gods were pleased with his plan.

Nathan crossed the open space to the office. Like the rest of the structure, it had been built of solid materials in an age that valued quality. Though the deep-red paint had peeled from the exterior walls, the heavy timber was still solid. He drew a key from his pocket and unlocked the door. A window high up on one wall filled the space with light. A doorway in the back led to a half bath. On a cot against the far wall, his son, Evan, reclined, one arm thrown over his back, the other attached to a support beam by a wrist manacle and chain. His son's wrist was raw where he'd struggled against the metal cuff. With the aid of the sedative Nathan had slipped him, Evan was sleeping deeply.

A sliver of guilt sliced through Nathan. Keeping his son prisoner was the hardest thing he'd ever done, but no one ever said parenting was easy. A father often had to make unpopular decisions for his child. Someday, Evan might forgive him. But as long as the boy remained healthy—and able to sleep—Nathan could live with the consequences. Nothing mattered more than his son. Modern medicine had no cure for the disease that waited in Evan's genes. Nathan would follow in his uncle's footsteps and try the old way. As his Druid ancestors had bargained with the gods to repel the Romans from the shores of Britain, he would make a deal for his and Evan's futures. No sacrifice was too great.

Nathan would walk through fire to save his son.

He watched, mesmerized, as Evan snored. His son was as yet unaffected by the sickness. Once afflicted, sedatives and sleeping aids only worsened the condition. Nathan should know. In the beginning of his illness, his uncle had been prescribed every known tranquilizer. Nathan thanked the gods he'd had the foresight to accumulate the medication.

How long would Evan be spared? Genetic testing had confirmed that his son carried the disease marker. It was only a matter of time.

He reached into his pocket and withdrew a lighter. A spin of his thumb generated a small flame. He held the flame to his opposite forearm. Hot pain licked into him, a physical release for the agony trapped in his mind. The smell of singed hair and skin filled the space.

A car door slammed. Nathan released the red button. The flame flickered out, and he withdrew from the room, carefully securing the lock. He moved to the shadow of the barn door and peered around the edge. His assistant was crossing the barnyard.

Nathan walked out into the sun. Inactive for years, the old farm had been searched months ago, while Nathan and his son hid in his assistant's basement. They'd moved here and set up headquarters after the manhunt had been abandoned. As long as the assistant didn't lead anyone back to the farm, Nathan was free to pursue his goal. "You're sure no one followed you?"

"Of course."

Nathan turned his face to the sun and closed his eyes. Warmth rejuvenated his skin.

"Danny Sullivan is back."

Fury rose in Nathan, as hot as the burn on his arm. "And?"

"And he's asking questions. He visited Mandy yesterday and again today. I've already reminded her to keep silent."

Nathan clenched a fist.

This could not be.

Come Beltane Eve, she was to be his May Queen, his flower bride, the pure one who signified strength, renewal, and growth.

Once the Bel-fire had eradicated Nathan's disease, he would tap into nature's energy through Mandy. Like the Green Man, Nathan would die and be reborn youthful and healthy. He would have a brand-new life after the ceremony. He could begin again.

With Mandy at his side.

Evan would be spared. He would be the first member of the family to escape the curse. The three of them could be a family.

Nathan had a beef with Danny Sullivan. It was his fault Mandy wasn't at Nathan's side right now.

Mandy was his. No other man would touch her.

"You've done well. She won't say anything. Her brother is too precious to her." Nathan always kept his affairs secret, a habit that had served him well over the years. The others had been married and just as determined to keep silent. Mandy had been harder to convince, but he was glad he had persevered. If people knew about their relationship, they might guess his plans. If anyone knew the extent of his love for Mandy, it would be all too obvious that he could never leave her. That couldn't be.

Plus, he had his assistant, but he might need another person in town to manipulate. He also couldn't take the chance that the police would interrogate Mandy about him. He didn't remember giving her too much real personal information, but he could have slipped in those more intimate moments. No question his memory was slipping.

No one must know that he'd been intimate with Mandy, that he loved her beyond all else, save for his son. Too many variables would be unleashed with that knowledge, and Nathan's plan didn't allow for variables.

Plus, he liked her knowing that he hadn't forgotten about her. There'd been nights he'd hidden behind her house and watched her stare out her bedroom window. Could she feel the depth of his love from across the yard? Was she looking for him, waiting anxiously for his return? They'd ended things on a sour note, but surely there was love for him burrowed deep into her soul. He turned to his assistant. "Beltane arrives in four short days. There is still much to do." It was almost a blessing that he rarely slept now. "I need some things." Nathan pulled a list out of his pocket.

"Where will I find stuff like this?" His assistant's brow knitted.

"The address is on the back of the list." The forest provided most of what Nathan needed. But since the police had confiscated all the treasures from his uncle's collection of spiritual objects, a few specific items needed to be procured. Homage must be paid to the gods who would be asked to cure him and spare his son.

"You want me to steal these things?"

"Those things are sacred. They belonged to my ancestors. Think of it as reclamation," Nathan said. "Besides, the power you wish to gain from the ritual comes with a price. No gain comes without sacrifice. It's time you anted up."

"I've hidden you for months. Isn't that enough?"

Nathan dismissed his assistant. "It's never enough."

CHAPTER SEVEN

Danny took the exit for Huntsville. On the country road that led into town, lunchtime traffic consisted of a tractor, three SUVs, and a few minivans. Irritation at Rossi churned in his gut. *Chill.* Begrudgingly, Danny admitted that the cop didn't have many options. Budget dollars and manpower were limited. The state of Maine had tried damned hard to find Nathan.

Maybe he really was dead. Maybe Danny was just paranoid. Maybe some hiker would come across Nathan's decomposing body this spring.

But something still felt wrong. The little antennae on the back of Danny's neck had been attentive way before he'd gone to Iraq. Danny had always known when shit was about to hit, which was how he'd avoided juvie and jail for ten years of troublemaking. Except for that last time, when he had gone too far and gotten caught red-handed. That had been a game-changer. But then, everybody's luck runs out eventually.

Just outside town, Danny glanced at his phone. Snap. He had bars. Last night he'd written down the number for the local pizza joint in town. A large pie would take care of lunch and dinner. He ordered, then turned the stereo volume up. The first drum beats of "Paradise City" emanated from the speakers. Danny tapped his fingers on the wheel. Green grass and pretty girls sounded like heaven.

Lights flashed in his rearview. Danny glanced at the mirror, then down at his speedometer. Nope. Not speeding.

Turning the stereo volume down to nothing, he pulled over and rolled down the window. A stocky cop in a tan-and-brown uniform stepped up to the side of the car. He removed his mirrored sunglasses and hooked them in his chest pocket. Under regulation short hair, small blue eyes glared down from a mean face. Danny bristled. He remembered this jerk from his last visit. Steroid Steve, aka Lieutenant Doug Lang, had been nasty to Danny's sister. Sullivans didn't forgive or forget when their siblings were concerned.

The cop leaned a veiny forearm on the open car window. "Heard that you were in town."

Danny glanced down at the badge pinned to the cop's shirt. It still read POLICE LIEUTENANT. Despite the death of the former police chief, the town had chosen not to put Lang permanently in charge. Good thinking on their part, but it still had to sting.

"Just for a couple of weeks."

"Staying at Reed's place?"

Danny hated it when people asked questions when they already knew the answers. "Yeah."

"Heard that, too."

Danny waited. Cops like Lang rubbed him rawer than a fresh blister. Small-minded men exploiting their power.

Danny breathed. *Green grass and pretty girls.* His mantra had gotten him through two tours in the desert and one year of complete hell. Surely it could stand up to one giant asshole.

The cop flexed an oversize bicep. "Where were you this morning?"

"Just running an errand." Did Lang know where Danny had been or was he fishing for information?

"You wouldn't be thinking about digging into Nathan's case, would you?"

"How the hell would I do that?" Danny flexed his sore hand. "The entire state of Maine can't find him. No one even knows who he was sleeping with."

Surprise flickered in the lieutenant's eyes, but he blinked it away in a second. "Well, I'm not done with my own investigation, and I won't tolerate any interference."

Danny would bet a hundred bucks this was the first Lang had heard about Nathan's unknown girlfriend. "I doubt I'd be any threat to your case. I hardly know anyone around here, right?"

Lang's brows knitted. He tapped the window frame. "I just want to make sure I've made myself clear."

"Crystal." Danny nodded. "Are we done?"

Lang's face pinched. "I suppose." He stepped away from the car. "Just remember what I said."

"How could I forget?" Danny swallowed his annoyance. *Green grass and pretty girls* might not cut it today.

Lang walked away, and Danny rolled up the window.

He turned Guns N' Roses back to full volume and wished it was warm enough to put the top down. A little sunshine on his head wouldn't hurt.

The cop car pulled out onto the road and drove off.

Why was the town cop interested in Danny? Weren't they on the same side?

Whatever. Obviously the guy enjoyed jerking people around. Today, Danny was his choice puppet.

He drove into town and pulled into the mini-mart gas station combo. While he filled his car's bottomless tank, he scanned the store's interior through the plate glass. The white-haired clerk stood behind the counter. Two other people perused the trio of aisles, the red-coated real estate agent and a tall, lanky guy who also looked to be in his fifties. The real estate agent spotted him at the pump. She bumped the arm of her companion and nodded toward Danny.

Not in the mood to socialize, he was tempted to skip the store, but the thought of coffee prompted him to suck it up. Besides, the real estate agent seemed nosey. He bet she knew a lot of things about a lot of people. He strode into the store. She pounced as he grabbed a shopping basket.

"Mr. Sullivan."

Danny looped the basket over his left elbow. "Ms. Fitzgerald."

She gestured to her companion with the can of cat food in her hand. "Let me introduce you to Dr. Ian Chandler."

"Nice to meet you." The doctor juggled a banana, a granola bar, and a cup of coffee to shake Danny's hand. "I remember your sister. Brave young woman. I hope she's well."

"Jayne's OK, thanks," Danny said.

"Glad to hear it." Dr. Chandler set his items on the counter.

"Let me know if you have any problems with the house." The real estate agent paid for her cat food and headed for the door. "Bye, Ian."

Danny tossed pretzels and bread into the basket, then moved to the coffee station at the back of the store. The weight of the basket dug into his left arm. The elbow seized suddenly. Danny set the basket down. He pushed it along on the floor with his foot and carried his coffee in his right hand. Getting in line behind Dr. Chandler, Danny set everything on the counter and massaged his elbow.

The news played on a small television behind the counter. On the screen a reporter stood in the woods holding a microphone. A river rushed in the background. "Tourist Kevin Dougherty and his ten-year-old son, Hunter, disappeared this morning while on a family fishing trip. When last seen by his brother, Mr. Dougherty and Hunter were angling on the banks of the Long River. Local rivers are unusually high and swift this year due to heavy rains. This morning's search of the immediate area yielded no clues, except a pile of belongings on the trail that leads to the cabin. With no sign of the father and son, rescue crews are concentrating their efforts downstream, where the river empties into Lake Walker. This incident serves as a reminder to stay out of floodwaters and be aware of unusually strong currents. Mr. Dougherty is an insurance salesman from New Jersey. His wife and three daughters anxiously await news on the search."

The reporter stepped closer to the camera. "This is Karen Stevens, reporting for Action-Packed News."

Unease trickled down Danny's spine. Tourists probably went missing every season. But as the cop said, disappearing people were never a good sign.

"You all right?"

Danny jerked. The doctor stared at Danny's hands. The fingers were doing their thing again. Shit.

"Fine, thanks."

"My office is right off Main Street if you need anything."

"That's not necessary."

Dr. Chandler pocketed his change and stepped aside. But he didn't leave. He waited by the door until Danny completed his transaction. They stepped out into the cool morning air together.

The doctor gave the Challenger a wistful whistle. "A car like that brings back a whole bunch of memories."

"She's a beauty." Danny opened his car door.

"I was serious about you coming into my office."

Danny studied the asphalt under his running shoes.

"Look. I'm the only game in town. I treat everything, and I've seen addictions before."

Danny's eyes snapped up. The doctor thought he had the shakes because he needed a fix? "I'm not an addict." Danny shoved his twitchy hand in his pocket while the doctor gave him a that's-what-they-all-say look. Danny sighed and pulled his hand out. He pushed the cuff of his jacket up a couple of inches to reveal the edge of the deceptively thin scar that ran from his wrist to his elbow. "It's nerve damage. Last year in Iraq, my patrol was hit with an IED."

"Oh." The lights went on in the doc's eyes. He pulled a card out of his coat pocket and held it out. "Well, the offer stands; if you need anything, call me. My office is open until five today, but I'm pretty much available all the time."

"Thanks." Danny accepted the card.

Dr. Chandler walked toward a beat-up SUV. Danny looked down at the business card. The doctor had likely treated Nathan at some point. Dr. Chandler probably knew more about the residents of Huntsville than anyone else in town. He didn't seem like the type of guy to blab on his patients, but maybe Danny could wheedle some info about Nathan's family out of him. As Mandy had pointed out, Danny didn't know squat about Nathan or this town.

Unfortunately, Danny's statement to the annoying lieutenant was all too accurate. Danny had a better chance of winning the lottery than finding Nathan, especially without Mandy's help.

Somehow, Danny had to convince her to work with him. She'd lived in Huntsville all her life, and she'd worked for Nathan part-time. She must know personal stuff about her former boss. Who knew what might provide a clue to his current whereabouts? Or who he'd been sleeping with.

Danny picked up his pizza and ate a slice as he drove toward the Black Bear Inn. Guilt twisted in his gut. Mandy was in for another reminder of the night she wanted to forget.

Mandy stowed the last clean pan and glanced at the clock on the oven. Eleven thirty.

The back door opened, and a tall, spare woman in her sixties let herself into the kitchen. Gray-streaked hair was pulled back in a severe knot from her ruddy face.

"Hello, Mrs. Stone," Mandy said.

"Good morning." The inn's only employee, Mrs. Stone, closed the door with red hands that had seen decades of hard work. She stowed her handbag in the closet. "How many rooms today?"

"Eight."

"Terrific." Mrs. Stone nodded. "You're nearly full. I was worried that ugliness over the winter would affect business."

"Me, too." The bookings had been a big sigh of relief to Mandy, and the guests actually showing up had been even better. It was hard enough to make ends meet with a ten-room inn. Winter was slow because Huntsville wasn't convenient to any of the major ski resorts. Three seasons of decent bookings barely generated enough income to keep the inn afloat. Luckily, tourists didn't have many options in this area. Last winter's killings had been written off as a bizarre, random event. But if Nathan turned up again, tourists might decide to try their hunting or fishing luck elsewhere.

And the Black Bear Inn would be in deep trouble.

"I'd hate to lose the supplementary income. Social Security just doesn't cut it these days." Mrs. Stone grabbed her bucket of cleaning supplies and headed upstairs.

Mandy wiped down the counters. Masculine voices drew her gaze to the window. Danny's convertible was parked next to Jed's truck. Jed was still on the ladder trimming branches. Danny stood at the base of the trunk, looking up at Jed.

What were they talking about? Would Danny's questions bring back awful memories for Jed? He didn't appear to be upset, but Jed excelled at concealing his reactions with a blank face. His lack of expression was one of the reasons most people discounted him as less than intelligent. But Mandy knew that behind Jed's poker face was a sharp mind, and that he'd had plenty of practice hiding his emotions. When Jed was growing up, his home life had been the main reason he'd spent so much time in the wilderness.

Opening a notebook on the counter, Mandy scanned her meal plan for the week. She went to the pantry and started taking inventory. Fifteen pounds of flour went on the grocery list. Everything that came out of the inn's kitchen was made from scratch. As she counted ingredient staples, she tried to summon up some anger for Danny but couldn't. Whatever irritation his persistence caused was canceled out by the excited flurry in her belly. Why was she glad to see him? He was a threat to her family. Danny and his questions were dangerous.

Hadn't she had enough risk?

———

Danny approached the ladder and stared up at the thin man pruning Mandy's tree. Next to the ladder, pieces of brush littered the lawn. "Hey, Jed."

Jed glanced down. Surprise, but not shock, flashed in his eyes. Mandy must have told him about the previous day's visit. "I'll be done in a second." He trimmed the remaining two branches that extended over the inn's gutter. Thin tree limbs fell to the ground. Jed climbed down, wiped his hand on his jeans, and held it out.

Danny accepted the shake. "It's good to see you."

"Yeah. You, too. Thanks again for what you did. I wasn't exactly awake when you came by the ICU."

"Hey, I know what that's like." Danny stared at his arm for a few seconds. Images of his own hospital stay, full of pain and fear, intruded on the beautiful day, and a needlelike sensation worked its way down his forearm. "I'm just glad I was there."

"I hate to think of what would've happened if you weren't," Jed said.

For a minute, the only noise in the yard was the squawk of an angry jay. Danny glanced at the back of the house. Would Mandy be alive if he hadn't been in that alley, totally by chance, looking for his sister? He doubted Jed would've made it. From the look on Jed's face, he knew that, too.

"Mandy says something's up with the case?" Irritation edged Jed's tone. He nodded at the inn. "The detective didn't call either of us."

"I imagine he only called us as a cop-to-former-cop courtesy thing," Danny said. His sister's fiancé, Reed, had once been a homicide detective. "Reed's been really edgy lately. I think the pressure of having Nathan still on the loose is getting to him. He doesn't let my sister out of his sight."

"I can appreciate that." Jed glanced at Mandy. "I worry about Nathan coming after Mandy. I've offered to stay at the inn, but she's too stubborn to let me."

And why was that?

"What about you?" Danny asked. "How do you feel about the cops not catching Nathan?"

"Pissed." Jed's jaw sawed back and forth. "If I run into him, I'm greeting him with a bullet to the head."

"Sounds reasonable to me." Danny didn't have much patience for killers either, insane or not. "If I see him first, I'll give him the message."

"Appreciate that." Jed grinned. He stooped down and gathered an armful of branches. Danny did the same. He followed the hunter to the rear of the property. They piled the small debris behind the garage and made a couple more trips. Then Danny helped him drag the larger limbs to the rear of the yard. By the time they'd finished, his entire left arm was shaking.

Jed leaned forward and placed his hands on his knees. His face had lost color and sagged with lack of air, pain, and disappointment. "I'll have to come back tomorrow and cut them up. Just can't seem to get back up to speed." He wheezed and pressed a hand to his belly.

Danny massaged his forearm. Fire shot from his fingertips to his elbow. "I'm done in, too."

Jed looked up. A wry smile crossed his face. "Not exactly prime specimens, are we?"

"Nope." Danny snorted. "We suck."

Jed barked out a laugh and straightened. "I need something to drink. Come on. Let's see what Mandy has in the kitchen, and you can tell us what the detective had to say."

Danny hesitated. He'd come planning on confronting her, but now that he was here, guilt poked him like a sharp stick. "She doesn't want to see me. She wants to forget the whole thing."

Jed shot him a hard look. Hard enough that Danny had no doubt there was some bad shit in Jed's background. "Well, she needs to face facts. It did happen, and pretending it didn't is stupid and dangerous."

OK then. Jed was a straight shooter, and Danny couldn't help but like him. Even if he was jealous as hell that Jed had Mandy and he didn't.

Danny followed Jed to the back of the house, and Jed used his key to open the door marked PRIVATE. They walked into the dated but clean and spacious kitchen. Notebook and pen in hand, Mandy turned away from the open pantry. Her eyes locked onto him and filled with regret. Danny could imagine what it would be like to be greeted by a smile on her beautiful face, and the fact that it would never happen was a big empty space in the center of his chest.

He fought the urge to apologize and back out of the room. Jed was right. Ignoring the possibility that Nathan was still around could be deadly.

"Hey, Mandy." Jed went to the fridge. He walked right past Mandy and did not stop to kiss her. Strange. That's the first thing Danny would have done. In fact, he wanted to do it right now, and she wasn't even his girlfriend. His gaze dropped to her lips. What would they taste like? Jed selected an orange sports drink and offered one to Danny.

"Thanks." Danny took it.

Jed twisted off his cap. "Danny stopped by to tell us about his meeting with the state cop."

Mandy gave Jed a what-the-hell look, but behind the laser glare was a whole lot of scared she couldn't conceal. So why was she so against digging the case up again? Danny had seen her courage. She had plenty to spare. Was she really unable to deal with the strain, or was there another reason she refused to acknowledge the possibility that Nathan was still a threat?

Mandy said, "I told you both that I didn't want to talk about it."

"You did," Danny answered, "but I thought you still might like to know what Detective Rossi said. Do you?"

"Not really," she said.

"Well, I sure as hell do." Jed pointed to Mandy with the bottle. "You're not the only one at risk here. Nathan gutted me like a brook trout. I won't rest easy until he's in the ground."

Mandy paled. She clutched her notebook to her chest for a few seconds. She focused on Danny, as if she was turning away from Jed and the memory of Nathan's attack. "Detective Rossi already told us he thinks Nathan is dead."

"That's just the official line he's toeing." Danny told them about the waterlogged SUV and the missing girlfriend, then summed up the rest of his meeting with Rossi.

Jed whistled softly. "Nathan ditched his wheels awfully close to home."

"That's because every police agency in the state was looking for his truck." Mandy shook her head. "He's not stupid. He knew his best chance was going out on foot. There's still no reason to think he stayed around here," Mandy reasoned. "Why wouldn't he have gone as far as possible from Huntsville?"

"Because he's nuts," Jed answered.

"And hung up on you." Danny remembered Nathan pointing at Mandy. The crazy man's words echoed in his head.

You're mine.

Jed chugged his drink. "So, who the hell was sleeping with him?"

Ignoring Jed's question, Mandy moved back to the pantry and pretended to count things, but she doubted Danny was fooled. Anything to avoid hypnotic contact with those sea-colored eyes. They made her want to confess everything. Her secret was a breath-robbing pressure in her chest, ready to burst free.

"There's more." Danny set his empty bottle on the counter. "Some fisherman and his kid disappeared this morning just a few miles upriver from where Nathan's SUV was found."

"Oh, no." Sadness curled in her belly. She swallowed the clog in her throat. "Do the police think foul play was involved?"

Danny's jaw tightened until it looked like it was going to pop. "No. They think the kid fell in the water and the dad went in after him."

Mandy fought to keep her voice steady. The pantry contents blurred in front of her. "It's horrible, but it happens every year." But it didn't make the loss of a child less terrible.

Danny looked to Jed.

The hunter shrugged. "Hard to say. Water's high right now from all the rain. The current is a lot stronger than usual, and the water's damned cold. But I don't like it. Not one bit. The last time two campers went missing and were considered lost, it turned out Nathan and his uncle killed one and imprisoned the other."

Mandy pointed her pen at Jed. "You can't blame everything bad that happens around here on Nathan."

"You better get your head on straight," Jed shot back. "As far as I'm concerned, until I see a dead body, Nathan is out there."

"What if they never find him?" Mandy asked.

"Then you'd better be prepared to take precautions for the next year. Now that the spring thaw is here, there's not much to keep Nathan from coming and going as he pleases."

Mandy's belly tightened. Jed's statement was uncomfortably accurate.

Jed rinsed his bottle and dropped it into a recycling container. "I have to go. Let me know if you come to your senses and want me to stay here. See ya, Danny." He shut the door harder than necessary. Mandy jumped. Plates rattled on the sideboard.

She turned around. Bumping into Danny's chest, she startled again. The muscles of his torso were as unforgiving as his persistence. She leaned back so their bodies weren't touching.

"Mandy, I'm not asking for much. Just tell me what you know about Nathan. Like who were his friends? Who should I talk to? Was he having an affair?"

"There's nothing to tell." She took a step back but bumped into the doorframe. The kitchen closed in around her. She was trapped by so many different things. Nathan. Her family. Jed.

Danny. The first three she was powerless to change. But Danny's mission conflicted with the well-being of those she loved.

But when he inched closer, eating up the space she'd so painstakingly put between them, the desire to lean on him overwhelmed her senses.

"Surely he must have some friends or family."

"No friends that I know of." She tried to swallow, but her mouth had gone dry. "And his only relatives are his uncle and son." Nathan's uncle had killed himself. Mandy assumed Nathan had taken his son, Evan, with him when he fled.

"Business associates?"

"I really wouldn't know." The funny thing was, other than the fact that she'd slept with Nathan, she really didn't know much about his personal life. Much of what Nathan had told her was lies. He'd played her. She'd been naive and lonely, swayed by a handsome face and the maturity behind it. At his insistence, she'd kept their affair a secret even though she'd wanted it out in the open. After a couple of months, the sneaking around bothered her enough to end it. Plus, she'd realized she didn't love him. It wasn't right to sleep with a man just because she didn't want to be alone.

"Did you ever see him with a female companion?"

Unable to verbalize the lie, she shook her head.

"You had no idea he kept a basement full of Celtic artifacts?"

"No." She tried to move sideways, but Danny caged her against the doorframe with one hand on each side of her head. His body was a millimeter from touching hers. She already knew his body was tough, and if she leaned on him, she could borrow a little of his strength. "I can't talk about it anymore." She looked away.

"That's bullshit, Mandy, and we both know it." He put a fingertip under her chin and gently turned her face back to his. "On the outside, you look all delicate and beautiful, but inside, you have a steel core. I know. I've seen that courage."

Mandy slid the notebook in her hand between them as a shield and hugged it close to her body. He leaned in. His chest pressed against her folded arms. But what she really wanted to do was touch him. To feel his arms around her. For his heat to melt her frozen heart. He said she was strong, but she felt as wobbly and weak as a newborn fawn.

He leaned closer. Was he going to kiss her?

"Trust me, Mandy," Danny whispered. His breath drifted across her cheek.

The dilemma was that she did trust him. He was an honorable man. Not only had he protected her from Nathan, he'd saved Jed's life. Then Danny had stuck around the hospital until her mother arrived, just quietly sitting in the background so she wouldn't be alone. And she'd learned later that he'd done all that with an injured hand and post-traumatic stress disorder. He was a hero.

She wanted to tell him everything and let him handle the fallout. She was damned tired of being strong.

The kitchen door slapped open.

"Mandy, what's for lunch?" Bill barreled through the opening. He stopped short, his eyes bugging when he saw Danny. "Are you OK, Mandy?" Bill's voice trembled with apprehension.

Danny eased back, slowly stepping away from her.

"I'm fine," Mandy breathed. Her heart pounded; everything inside her fluttered like moths in the porch light. This was no good. She needed Danny and his solid body out of her kitchen. As much as she wanted his help, he couldn't fix the problem. "Bill, this is Danny Sullivan. He's a...friend."

"Nice to meet you, Bill." Danny must have known about or sensed Bill's discomfort. He didn't move any closer or hold out his hand to her brother.

Bill's eyes bugged. He wasn't convinced, but he bravely stayed in the kitchen though the tension in his body told Mandy he wanted to bolt. Watching Bill fight his fear of strangers for her, Mandy's heart swelled. She should be ashamed she'd ever thought of Bill as a burden. He loved her unconditionally.

"Danny was just leaving." Mandy walked to the back door and opened it. "I'll see you out."

The desire in Danny's eyes shifted to irritation. He spun around and walked out the door. Mandy followed him onto the back porch. "Thank you for not scaring Bill."

Danny pivoted. "I don't want to scare anyone. I just want information."

"Which I don't have."

His eyes narrowed. He didn't believe her. She couldn't blame him. She'd never been a good liar. He jogged down the wooden steps. "I'll be back, Mandy."

The look he shot over his shoulder was *challenge accepted*.

He got into his car. The engine started up with a deep rumble. She stood on the porch until he'd driven away. This was not good. Not good at all.

Danny was not the sort of man to step down from a confrontation.

What was she going to do? Ignore him and hope he went away?

Mandy turned back toward the kitchen door. A tingle shot down her spine. She whirled around, certain that Danny had returned, but there wasn't anyone behind her. She scanned the rest of the yard. Except for a squirrel clambering up the trunk of the big oak near the garage, the yard was empty.

She went back into the kitchen and locked the door. Bill was opening the refrigerator. He pulled out a gallon of milk and set it on the counter. She smiled at him. "How about a grilled cheese to go with that?"

"Yes, please."

As she lifted her frying pan from the overhead rack, she gave the yard one more glance. Was there something out there? She thought of the notes under her mattress.

Could it be Nathan? She didn't think he'd take the risk of coming into town, especially in daylight. So who was it? Who was helping Nathan?

CHAPTER EIGHT

Kevin lifted his head. It weighed about a thousand pounds, and his neck felt like cooked penne. His mouth had never been so dry. His lips stuck together.

What happened?

He felt like he had the worst hangover in his life.

And the flu. Avian flu.

He opened his eyes and squinted in the dim light. His eyes focused. Over his head was solid wood. Evenly spaced four-by-fours comprised the sides of his prison. Bars? Shock sent adrenaline chugging through his system. He was in a cage.

An image flashed in his mind. A man. Blond and thin. Pointing something at him. Oh, no.

Hunter!

Kevin turned his head. A small body was curled behind him. He tried to push to his hands and knees but collapsed. His chin struck the ground. *Ow.* Letting the waves of pain clear his head, he belly-crawled forward and placed a hand on his son's chest. An agonizing few seconds of stillness preceded the shallow rise and fall of Hunter's ribcage.

Relief rushed through Kevin with dizzying speed. Nausea followed. He rested his forehead on his son's arm. Several deep breaths passed before he was able to lift his head again to scan their surroundings. The cage that housed them was only about four feet high. Kevin would be able to sit up but not stand. The enclosure sat in the middle of an old, dirt-floored barn. The building was two stories tall. In Kevin's half, the space was unobstructed from floor to roof; a loft divided the remainder. The barn doors opposite him were closed. High up on the opposite wall, a few sunbeams poked through broken boards. Dust floated in the skinny rays of light.

Kevin squinted into the shadows. A tractor hunkered in the corner. An ATV and a small boat on a trailer sat next to it. Rusted tools hung on the wall. A pile of lumber and some odd objects occupied the area under the loft. A birdcage-like head decorated with a carved mouth, nose, and eyes. Two long and thin branches bent like arms. Strewn on the dirt floor, they looked like giant snowman parts after the thaw. But he didn't see the blond man or anyone else. His ear strained for sounds of human occupation, but none came, except a soft snore from Hunter.

Thank God.

He patted down his pockets. Empty. Even his breath mints were gone.

Where was the blond man, and why had he kidnapped them? Whatever the reason, it couldn't be good. Kevin looked for a lock to pick. He swiveled his head in both directions. Fear rolled through his belly as he crawled to the edge and put both hands on the thick wooden posts that served as bars. No give.

His cage had no door.

There was no escape.

Danny juggled the pizza and unlocked the front door. In the kitchen, he set the box on the granite counter. The smells wafting from the box didn't do anything for his nonexistent appetite. He couldn't get the missing father and son out of his head. He'd spent the afternoon driving around to get a mental map of the town in his head. The latest news updates on the radio made it clear no one expected to find the pair alive.

He glanced out the window. Plenty of light left for a run. He changed into sweats and a T-shirt.

Danny jogged down the long driveway and slipped around the gate. On the main road, he opened his stride. His feet hit the pavement with reassuring firmness. With his bum hand, the sports of his youth were out of the picture. No more boxing as an outlet for stress. Pickup games of baseball or basketball were a thing of his past. But running made him feel competent and athletic again. Running was freedom. He'd always been fast, but now he was outrunning his memories instead of the cops.

It was a race he couldn't win.

A mile or so down the road, his leg muscles warmed, and Danny hit his stride and pushed harder. The pain in his hand, the visions of blood and bombs, the threat to his sister, everything faded away as his body focused on its basic need for oxygen. When his thighs burned and his lungs complained, he slowed to a jog.

He scanned his surroundings. Nothing but trees in sight. Where the hell was he? He'd gone farther than he'd planned. The deep, dark woods were creepy as shit. He turned and headed back.

Past the point where he needed to drive himself to exhaustion to battle his stress, Danny took it easy on the way back. The return trip took considerably longer since he wasn't kicking five-minute miles. He slapped an insect off his sweaty neck. Full dark had fallen on the house by the time he hit the driveway. Of course, he'd forgotten the freaky-deaky dark-as-a-subterranean-cave that smothered the forest at night. The crescent moon hanging over the treetops was barely a nursery nightlight. Just enough so Danny didn't fall on his face. Not enough to see what was lurking in the shadows.

He slowed to a walk at the end of the driveway. The hairs on his neck quivered. He ducked behind a fat tree trunk and listened.

The distant, high pitched whine of a dirt bike or ATV floated on the wind. But Danny heard nothing close by except for tree branches rustling in the breeze. A shiver passed through his muscles. The temperature had dropped while he was running, and his sweat-soaked clothes didn't help. The house and a hot shower beckoned.

Still, careful had kept him alive in Iraq. He circled the house and approached the back entrance. He unlocked the door and went through the mudroom into the kitchen. His ears strained for sounds of an intruder, but only quiet greeted him.

He flipped the wall switch. Light gleamed off stainless steel. Danny moved from room to room in a methodical search of closets and shadows. Satisfied the house was empty, he took a hot shower and put on fresh clothes. Back in the kitchen, the chill returned. The spring damp had permeated the house, and Danny had depleted his calorie stores on his run. He found a cookie sheet and put half of the pizza in the oven. The other half went into the fridge. In the living room, the woodstove caught his eye. Danny checked the back porch. Seasoned wood was stacked neatly against the far wall.

He piled wood next to the stove, then opened the door and peered inside. Looked simple enough. He'd never used a woodstove, but it didn't seem much different from a fireplace. He stacked crumpled paper and kindling. Lighting a match, he held it above the pile to check the draw before igniting the paper. When the kindling had caught, he added a couple of small logs.

Satisfied it was burning, he returned to the kitchen and brought his hot pizza into the living room. He sat on the floor in front of the stove and switched on the TV. Several stations ran clips about the missing fisherman and his son, but there were no new developments. No bodies. No clues in their disappearance. If they had drowned, wouldn't their bodies have been found downstream by now? And why was all their stuff found on the trail to their cabin?

Danny added a larger log to the stove. Between the heat pouring from the iron box and the food in his belly, the chills faded. He moved to the couch and flipped through the sports channels. He settled on baseball and watched the last four innings of the Phillies game. When it was over, he added more logs to the fire, which was burning nicely, and closed the stove door. The fire had taken the moisture from the room. Hopefully by morning the dampness would be banished from the rest of the house as well.

He checked the locks and turned off the lights and TV before heading to bed. As tired as he was, sleep eluded him for a long time. He and his brother Conor shared an apartment over the family tavern. The military had taught him to sleep through all sorts of noise, too. The dark quiet of the woods was alien. Danny needed a noise machine with honking horns and swearing drunks.

A flat-screen TV hung on the wall opposite the bed. Danny turned on the weather channel and lay in the dark listening to storm reports.

He lay awake for a long time. Even with background noise and flickering light, something still felt wrong.

———

Soft light glowed from the back windows of the contemporary house as Nathan crept soundlessly through the trees. To avoid announcing his presence, he'd left the ATV a mile down the trail. Though he preferred civilized life over the wilderness, his uncle had taught him well. Being in the woods felt like a return to childhood. When they'd moved to Huntsville after the deaths of Nathan's parents, the forest had healed them.

Smoke rose from the chimney. The woodstove was in use. Perhaps he wouldn't need the gasoline he'd found in the shed on his earlier visit.

Nathan approached the rear of the house and listened. Blessed silence greeted his ears. Moving closer, he peered into the window, the same window he'd nailed shut earlier. Danny Sullivan was stretched out on the king-size bed. His body was still, his eyes closed. Nathan watched the young man sleep for a long time. Anger festered in his belly. There lay the reason Nathan was alone, the man who dared to stand between Nathan and his May Queen. That was reason enough to pay a penalty, but the thought of the younger man charming his way into Mandy's good graces—and her bed—lit Nathan's gut on fire.

There was no question. He had to get rid of Danny Sullivan.

Nathan stole along the foundation to the back door. He inserted the key into the lock and turned it. The deadbolt clicked open. He listened for the telltale chime of an alarm system. When nothing but quiet greeted him, he stepped inside. No one expected middle-of-the-night intruders this far out in the woods. At least not the kind on two feet.

He passed through a large, slate-floored kitchen into the living room. Embers glowed orange through the slits in the woodstove door.

Perfect. There was no better way to slow an arson investigation than to make the cause obvious. Accidents were bound to happen when city people tried to live in the country. Woodstoves and fireplaces caused fires all the time. Plus, Nathan had had good luck with fire in the past. Flames were cleansing in many, many ways. A few tweaks to a space heater had rid him of a pesky police chief. No one had been the wiser. He was sure many people had figured out that Nathan was responsible, but at the critical time, the chief's death had been attributed to accident.

The green light blinked from a smoke alarm on the ceiling. Nathan stopped to remove the nine-volt battery. He did the same in the kitchen. By the time smoke hit the master bedroom, the fire would be well advanced. He hoped.

He opened the woodstove door slowly to avoid the squeak of metal. Using the tongs from the nearby stand, he removed a few embers and set them on the closest area rug. The material caught. Smoke licked from the growing blaze. He leaned forward and put his hand into the flames. Fire wrapped around him, soothed him with blessed pain. Reluctantly, he pulled his hand free before the heat seared his skin.

There was no time for indulgence.

Nathan scattered a few more glowing coals on the hardwood. Then he backtracked through the kitchen and slipped outside.

The trees welcomed him. He took a deep breath. The scents of pine and loam, the sounds of bugs and bats, calmed him. In the forest, all his senses reminded him of his uncle, the true Druid. Nathan should have embraced his uncle's ways sooner. To turn his back on his heritage was wrong. Maybe the gods were angry with him. Maybe that was the reason the family curse had been invoked.

Nonetheless, he was glad he was following his uncle's path now. From behind a thick bush, he turned to watch the growing glow in the windows of the house. A flame licked into sight. Then another. The faint smell of smoke drifted toward him.

Satisfied, Nathan made his way to the game trail. His boots made no sound on the soft spring grass.

Tonight, Danny Sullivan would regret returning to Maine. If he survived, he'd learn a valuable lesson. Mandy belonged to Nathan. Anyone who came between them would suffer.

CHAPTER NINE

An alarm shrieked over Danny's head. He leaped out of bed. The heavy comforter and sheets tangled around his feet. He flung his hands out to brace his fall. Pain shot through his left wrist and hand as his weight crashed to the hardwood. He righted himself and yanked his legs free of the twisted linens.

Smoke!

The alarm's wail faded as the memories of screaming men took over. Instead of a smoke-filled hallway, Danny saw bodies and blood and fire. Heat seared his skin. The pungent odor of burning motor oil filled his nose. His heartbeat slammed through his chest. Lights danced across his vision like a swirling disco ball.

Stop! He shook his head and blinked hard. *You are in Maine, not Iraq.* He wasted a few precious seconds sorting reality and flashback. If he didn't get out of this house, it wasn't going to matter much. Dead was dead, no matter where it happened.

He padded to the doorway barefoot and in his boxers. Down the hall, flames engulfed the living room. Smoke filled the top half of the space. He was not going out that way. Coughing, he stepped into his jeans and running shoes, then swiped his keys, cell phone, and wallet from the dresser. He threw everything into his still-full duffel bag on the floor. His shaving kit, neatly packed on the vanity by the sink, followed. Eight years in the military had made him neat and ready to bug out at any moment. Good thing.

He crossed the room in two long strides. Three wide windows banked one side of the bedroom. He unlocked the first and pulled up on the sash. Nothing moved. Danny pulled harder, but the window wouldn't budge. Was the wood swollen from the harsh winter? He glanced over his shoulder. Smoke was pouring into the room, obscuring his view of the doorway. His eyes burned and watered, and his lungs protested with a wracking cough. The remaining two windows were also stuck.

He dropped the duffel and picked up a heavy bronze lamp from the nightstand. He swung it like a baseball bat at the center of the window. Glass shattered. He swung again and again, until he'd knocked out the entire pane.

Danny tossed his duffel bag out onto the grass. He snagged the comforter from the bed and laid it across the bottom sash so any stray shards wouldn't slice his body on the way out. He gripped the window frame and carefully eased out feetfirst. He dropped to the grass, fell to his knees, and rolled away from the house.

Danny gathered his stuff and jogged to the rear of the yard. At the edge of the trees, he stopped, rested his hands on his knees, and coughed until his lungs threatened to evict themselves from his chest. Gradually, the damp air soothed his throat, and his frantic heart calmed the hell down.

He lifted his cell phone and squinted. The display blurred, and his eyes burned. He blinked until they cleared. Damn. No bars. He glanced up. Flames were dancing in the living room windows. The smoke alarm screamed over crackling of burning wood. He wasn't going back in the house to use the phone.

Simultaneously sweating and shivering, he ran around the house to the driveway. Tossing everything into his car, he backed away. Halfway down the drive, he stopped to fish a sweatshirt from his duffel bag.

How far was the nearest neighbor? A mile and a half down the road, Danny asked the elderly man to call the fire department.

Several hours later, Danny stood on Reed's front lawn. The house still smoked. The smell of wet ash tainted the air, and the house was a soggy, burned mess. Unlike in the city, the mostly volunteer fire department wasn't on the next block.

The fire chief approached. He raised the clear shield from his soot-streaked face. "Sorry, the house was too far gone to save much."

Danny blinked. His eyes still stung from smoke. "Any idea how it started?"

"Can't say for sure yet, but the origin appears to be the woodstove."

"Shit."

"Woodstoves start fires every year." The chief coughed. "Creosote buildup in the chimney, or someone leaves the door open. Embers pop out onto a rug or curtain."

He'd closed the door, hadn't he? Danny scrubbed a hand down his face.

"You have a place to stay for the rest of the night?" the fire-man asked.

The closest motel was out on the interstate, a thirty-minute drive away. Exhaustion weighted Danny's body at the thought of driving that far. There was only one place to stay in town. Nothing would suit him more than being that close to Mandy. But she wasn't going to be happy to see him. Would she let him stay?

Mandy jerked awake. The phone rang next to her ear. She glanced at the clock as she grabbed the receiver before it pealed again and woke everyone. Calls at three in the morning meant accident, death, or other dire emergency. Instant apprehension jump-started her heart. "Hello?"

"It's Danny. I'm on your front porch. Could you open the door, please?"

His voice gave her nerves another boost. "Are you all right?"

"Yes."

"I'll be right there." Mandy tossed back the covers and swung her feet to the floor. She tugged her robe over her flannel pajamas and slipped the .38 into the deep pocket from habit.

The house was silent as she left the family apartment and walked into the foyer. She squinted through the peephole. Danny stood on the front porch. Sweat and soot were smeared across his face. His black hair was askew and his clothes were rumpled as if he'd jumped out of bed. Disheveled looked sexy on him, but then Danny would look hot no matter what. She opened the door and let him in. The faint smell of smoke followed him into the house.

"There was a fire." He coughed.

"Let's go in the kitchen." She walked through the doorway, flipped the wall switch, and blinked at the bright overhead light. "You're sure you're all right?" She scanned him from blackened sneakers to bloodshot eyes.

Danny hacked again. "Fine."

Mandy filled him a glass of water. "Here."

"Thanks." He downed half of the liquid. "Looks like I burned down Reed's house with the woodstove, though I'm not sure how it happened. I need a place to stay."

No.

She didn't want him here. She wanted Danny to go home to Philadelphia so she could forget about Nathan and whoever didn't want him found. A threat had followed Danny's arrival. If he left, would that be the end of it? Could she go back to pretending to be normal? She wanted everything to go away, including the emotions and desire Danny stirred up inside of her. She couldn't miss what she'd never had. But once she let that heat build, how would she go back to the cold?

She opened her mouth to tell him the inn was full. The door to the family quarters opened.

"Of course we have a room for you." Leaning heavily on a cane, Mandy's mother walked in. Pain lines around her eyes and the deliberation in her gait tightened Mandy's chest.

"I'm sorry I woke you, Mrs. Brown." Danny held out a hand.

"I wasn't asleep." Mandy's mother took his hand in both of hers. Gratitude shone from her pale face. "You saved my daughter. There isn't anything I wouldn't do for you."

"I'm just glad I was there to help." Danny smiled, but concern flashed across his face. He'd noticed her mother's fragile appearance.

"Mom, why don't you sit down?"

"I'm not an invalid, Mandy," her mom protested, but she was two-handing the cane. She shuffled to the medicine cabinet, unlocked it, and squinted at a prescription bottle of pain pills. She swallowed a tablet with tap water and gave them a weak smile. "Please excuse me. I'm going to go back to bed. I'll see you later, Danny. Let us know if you need anything. Mandy will take good care of you."

"Thank you, ma'am."

"Let's get you checked in." Mandy faked a smile and led Danny back into the foyer. At the registration desk, she pulled out a new guest card, slid it across the counter to him, and then booted up the inn's laptop.

Danny filled out the empty boxes and handed her the card. "Is she all right?" he asked in a low voice.

She typed his name and address into the system. "My mother hasn't been feeling well."

"I hope it isn't serious."

Mandy tapped computer keys. "She had a heart attack over the winter."

"I'm sorry to hear that. She's on the mend?"

"Yes. Her recovery is slow but steady." Slow being the operative word.

"I'm glad to hear it." Danny handed her his credit card. "So, you've been running the place by yourself?"

"It's just temporary." Mandy stared at the card. The familiar panic welled up inside her. Her mother was going to be OK. She had to be. Mandy couldn't take over the inn and Bill and everything. She'd only been doing it for a couple of months, and she was exhausted already. Her stress level was busting through the roof, even without Nathan hanging over her head for the next year. "How many nights will you be staying?"

"I'm not sure. Could be a couple of weeks. I feel responsible for Reed's house. I'll have to arrange for the repairs or cleanup or whatever." Of course, Danny would do the honorable thing.

"Oh." Two weeks of looking at him, the hero, and being reminded of what she'd done. Two weeks of not letting her thoughts slip out of her mouth no matter how much his eyes tempted her to spill everything. Two weeks of resisting the heat simmering deep in her belly right now.

"Is that a problem?"

"No, of course not." She smoothed the anxiety from her face and handed him a key. "The room should be all set. Let me know if you need anything."

"I will." He pocketed the key and picked up his duffel bag from the floor. "Try to get some sleep. You look tired."

"You, too." Mandy watched him ascend the stairs until his long, jeans-clad legs disappeared from sight.

What was she going to do? She'd barely resisted him when he wasn't living under the same roof. Now she didn't stand a chance. After two weeks, his constant questions about Nathan were going to feel like a barrage.

CHAPTER TEN

Danny closed his shaving kit and dried his face with a fluffy, white towel. He left the steamy bathroom. The room was small, the furniture probably antique but not fussy. The décor was Yankee sparse, nothing taking up space that wasn't useful. The wood floor chilled his bare feet. Spring mornings in Maine felt like freaking winter. He massaged his hand. After last night's batting practice with the lamp, his arm was stressed. Fiery pinpricks shot from his elbow to his fingertips, and it wasn't even six a.m. Not a good sign.

He dressed in jeans that didn't smell like an ashtray and grabbed a pair of socks from his bag.

Coffee. He needed coffee and food. Three hours of lying in bed not sleeping had left his whole body cramped and his head achy. Yeah, right. His crankiness had nothing to do with the erotic thoughts that stemmed from seeing Mandy in her pajamas and robe. He was ridiculous. She'd been covered from head to toe in more flannel than Mrs. Walton, for crying out loud. There was nothing sexy about flannel. Except on her. Her mussed hair and sleepy eyes had given him a clear image of her in bed, which was great until he remembered she had a boyfriend.

Disappointment crawled into Danny's chest and got comfortable. He'd known coming up here that she was taken. Hell, he'd saved her man's life. So what was his deal? Jed may not be fully recovered, but he had a business breeding and training hunting dogs and, hopefully, a future that included a return to guiding tourists through the wilderness. Danny was a damaged veteran with no immediate prospects. His siblings didn't really need him to run the tavern, and Sullivan's could only support a limited number of people. Returning to the army wasn't an option. So what was he going to do with the rest of his life?

The only goal on his horizon was figuring out what happened to Nathan Hall. As far as goals went, it was a huge freaking long shot. The only things he'd managed to accomplish so far were pissing off Mandy and burning Reed's house down. The phone call to Reed should be fun.

He turned on the TV and checked the weather. Same as yesterday. Sunny. Cold in the morning. Warmer in the afternoon. Possible rain later in the week. Danny flipped to the news. Stalling. Yup. That's what he was doing.

Shit.

He could skip breakfast and slip out without seeing her at all. No. Being love-struck as a high schooler over Mandy Brown didn't give him an excuse to backslide. According to his therapist, avoiding uncomfortable situations wasn't healthy. His recovery from post-traumatic stress was more than a slippery slope. As last night's trip to flashback land had demonstrated, it wouldn't take much to send him careening over the cliff he'd clawed his way up last winter. Discipline had been a key to his recovery. So he would eat regular meals, exercise, and attempt to get enough sleep. In a couple of hours, he'd make the call to Reed and fess up. And he'd face Mandy Brown.

Dammit. He'd be healthy even if it killed him.

A news clip showed a reporter standing outside a large brick building. The caption read MUSEUM THEFT BAFFLES BANGOR PD.

"The theft of a collection of Celtic artifacts baffles Bangor police. Last night, thieves bypassed more valuable pieces to steal items from a Celtic collection on loan from a Scottish museum. With no sign of a forced break-in, detectives are trying to determine how the thieves gained entry to the building." When the clip ended, Danny switched off the TV. Anything Celtic set off his internal sensors. He needed access to a computer. Maybe Mandy would let him use her laptop. And on that note, it was time to get moving.

He grabbed his running shoes from the corner and shoved one foot in a sneaker, then the other. Dropping to one knee, he tied shoe number one. By the time he got to number two, his bum hand was shaking so hard he couldn't hold on to the laces.

His chest burned. Sometimes, the smallest roadblocks were the hardest to overcome. He swallowed his frustration. This was what he wanted when he volunteered for this trip, wasn't it? To be on his own. To not have his siblings there to jump in and help him with everything. More than a year after his war injury and medical discharge, Danny had come to the conclusion that the only way to reenter the pool of self-reliant humans was a giant swan dive. Testing the waters with a pinky toe only gave him more opportunities to quit.

After three more attempts, Danny gave up. If he rested his hand, the muscles would calm down. He tucked his laces into the top of his running shoe, but only because his stomach was audibly growling. As his siblings kept telling him, Sullivans weren't quitters.

Most of the time, Danny believed them.

But right now, packing up his shit and going home was hugely tempting.

He left the room and jogged down the stairs. The clinking of utensils on dishes drew him through the doorway at the back of the parlor. The dining room held eight square tables with four place settings apiece. On the far wall, a long oak sideboard boasted an assortment of breakfast foods. Beverages in urns and glass pitchers were lined up on a buffet on the adjoining wall. In between was a doorway Danny assumed led to the kitchen. Only two tables were occupied. An older couple dressed for some sort of outdoor pursuit were finishing up close to the door, and four old guys in fishing hats were tucking in to full plates in the corner.

Danny grabbed a thick mug from the closest table and filled it with coffee. Sunrise peeked through the side windows as he perused the chafing dishes. He loaded a plate with pancakes, bacon, and whole wheat toast. One-handed, the process took him a while. Once seated, he ate with rapid efficiency, keeping one eye on the doorway.

When he was finished, he bent down and slowly tied his laces on the first try. Patience was a virtue he often neglected.

Mandy didn't appear. Danny drained his coffee. He wasn't sure if he was relieved or disappointed. An angry Mandy was better than no Mandy at all, which was just pathetic.

"Mom, you're not supposed to be working." Mandy loaded coffee mugs into the dishwasher. Sweat beaded on her forehead. A strand of hair escaped her ponytail and fell across her cheek. She tucked it behind her ear. "There's oatmeal in the dining room."

"I'm just helping you with the pancakes." Standing in front of the stove, her mother added a lump of butter to the griddle with one shaky hand. With the other, she gripped the edge of the counter.

"The doctor said it would take several months to recover. You have to be patient."

"I'm tired of being useless." Mae raised a defiant chin.

"I know. It's only temporary. Sit down. I'll make you some scrambled egg whites and wheat toast."

Mae ladled pancake batter into the hot pan. "You have enough to do. You don't need to wait on me." Despite her protest, Mae leaned harder on the counter.

Mandy started the dishwasher, crossed the kitchen, and wrapped an arm around her mother's shoulders.

"I'm not good at sitting around." But Mae's face was pale, her voice breathy. Clearly, the small effort of standing at the stove, flipping pancakes, was draining her. "You can't make breakfast alone every day. Running this inn is too much for one person."

"You did it for years," Mandy said.

"Which is how I know how hard it is," her mother quipped.

"How about I give Mandy a hand this morning?"

Mandy whipped her head around. Danny was standing in the doorway. His black hair still damp from the shower, worn jeans and a snug T-shirt outlined his hard body. No one should be allowed to look that good after less than three hours of sleep.

She cleared her suddenly constricted throat. "Guests don't work in the kitchen."

"I'm not really a guest, am I?" Danny asked with a bad-boy grin. He sauntered across the kitchen and looked over her mother's other shoulder. "Mm. Mm. Those sure look tasty."

Even in pain, Mae gave him a smile. Oh, no. Her mother was falling for Irish boy's charm.

"We'll manage, but thank you." Moving closer to her mom, Mandy pulled a stainless steel bowl from the wall shelf. She separated four eggs and beat the whites with salt and pepper.

Instead of yielding to Mandy's attempt to claim her space, Danny took her mother's arm. "How about I take over the griddle, Mrs. Brown? It would make me feel better knowing I was helping Mandy after I interrupted her sleep last night."

"Well, all right." Her mother moved aside. She pulled a mug down from the cabinet and filled it with decaf before sagging onto a stool at the center island.

Mandy looked over at Danny. Clearly this wasn't his first time in a kitchen. Even one-handed, he handled the spatula like a pro. Mandy wiped a hot pan with vegetable oil and poured the beaten egg whites in with a sizzle. A few minutes later, she slid the low-fat breakfast onto a plate, added some fresh berries, and set it in front of her mother.

While Danny flipped pancakes, Mandy went into the dining room to check on the guests and the coffee supply. The first wave had finished. Mandy cleared their tables. She walked back into the kitchen and collected the stack of pancakes. By the time she'd refilled the chafing dish in the dining room, Danny was drying the clean griddle with a dishcloth. "Your mother went to rest."

"OK." Mandy loaded the dishes into the second dishwasher. "You don't have to do all that."

"I know. I want to." He set the griddle on the stove. "You took me in last night. Now it's my turn to help you."

"Thank you." But working side by side with Danny proved distracting. Had the kitchen been this warm earlier? Mandy poured a glass of cold orange juice. "Did you eat?"

"I finished breakfast before I came into the kitchen."

Had he been looking for her? Needing space, Mandy filled a pitcher with orange juice and returned to the dining room. By nine, the few late sleepers trickled out. Most guests liked to get a jump on their chosen outdoor activities. Mandy bused the last tables. With Danny's steady help, kitchen cleanup took twenty minutes instead of forty.

"Thanks again."

"Anytime." Way too comfortable in her kitchen, Danny wiped the countertops.

"I appreciate the help this morning. I slept through my alarm—"

"Which was my fault," Danny interrupted.

"It was," Mandy continued. "But tomorrow, I should be fine."

Danny took a step closer. He tossed the sponge into the sink. "Why don't you want my help?"

"It's just that you're a guest, and guests don't work in the kitchen."

"That's the only reason? It's not because of Jed?"

"What does Jed have to do with it?" Mandy inched away. Her back pressed into the countertop. She didn't want to bring up Nathan because, well, she didn't want to talk about the case.

"He's not jealous?"

"Why would he be jealous? We're just friends. Jed's been my best friend since we were kids." Mandy gave herself a mental head slap. First her mother, now Danny. "Jed and I aren't in a relationship."

"Really?" Danny frowned.

"Really." Why was everyone trying to hook her and Jed up?

"That's good to know." He flashed a wicked smile that brought to mind all sorts of things good girls didn't do. A sigh worked its way up from Mandy's toes. Why did things that were wrong for her always look so good?

"Hold still. You have some dough…" He reached out and brushed a finger across her cheek. Nerves twittered in her belly. Her mind went blank. Why did she want him to go?

Danny leaned in. His body caged her against the cabinets.

She couldn't back up any more. And if she moved sideways, she'd rub against the lean hips that were blocking her exit. Not that she really wanted to move at all. But she angled her body a bit so he wouldn't feel the gun nestled behind her right hip.

His eyes darkened and dropped to her mouth. He licked his lips, as if contemplating the taste of her.

"Do I make you uncomfortable?"

Uncomfortable just didn't cover it. The kitchen was warm, but the external temperature had nothing to do with the lava flowing through Mandy's veins. Never had a man made her feel like every inch of her skin was alive.

"Mandy?" The door opened, and her mother stepped into the room.

She felt the disappointed sigh roll through Danny's whole body. He backed off. But regret didn't dim the intensity in his eyes.

"Thank you for helping me with breakfast." Her voice came out way too Marilyn Monroe breathy. She was practically panting. Ugh. *Get a grip.*

"Anytime." He left the kitchen.

Her mother crossed the tile to the coffeepot. She emptied the decaf into her mug, then took the pot to the sink and filled it with soapy water. "Did I interrupt something?"

Mandy gulped orange juice. It wasn't nearly cold enough. "No."

"Sure looked like I did."

And now her humiliation was complete.

"Well, you didn't." Mandy set her glass on the counter. "Danny was just helping me to say thanks for taking him in last night. That's all."

"Look, Mandy. You're a grown woman. I can't tell you what to do," her mother said as she scrubbed the glass pot clean. "Danny seems like a nice man, and God knows I'm grateful to him for saving you and Jed, but he's not going to stay here. Half the people who live in Huntsville don't want to stay here. You can't expect a city person to be content living in the middle of nowhere."

"I know that. There's nothing going on between us," Mandy insisted.

"Good. Maybe Jed would come and help you with breakfast."

"Mom, please stop calling Jed to help me. He can barely take care of his own place, and I can handle breakfast by myself. No, it's not easy, but I can manage."

Her mother shook her head. " I don't want you to work yourself to the bone like I did. You should just marry Jed. If he moved in here, he wouldn't have a separate place to keep up."

Mandy took her glass to the sink. "We've been over this before. I don't want to marry Jed. Besides, he hasn't asked. He hasn't made one move to suggest he has anything but platonic feelings for me. Ever."

"He would if he thought you were interested."

"I don't love him. Not like that." Sadness doused her desire like a bucket of cold water. "I'd rather be alone than settle for a marriage without love."

"Love can grow out of friendship." Mae looked over the half glasses perched low on her nose. "Marriage isn't about romance. It's about commitment through the drudgery of everyday life, when the moonlight and roses have turned to sick children and medical bills." Mae's voice turned bitter. "I wish I'd have used some sense in picking a husband instead of following my heart. This heart attack has made me worried about your future. I'm not going to be around forever."

Mandy looked away. Her father's betrayal had left a deep imprint on all of them. "I'm sorry Dad left us, but that doesn't mean I should marry Jed."

Mae was right, though. Jed had always been there for Mandy. He was her best friend. The person she called if she needed help with anything.

But was friendship enough? After the disastrous affair with Nathan, maybe that's exactly what Mandy needed to do. To use her head instead of her emotions. To ignore the flash of desire that heated her blood. The tension coiling in her belly made her forget the reasons she needed Danny to leave. Desire was dangerous, addictive, and should be doused at its first spark. He was hypnotic, like truth serum. Unless she could figure out who was threatening her and why, the absolute last person she could get involved with was Danny.

CHAPTER ELEVEN

In the lot behind the inn, the spring air was still morning cold. Today, Danny welcomed the chill. He tossed his jacket in the passenger seat. He needed to cool the fire rushing through his body. Being that close to Mandy made him want things he hadn't had in a long time, since before his last tour. He could imagine Mandy's soft body under his far too clearly.

Now that he knew she wasn't Jed's girlfriend, his imagination was doing all sorts of speculating. He brushed away the prickling of guilt. How could she not see Jed was in love with her? Maybe she was too close to the situation.

He needed to think. He also wanted to do some research. There was no way he was going back into the inn to ask Mandy for her laptop. Did Huntsville have a library? If it did, it couldn't be that hard to find.

Danny's car roared to life. The engine coughed a few times while it warmed up. He turned onto Main Street. The two-block-long business district quickly gave way to residences. Houses grew farther apart along the long, winding road that led out of town. Danny drove to the Quickie-Mart and grabbed a candy bar and a Coke. The elderly clerk was watching a game show on the small TV behind the counter.

The clerk rang up his purchases. Danny handed him a five. "Is there a library in town?"

"Sure is." The clerk handed Danny his change. "It's right next to the grammar school on Sixth Street. We have computers and everything." His voice rang with pride.

"Great. Thanks."

Danny cruised back into town. Sixth Street was an easy find. Next to a small park, a converted two-story Colonial housed Huntsville's library. He parked at the curb and went inside. The transformation process from house to library consisted of lining all the walls with bookshelves. Chairs and a table or two were assembled in the center of each room.

Danny wandered around.

"Hello," an elderly woman greeted him. "I'm the librarian, Mrs. Proctor. Can I help you find something?"

She was about a thousand years old and had the same skin tone as the tortoises at the Philadelphia Zoo. The baggy dress, support hose, and orthopedic shoes didn't help.

Danny turned on the charm with a wide smile. "I'm looking for a computer."

Unswayed, she frowned at him with less humor than his high school principal. "Our media room is upstairs. Follow me." Could she even get up the stairs? Spryer than Danny expected, she led the way back to the foyer and up a narrow staircase in the center hall. The media room was an empty bedroom with three desktop computers on a trestle table. Mrs. Proctor booted up the first machine. "Our system is slow. I hope you're not in a rush."

"I have some time." He was avoiding the inn and Mandy and her mother, who had just witnessed Danny making moves on her daughter. Being caught by angry parents was nothing new to Danny. With his reputation for trouble, he'd never been welcomed into a girl's home in his youth. In adulthood, his army career had made long-term relationships difficult. How did a man talk to a woman's parents while he was thinking about getting their daughter naked?

And why was he suddenly pondering parents and long-term relationships? Neither was part of his MO.

Wishing he'd borrowed a laptop for the trip, Danny waited for the browser to open. He called up a search engine. The aged computer chugged along. Web pages loaded at cyber snail's pace. He started with getting an update and details on the fisherman's disappearance. Nothing on that front except head scratching from rescue crews. The search was being expanded, but so far, nothing indicated foul play. Lake Walker was deep. Dragging its bottom would be a lengthy process. Danny stared at the grainy pictures of a pudgy, smiling man and his freckle-faced son. Danny wanted to believe the pair was too happy, too innocent to be gone, but he knew otherwise. Death didn't discriminate. Suppressing his pity for the victims' family, Danny took a few pertinent notes and moved on.

Danny googled the museum theft and was rewarded with a number of articles. Ignoring the NO CELL PHONES sign hanging on the wall, he dialed his brother.

"Yo," Conor answered.

"Yo, yourself," Danny retorted.

"Everything OK?"

"Sort of." Danny sucked up his pride and told Conor about the fire at Reed's house.

"I'm coming up there," Conor said in his chronically rude older-brother voice.

"Because I clearly need a babysitter."

"You almost set yourself on fire."

"No shit. Thanks for pointing out my latest failure. I feel useless enough," Danny shot back.

"Look, I'm sorry." Conor sighed. "But we're all worried about you. None of us wanted you to go up there by yourself in the first place. Honestly, we figured the chance of you actually discovering something was pretty slim, and therefore, you weren't in any real danger."

"Thanks for the confidence."

"I only meant that there doesn't seem to be anything to find."

An ache gathered behind Danny's temple. "I need to do something, Conor, without one of you to jump in and fix it for me." He rubbed his eyes. "Jayne is never going to feel safe unless Nathan Hall is found, and the police up here have given up."

"Maybe you should give up, too. Maybe the police are right, and he's gone," Conor reasoned. "The dude did have a fatal brain disease."

As usual, Conor's coolheaded calm irritated Danny's sensitive nerves. He fell right into his assigned sibling role as family hothead. "Do you really want to take that chance with Jayne? This guy could be a threat for another year."

"We can protect Jayne." Conor's voice hardened.

"That's not the point. Jayne deserves some peace and happiness, don't you think?" Danny shouted. "She shouldn't need a bodyguard for a fucking trip to the grocery store."

"Is everything all right up here?" The librarian stuck her head into the room. Disapproval scrunched her wrinkled face into a giant prune.

Danny turned toward her and covered the phone with a palm. "Yes, I'm sorry."

Not assuaged, she raised a brow and pointed to the sign. "You'll have to take your call outside."

"There's no one else in the whole building," Danny protested. Wrong move. Mrs. Proctor crossed her arms.

"Rules are rules." Under her thinning, snow-white hair, her eyes were solid, clear, and filled with the superiority of the aged.

"OK, OK. I'm going." Annoyed with rules, tight-assed old people, and his arrogant brother, Danny spoke into the phone. "I'll call you back in a few. I have to go outside."

Over the line, he could hear Conor chuckling. "You've been served, baby brother."

Danny hung up on him. "Can I print this article?" he asked the librarian.

"It'll cost you a dime per page." Unbelievably, Mrs. Proctor's posture stiffened.

"That'll be fine, ma'am."

She turned on an old printer in the corner of the room and entered a passcode. Then she supervised his use of the machine. Danny shelled out the fifty cents, took his pages, and bolted for the exit.

One curse and he was on the librarian's shit list. Small town life was going to take some adjustment. As soon as his sneakers hit the sidewalk, he was dialing Conor's number. His brother picked up.

"Stop laughing." Danny got into his car and flipped through the article.

Conor snorted. "Sorry."

"How can you irritate me eight hundred miles away?"

"It's a skill. Now what's up?"

"The Winston Museum of Art and Archeology in Bangor was robbed last night," Danny started. "The only objects stolen were part of a Celtic History exhibit."

"Is there a list of what was stolen?"

Danny skimmed the text. "No, but the thief bypassed more valuable pieces to lift the Celtic stuff. The journalist speculates about it being an inside job, based on the assumption that if there's no forced entry, the thief had a key."

"You know what happens when you assume. Criminals know lots of clever ways to get into buildings."

"But they usually go for stuff that's easy to fence." Danny always had. He waited for the slap of guilt that usually followed memories of his dark teen years, but all he felt was a nudge. "Celtic artifacts are not easy cash."

"What are you thinking, Danny?"

"That the police confiscated Nathan's collection of Celtic objects back in December. Maybe he needs stuff."

"For what?"

"No idea," Danny said. "But it's weird, and weird shit gives me hives. It makes me worry about Jayne." *And Mandy.*

"How far is Bangor from Huntsville?" His brother's wheels were turning.

Danny checked his map app. "Couple of hours by car."

Conor was quiet for a minute. He'd be at the bar at this hour, but from the lack of noise behind his voice, he was probably sitting in the tiny back office with the door closed. Though on a weekday between lunch and dinner, the tavern would be fairly quiet. His siblings would be preparing for the evening rush. "You really think this museum robbery could be connected to Nathan's disappearance?"

Through the windshield, Danny scanned the quiet street. Solid homes, mature trees, and well-tended yards should give him a case of the warm and fuzzies. But the bright sun shining down on Huntsville couldn't chase away the bad vibes buzzing through the fresh air. "I can't figure out how Nathan could possibly have pulled it off, but I do. Don't forget he's had four months to get his act together. Something bad is going to happen here."

And there it was. Danny had said it. He hadn't experienced this sense of impending doom since he'd left Iraq, where people were trying to blow him up every minute of every fucking day.

"How are you?" Conor asked the hard question. "Maybe you need to come home for some more therapy."

Danny thought about it. "It's not post-traumatic stress. This is different. The best way I can explain it is that my PTSD is like a nightmare, and I'm wide awake. There's danger here. How are things there? How's Jaynie?"

"She's holding up." The heavy breath on the other end of the line signaled he'd hit the mark. Conor was giving in. Jayne did a damned good job of putting on a happy face, but behind the mask, fear lurked. The three Sullivan brothers had a pact to take care of their sister. "What do you want me to do?"

"Can you go to Bangor and see what's what?" Danny started the engine. "I'm still nosing around here." He told Conor about the disappearance of the fisherman and his son.

"So, you burned down Reed's house, and a couple of people vanished?"

"Yeah. That sums it up."

"I can clear my schedule tomorrow and head to Maine the day after. Does that work for you?"

"Thanks, Conor."

"Be careful, Danny. It would kill Jaynie to lose you." Conor tossed Danny's strategy back at him.

"Is Reed there?"

"Yeah. Let me get him."

Danny apologized for setting Reed's house on fire, but his almost-brother-in-law wasn't angry, just worried. They sorted through a few insurance details, and Danny told Reed about his meeting with the detective. Reed wasn't happy but thanked him for the information. He punched END.

Danny hadn't exaggerated to his brother. He'd simply verbalized the persistent itch between his shoulder blades. There was no need to convince Reed that Jayne was still in danger. The former cop's instincts were in line with Danny's.

The state police detective could rationalize all he wanted, but Danny knew in his soul that the danger still centered in

Huntsville. The quaint little town, with its postcard-perfect views, was the hub for something evil.

Mandy pushed the lawn mower. The smell of gasoline and fresh-cut grass filled the air around her. Happy to be outside for a change, she hummed the last song she'd heard while doing the lunch dishes.

Jed pulled into the parking area and got out of his truck. Honey jumped down from the passenger seat, raced to the house, and barked at the back door. Bill let her in and knelt to give her a hug. The dog's tail wagged on overdrive. Mandy warmed as she watched the happy greeting. Jed stomped toward her, and her feel-good moment deflated. The huge scowl on his face didn't hide the gauntness or dark circles. Did he sleep at night? He shouted something that Mandy couldn't hear over the engine. She shook her head at him, hoping he'd go away. He didn't.

With a heavy sigh, she shut off the mower. The rumbling cut off abruptly.

"I said," Jed yelled, then lowered his voice, "why are you cutting the lawn?"

Mandy shot him an *isn't it obvious* look. "Because it needs to be cut."

"You should've called me."

"Seriously?" Mandy crossed her arms. "This is hardly beyond my physical ability."

"You have enough stuff to do."

She couldn't argue with that, but the inn's lawn wasn't that big. She and her mother had taken turns mowing it weekly for as long as Mandy could remember. Why was Jed suddenly stepping in? "Well, the grass was high after all the rain and that warm spell last week."

"Here, I'll take over." Jed reached for the mower.

Like he wanted to take over everything. Mandy was tempted, but she knew Jed. If she let him do this, he'd be back tomorrow to do more work. Physically, he could barely keep up with his own place and care for his dogs. He couldn't possibly maintain the inn as well. Mandy blocked him. "I'm halfway done. I'll finish it up."

"This isn't the kind of work you should be doing," he protested. "You aren't cut out for manual labor."

"Oh, really." Mandy propped a hand on her hip. "And what should I be doing?"

Jed shifted his weight as if he knew he was about to say something wrong but just couldn't stop himself. "You know. Woman-type work. Cooking and cleaning and stuff."

"So, women are only good for housework?"

"Not all women. Your mom's sturdy enough." Jed's gaze dropped to his work boots. "But you're…"

Mandy tapped a boot toe on the grass. "I'm what?"

"Delicate." Jed swallowed. "And you're such a good cook. You belong in the kitchen."

Mandy glanced down at her thin but muscled forearms and fingers. Running the inn was hard work, inside and out. She took a couple of calming breaths. "I know you don't mean that exactly the way it came out."

Jed's eyebrows scrunched together. "But I do."

"You want to go down to the gun range and see who belongs in the kitchen?"

He didn't answer, but annoyance flashed across his face.

"And why don't you ever volunteer to help with the cooking and cleaning?" she asked. Jed's horrified look said it all. He was her best friend, but he was a Neanderthal when it came to gender roles. Mandy glanced at her watch. It was nearly time to put out the afternoon refreshments. "Thanks for the offer, Jed, but I can finish the lawn. It feels good to be outside."

"Dammit, Mandy. You're only saying that because you think I'm weak."

"I didn't mean that." She didn't, though the reference to her superior shooting skills had been an unnecessary poke to Jed's sensitive male pride. His injury had upset his expectations in life. He might never be able to return to his career as a hunting guide.

"You didn't have to." His head swiveled as Danny's car parked next to his truck. Jed gave Mandy a hard look. His gray eyes bored into hers. Something dark lurked behind his gaze. Jed was usually serious and quiet. When they were alone, he could also be fun in his own gruff way. He was never hostile toward her. Could her mother be right? Was Jed jealous of Danny? Had she been wrong all these years? She searched her memory. They'd known each other since first grade. Mandy's father had left. Jed's mother ran out on his dad soon after. Mutual sadness and loneliness created a strong bond between them as children, but Mandy couldn't remember treating Jed like anything but her best friend. No other relationship had ever occurred to her. "Fine. Mow your own damned lawn. I'm going home."

He stopped at the house and called for his dog. The lab followed him to the truck but kept glancing back toward the house.

With a quizzical glance at Jed's retreating back, Danny crossed the grass. "Is everything all right?"

"Yes." Mandy pulled off her gloves. The lawn would have to wait until later. "I was just about to put out lemonade and cookies."

Danny followed her to the back porch. She left her grass-stained work boots by the door and slipped into her sneakers before going inside. At the sink, she scrubbed her hands and forearms, then donned an apron. She retrieved the pitcher of homemade lemonade from the fridge and set it on the counter next to the platter of cookies she'd prepared earlier. Danny leaned on the wall, and she tried to ignore how comfortable he looked in her kitchen.

Right on time, her brother burst into the kitchen. Bill liked to get his cookies before the guests appeared. "Are they ready?" He spotted Danny and slid to a stop.

"They are," she answered.

Bill gave Danny a worried look and inched backward toward the door. Mandy poured them both glasses of lemonade. She smiled at her brother. "Want a cookie?"

Her brother's gaze shifted from Mandy to Danny. Watching Bill struggle, Mandy's heart ached.

"Oh, Bill. I almost forgot. I have a present for you." Danny shrugged his shoulders nonchalantly. "If you don't like presents, then don't worry about it."

Curiosity kept Bill rooted in place, his big body taut with indecision. "What is it?"

"I don't know. It's from Reed." Danny set his glass down. "Let me run to my car and get it. Good thing I left it in the trunk. Don't go anywhere, OK?"

Danny hurried out of the kitchen. Mandy put a few cookies on a plate and slid it in front of her brother, but Bill didn't notice. He stared at the door. When Danny returned, he held a box in his hands, bright and shiny with bright-red wrapping paper. Curling silver ribbons cascaded over the sides.

Bill inched closer, eyes locked on the present. "It's from Reed?"

"It is." Danny set the box on the counter. "He's going to marry my sister, so we're almost related."

"Reed sent me a present?" Bill's eyes brightened with disbelief.

"Yes, he did." Danny was biting back a grin.

Bill stared at the package. "Wonder what it is."

Mandy's heart pinged. Wood sculptor Reed Kimball used to live in Huntsville. Reed had been one of her brother's only friends, a pseudo father figure, before Reed had fallen in love with Danny's sister and moved to Philadelphia to live with her.

Danny nudged the gift toward Bill, who forgot his distrust of strangers and plucked it from Danny's hand.

Danny grinned as Bill took his prize to the other side of the room. He bent over the package, ripped the wrapping paper off, and opened the box. Reverently, he lifted a wood carving of a Labrador retriever.

"It looks exactly like Jed's dog, Honey. I always wanted a dog." Cradling the small statue in both ham-sized hands, Bill looked up at Danny with the guileless eyes of a child. "Thanks for bringing me this."

"You're welcome." Danny reached into his back pocket and pulled out his cell phone. "Do you want to call Reed and thank him?"

"I can call Reed?"

"Sure, why not?" Danny dialed and handed the phone to Bill.

"That was sweet of Reed." Mandy wiped her moist eyes.

"Reed's a good guy." Danny leaned a shoulder on the wall. "If he had any idea how much Bill missed him, he would've called. Bill could've called him anytime."

"Sometimes it's best to let things go that aren't going to come back. I'm going to put the snacks out in the dining room." With a backward glance at her brother, who now seemed perfectly comfortable with Danny, Mandy retreated to her chore. She laid out the lemonade and cookies, then stocked the sideboard with ice, glasses, plates, and napkins. When she couldn't find anything else to keep her away from the kitchen—and Danny— she went back in. The room was empty.

Movement drew her gaze to the window. In the backyard, Danny was starting up the mower. She went out onto the porch, determined to tell Danny his help with the grass wasn't necessary. But it wasn't Danny pushing the mower across the yard. Bill gave her an excited wave as he cut a fresh swath in the grass.

Mandy's heart swelled at her brother's simple joy. Who would have thought he would enjoy yard work? Her eyes flickered to Danny. Still watching Bill, Danny walked across the yard and joined her on the porch.

"Do you think it's safe for him to do that?"

"I'll keep an eye on him," Danny said, "but it's not that complicated. I gave him the safety spiel."

Doubt and fear lingered in Mandy's belly. "He could hurt himself."

"He could. But he could also accomplish something and feel good about himself," Danny pointed out. "Everyone needs to be useful, Mandy."

Her brother turned the mower and started a new row. Jed was nice to Bill, but he never let him help with chores. Single-minded with work, Jed wanted to get things done. Letting Bill help often meant the work took twice as long.

"It's going to take him a long time to finish," she pointed out.

"That's all right. I don't have anything else to do." Sadness darkened Danny's eyes as he tracked Bill's progress. "And I like the smell of cut grass."

Mandy backed away and reached for the doorknob. "You'll watch him until he's finished?"

"Don't worry. I'm not going anywhere."

In the kitchen, Mandy leaned on the closed door. What was she going to do about Danny's persistent presence?

Jed crossed the inn's lawn, stifling the urge to run away from the sight of Mandy and Danny talking. His gaze strayed to the metallic purple muscle car. He hated to admit it, but the car was a damned nice ride.

Just as Danny Sullivan was a damned nice guy.

Jed opened the door to his truck. Honey jumped into the cab. She settled on the passenger seat with her head on her paws and heaved a depressed sigh. Even his favorite dog didn't like him best. Honey's bond with Bill grew stronger every day. That was what he wanted, wasn't it?

"I know you wanted to stay and hang out with Bill. I didn't want to leave either, but we aren't needed." Or at least Jed wasn't needed at the inn, not as long as Danny was there. He had no right to be jealous or angry. If it weren't for Danny, Jed would be dead, and God only knew what would've happened to Mandy. Nathan would've gotten her for sure.

He settled behind the wheel and pressed a hand to the never-ending ache in his gut.

He was grateful. He was.

But why did the guy have to come back here? Watching Mandy get all flustered over some other guy was rubbing Jed's ego raw.

After all these years she didn't see him as a man. She thought of him as a brother. Jed's feelings were anything but brotherly. What could he do to change the way she felt about him? She wouldn't let him do much around the inn, except to help out with Bill now and then. But Christ, he could barely lift a ladder. Bringing Honey to visit Bill was about the most useful thing Jed had done for Mandy in ages.

Jed shifted into drive and pulled out onto the road. He cruised to Main Street and turned right, heading out of town. He drove back to his house in silence. Honey sat up and put her nose to the window as they neared his home on the outskirts of town. The truck bounced on the rutted drive and sharpened the pain in his belly. He parked and got out of the truck. From the kennels on one side of his compound, a chorus of barking greeted him. Each dog had an insulated doghouse and a run. His labs were tough hunting dogs, not pets. They lived outside in all but the worst weather. Except Honey. His hand rested on the golden head at his side. She'd always been meant for something more.

Exhaustion and pain clawed at his body, but the dogs came first. As much as he faked wellness in front of Mandy, Jed was not 100 percent. Shit, he wasn't 60 percent of what he'd been, and the doctors hadn't made any promises. Between the original wound and the sepsis that had invaded his body in the weeks after, Jed knew he'd cheated death. He'd all but high-fived the Grim Reaper. His heart had stopped twice. The doctors were surprised he was still alive. This could very well be Jed's new permanent reality. Mandy blamed herself, but he didn't. He'd do it all over again in a heartbeat to save her.

He'd do anything for Mandy.

In the shed behind the kennels, Jed lined up stainless steel bowls and filled them with kibble. He gave each dog a bowl of food and fresh water, then did a quick cleaning of the cages. Following him, Honey wagged and sniffed at each kennel door. Bear, the young chocolate lab in the first cage, was the next up-and-comer. Smart, willing, energy to spare. Jed had already received several very nice offers for the dog, but he had to have one dog in competition at all times. Plus, Bear was going to make a fine stud. This fall would be Bear's year.

There'd be no more field trials for Honey.

Jed patted Bear on the head and secured the door. Too many kennels sat empty and dark. If he wasn't going to breed Honey, he should invest in another bitch, but the future just didn't feel bright enough to plan very far ahead.

Full dark had fallen on the clearing by the time he crossed to the house. A brown package sat on his porch. He carried it inside, pulled his folding knife from his pocket, and slit the tape securing the end. He sat down at his desk. Inside a nest of packing peanuts sat a black box with a large white button. Honey rested her head next to the box as if she knew it was for her.

He fed Honey in the kitchen before heading for the shower. He stepped under the spray and turned his back to the pulsing water. The long, ugly scar that wrapped around his midsection was too tender for direct contact. Jed put his head under the cascading water. How much of a chance did he have of convincing Mandy he was a man, not just a friend? His fingers strayed to the puckered skin on his abdomen. He didn't feel like much of a man, not when picking up a ladder felt like he was trying to lift a Chevy.

He turned off the shower and toweled off. Wait. He froze. There was one thing he could do for Mandy. Something that might convince her that what he felt for her was beyond brotherly affection.

He could find Nathan. Ha! If only his ruined body would hold up to the task, Jed could put an end to this whole thing. But Nathan's knife had rendered Jed useless, emasculated him as surely as if the cut had been eight inches lower.

The memory of lying cold on the pavement, blood flowing out of his body like a hung deer, wasn't the only thing that haunted Jed. Right after he'd stabbed Jed, Nathan had declared Mandy as his own. The cops could claim he was long gone till they ran out of wind. But Jed knew the truth. He wrapped the towel around his waist and went into the adjoining bedroom.

Finding Nathan for her wasn't possible. Not for Jed.

His eyes strayed to the window. Just beyond the outdoor lights, the trees surrounding his cabin formed a black, impenetrable wall. Nathan was out there. Somewhere. He wanted Mandy, and if anyone got in his way, Nathan wouldn't hesitate. He'd shown his true nature. Under all his polish, Nathan was a killer.

CHAPTER TWELVE

Boston, May 1975

A high-pitched scream jolted Nathan from a dead sleep. He rubbed his eyes. Was he dreaming?

Moonlight streamed through the window, illuminating his room in silvery gray and casting long, boogeyman-type shadows from the furniture. But Nathan wasn't afraid of anything creeping up on him. He was too old to be afraid of the dark, and stark reality had replaced any nightmare that could spring from his imagination. No dream could possibly be worse than real life.

Another scream pierced his eardrums, and Nathan cringed. Hopelessness was a freezing hand on the back of his neck.

Mom!

He threw back the covers and tiptoed through the doorway. He stopped in the middle of the hall. The wood floor was cold under his bare feet, but that wasn't what made him tremble. It was thinking about what had caused the scream that made his knees go wobbly. The urge to run back to his room and hide under the covers almost won.

But he needed to know what was happening.

He eased to the threshold of his parents' room. The door was ajar. Dread slid through his belly like an icy eel as he gave the door a two-finger nudge.

His parents were huddled on the bed. Mom's head rested against Dad's chest. His mother sobbed. Something about bugs.

Bugs on the bed. Bugs crawling on her. Thousands of them. Her shoulders shook. Between the thin straps of her nightgown, her backbone protruded through the skin like a snake's skeleton.

"Shhh." Dad stroked her hair and murmured things too softly for Nathan to make out the words. The words didn't matter anyway.

Moonlight deepened the shadows across his mother's face. One eye twitched. Without seeing, he knew the pupil was just a tiny pinprick, nearly lost in eyes the color of the ocean in winter. Her freckled skin had gone sallow and slack.

Dad hadn't slept much either. His face was haggard; shadows under his eyes made him look like one of the zombies in Night of the Living Dead, *the movie Nathan and his friend Eddy sneaked in to see last Saturday when Dad took Mom to another doctor, some big-time psychiatrist who wanted to put Mom in an asylum.*

Nathan wished he'd gone with them. He'd have told the doctor he was wrong. His mother wasn't crazy. She just couldn't sleep.

Ever.

He swiped a hand under an eye. Guilt pricked at his conscience. He shouldn't've gone. He should've said no to Eddy. Instead he'd disobeyed his dad. But he'd just wanted to escape his life for a while.

But the problem was, the movie hadn't been much of an escape.

Feeling like an intruder, he retreated. He backed slowly down the hall to the darkness of his room and covered his ears, but it wasn't enough to block out his mother's cries. Dropping to his knees at the side of his bed, he fished in the nightstand for his rosary. He began the litany, pushing the beads through his fingers as the words tumbled from his mouth.

He focused harder. Surely if he prayed hard enough, God would save his mom. He squeezed his hands together until the cross bit into the flesh. He repeated the prayer, over and over, hoping the words would drown out Mom's despair.

But her sobs still crept into the bedroom.

The floor behind him creaked. He glanced over his shoulder. A huge, familiar shape filled the doorway. His uncle lowered his bulk to his knees beside him. Their shoulders pressed together, and Nathan took comfort from the strength that flowed from his uncle's body.

"What are ye doing?" Uncle Aaron's accent, once strange, was now strangely soothing.

"Praying for her." Nathan reached into the nightstand and produced another rosary. His breath caught in his throat, and he had to swallow before the words would come out. "I know you don't go to our church, but would you say it with me?"

"Aye. You just tell me what to say." The beads looked tiny, like shelled peas, passing through his uncle's thick, sausage-like fingers. Nathan looked up into piercing blue eyes. Trust and relief bubbled up inside his chest. He knew Uncle Aaron didn't go to the Catholic church. But it didn't matter. His uncle would always be there for him.

As Uncle Aaron always said, blood was thicker.

Nathan inhaled the scents of the forest, only mildly tainted by the smell of gasoline. The ATV beneath him bounced as it ran over some rocks on the moonlit game trail. The vehicle was noisy, but Nathan had much ground to cover this night.

So many tasks. So little time until Beltane, the annual fire ceremony that marked the end of winter and the beginning of spring. Just three more days.

Luckily, he was in an isolated area. There was no one around to hear the engine scream. He stopped the vehicle at the edge of a clearing. Before him sat his uncle's old house, now dark and gloomy with neglect, but in his mind's eye, Nathan could see the home of his youth, the place his uncle had brought him after the dual tragedies that had ripped the innocence out from under his childhood.

A semicircle of trees rimmed the property: oak, ash, rowan, birch, alder, willow, hazel, holly, and hawthorn. Though not all native to Maine, his uncle had cultivated the nine sacred trees on his property. Nathan would need some of each to maximize the effectiveness of his Bel-fire and gain the favor of the fire god, Belenos. He got off the ATV and untied the sickle from behind the seat.

He collected two thin branches from the first eight species and bundled them together with nylon cording. Standing before a small stand of rowan, or mountain ash, Nathan snipped a half dozen narrow limbs from the sturdy trees. The most sacred of all should have the most impact. He carefully dug up a rowan seedling sprouting near the base of the tree. Cradling the tiny root ball, he placed it lovingly in a burlap sack.

He secured his cargo behind the seat and got on. Darkness inhibited his speed. More than an hour passed before he reached the edge of town. Nathan concealed the vehicle in a stand of evergreens and traversed the last mile into town on foot. He carried a short piece of rowan, along with the contents of his special bag. A few blocks from the inn, he took care to keep to the shadows. He touched the knife in the sheath at his waist. The town's one remaining policeman wasn't much of a threat, but a missing or dead cop would bring unwanted attention to the town and ruin Nathan's plans.

He only had one shot at a new life for him and his son. All of his acquisitions must be attributable to accident or misadventure.

Still, tonight's activity was risky. But Mandy must be claimed as his. She mustn't be allowed to forget about him. From the darkness beneath the mature maple in the inn's rear yard, Nathan gazed up at the house.

She was inside. His May Queen. The pure maiden who would give him life anew once the disease inside him was destroyed. Emotions surged in Nathan's veins. Love, gratitude, and anger swirled into a heady cocktail that energized him more than sleep ever could. No man would come between them. Danny Sullivan must be stopped.

Nathan stole soundlessly across the grass, the dewy blades dampening the toes of his boots and the hem of his pants. He left his gift on the back porch: a small cauldron depicting the god who would grant Nathan salvation, Belenos. In the pot, Nathan had included hardy plants to signify new life. They were Mandy's favorites. Small but strong flowers that belied their name and bloomed right through a spring snowfall. The perfect flower for the perfect woman.

Thus, nature could give Mandy the message that Nathan was unable to verbalize.

With twine, he affixed the rowan branch above her doorway to protect her from evil spirits.

Turning, he spied the old convertible sitting near the garage. That must be Danny Sullivan's car. No outdoor enthusiast would drive such a vehicle. The temptation to sabotage the convertible flickered in his mind. He could damage the brakes or the wheel alignment, render the car inoperable or dangerous through any manner of procedure. But the risk of killing Sullivan was slim, and he'd need his car to leave town.

The best way to get rid of him was to have Mandy kick him out. Nathan's mental gears clicked. He'd have a new job for his assistant tomorrow. Thank the gods he'd had the foresight to force her to conceal their relationship. Having two members of the Huntsville community to do his bidding was proving useful.

He jogged empty-handed back to the ATV. One more stop. With a worried glance at the brightening sky, Nathan drove forward. Fortunately the public cemetery was on the way back. He only needed to be back in the deep woods before morning overtook the night.

He stopped in front of a plain marker. No inscription other than his uncle's name and the dates that encompassed his life. Nothing about devotion to his family or his skill as a Druid. Sadness filled Nathan's soul. Beneath the earth at his feet lay the man who had given his life for Nathan and his son. Uncle Aaron had embraced pain, loss, and death for one chance to save his family. There wasn't anything Nathan could do to correct the injustice that fate had brought upon his uncle, but Nathan could ensure his passage into the next life was smooth. Nathan took the sapling from his saddlebag and planted it on the gravesite. The sacred tree would ensure his uncle's final resting place would not be haunted by the dead.

It was the least he could do for the man who had given his life to show Nathan the true path to salvation.

CHAPTER THIRTEEN

The coffeepot gurgled as Mandy pulled raw loaves of cinnamon bread from the refrigerator. She slashed the tops and glazed them with an egg wash. While the oven preheated, she finished the dining-room setup. Once the bread was in the oven and the timer set, Mandy poured an enormous mug of coffee and drifted to the window. Dawn washed the yard in pale, peaceful morning light.

All looked serene now. Last night, during a fit of wakefulness, the trees had cast ominous shadows only her imagination could penetrate. Would she ever sleep through the night without being shaken by her paranoia?

Mandy sipped the strong brew while staring out the window and watching the morning brighten. Caffeine cleared her head. The timer dinged, and she pulled the baked bread from the oven and set the loaves on a wire rack to cool. The scents of warm cinnamon and sugar filled the room. She refilled her mug and went out onto the back porch.

The kitchen door smacked into something metal. Mandy looked down. Next to the flowers Bill had brought her the other day, a container of pansies sat in the middle of the porch. The metal was antiqued and dented, as if someone had drop-kicked it from a garage sale to her back porch. The image repeated around the outside side was of a man's face. His beard and hair flowed around his head like fire, or maybe rays of the sun. Despite the odd, almost intimidating depiction, Mandy smiled at the purple-and-white blooms rioting in the soil.

Had Bill left this for her? How sweet. As one of the earliest colorful annuals, pansies were her favorites. The hardy little flowers could endure the blasts of winter so common in a New England spring.

"Good morning."

Mandy startled. She spun around. One hand went to her throat. Coffee sloshed onto the porch floorboards. Danny was standing in the doorway. His damp hair invoked thoughts of a warm beach and a rum-spiked drink. The only beaches she'd visited were rocky, the water a toe-numbing cold that did not invite the rest of her body to wade in.

"I'm sorry. I didn't mean to scare you." He retreated to the kitchen for a second and returned with a dish towel. "Let me get that." He bent down to mop up the spill.

Putting aside visions of places she'd likely never see and a vacation she'd never take, Mandy recovered. "It's not your fault. I was looking at this pot of flowers. Bill must have put it there for me."

Staring at the pot, Danny straightened. "It's, um, different."

Mandy laughed. "I've no idea where he dug up the pot, but pansies are my favorites."

He tilted his head. "I'll remember that."

The comment drifted on the silent morning air. Mandy cleared her throat. "I have to get back to work. There's coffee if you want it." She reached for the doorknob. A strange branch was tied over the entrance. She paused. "What on earth has Bill been up to?"

Danny reached around her and opened the door. "Why would he hang a stick over your door?"

"I don't know. Even for Bill, that's strange." From just a few inches away, Danny's aftershave drifted to her nose. Light and fresh, it reminded her of the woods in midwinter, and tempted her to lean in for a better whiff.

Probably not the best way to discourage Danny's advances. But she really wanted to. If only they'd met under different circumstances, like the kind that didn't include threats to her family members' lives. It wasn't meant to be. Reluctantly, she moved away from it, and him, into the safety of her kitchen. The smell of freshly baked cinnamon bread camouflaged his scent.

A glance at the clock told her she needed to get breakfast rolling. She moved to the fridge and pulled out a dozen eggs. When she turned around, Danny was tying a plain black apron around his waist. She raised an eyebrow. "What are you doing?"

"Thought I'd help with breakfast." He washed his hands at the sink.

"I don't think that's a good idea."

"Don't worry. I promise not to ask you any questions about the case."

"I'm very particular about the food that comes out of my kitchen."

"Seriously, breakfast food isn't that tough. As long as it's simple, I can cook it. Short order is my specialty. My family owns a tavern. My brother Pat put me to work in the kitchen at a young age. He was trying to keep me out of trouble."

"Did it work?"

"Not a bit." His face split into the sexy bad-boy grin that melted her resolve faster than butter on a hot griddle. He dried his hands. "What are you serving this morning?"

"Waffles, scrambled eggs, and bacon." Mandy grabbed her own apron and washed up. "Plus the basics."

Danny lifted a large skillet from the overhead rack. "I'll take the scrambled eggs. Do you do anything special with them?"

"I've made herbed cream cheese to fold in at the end."

"Nice." Danny lit the burner under the pan and went to work cracking eggs like a pro.

Mandy started on the waffles. "Tell me about your family."

Danny tossed a slab of butter into the pan with a sizzle. "My parents died when I was eleven."

"I'm sorry. That's awful." Mandy paused, a ladle of batter suspended over the waffle maker.

"For a long time it was," Danny said. "Anyway, there are four of us. I'm the youngest. Jayne's a year older. Then there's Conor and Pat. Poor Pat. As the oldest, he took over running the family business and raising me and my sister. In exchange, I made his life hell."

Mandy poured batter into the machine, closed it, and set the timer. "I'm sure you weren't all that bad."

"Oh, I was." Danny selected a whisk and whipped eggs with an angry zeal. "I skipped school, barely stayed out of juvie, and dragged my sister into my nefarious exploits whenever I could. That's what I feel the worst about. It was one thing to self-implode, but to pull Jayne into my downward spiral with me was selfish."

"You were angry." With a sad pang, Mandy remembered the night her father left. No argument, just exited with a simple declaration. *I can't take it anymore.* She'd had her mother to help her through the anger and helplessness.

"That I was."

"What happened?"

"Eventually, I got caught doing something I couldn't weasel my way out of. Only I wasn't a snot-nosed little neighborhood brat anymore. I was a legal adult, and the local beat cops had had it with me. I think they ignored the petty shit I'd done in the past because they had so much respect for my brother Pat. But at twenty, it wasn't acceptable anymore. They grabbed me outside an electronics store with an armload of DVD players."

Mandy stared, open-mouthed. "You were stealing them?"

Danny sighed. "I was."

The timer dinged. Mandy transferred the first four Belgian waffles to a plate. "Did you go to jail?"

"No." Danny stirred the herbed cream cheese into the eggs. He was silent for a minute, as if he was trying to decide if he should tell her any more. "The cop who caught me put me in his squad car." Danny paused, scanning the kitchen. "Where can I find a chafing dish?"

"Bottom cabinet to your left."

He pulled out the dish and set it on the counter next to the stove. "The cop was pissed. Kept asking me how the hell a man as good as Pat could have a brother as worthless as me."

Mandy refilled the waffle maker. "That's terrible."

"Hey, I deserved it. I was worse than worthless." Danny dumped the eggs into the silver dish and covered it. He set the pan back on the stove and turned off the burner. "Anyway, the cop said this was the end of the line. I was shaking in the back of the car. Thought I'd finally done it. Either he was going to beat the shit out of me, or I was going to prison." Danny looked up at her. "I think your waffles are done."

"Oh, geez." Mandy rescued the food just in time. "Thanks. What did he do?"

"What?" Danny pulled another dozen eggs from the refrigerator.

"Did he beat you or arrest you?" Mandy asked impatiently.

"Oh. Neither. He drove around until morning. Then he took me to the army recruiting center. My choice was to enlist or go to prison. Either way, he was not dealing with my ungrateful punk ass committing crimes in his neighborhood again."

"What did you do?"

"I spent the next eight years in the army and served two tours in Iraq," Danny said. "I'd still be in the army if I hadn't been injured." He took a heavy breath. "We'd better get this food out, right?"

Mandy checked the time. Breakfast officially started in less than five minutes. "Are you mad at that policeman for making you go into the army? If you hadn't, your hand wouldn't be injured."

"True, and I catch myself blaming that cop even now. But I was headed in a dark direction. Joining the army turned me into a man instead of a future ex-con while I was young enough to change. God knew I needed the discipline. I needed to leave my pain behind and start fresh, where nobody knew me. At some point in your life, you have to let go of the past. I carried the anger for my parents' deaths for almost a decade. That's a long, long time to be mad. I don't want to live like that anymore. I want to move forward."

"I know what you mean." Mandy shot him a look. All she wanted was to get through this next year. After that, she'd be relatively certain Nathan couldn't harm her family.

And apparently, moving forward meant blathering about his emotions like he was a guest on Oprah or some shit. *Is there anything else you'd like to share about your pathetic life?* Ten months of therapy, and he was sliding into the touchy-feely zone like it was home base.

Danny carried the eggs to the dining room and lit the burner. A trio of pretty college-age girls chattered as they took a table. Two brunettes and a blonde. They were dressed for the trail in thick boots and expensive-looking synthetic pullovers in bright pink and yellow. A trio of backpacks was stacked on the extra chair.

"Coffee?"

They nodded. Three ponytails bounced. "Yes, please." One of the brunettes answered with a flirty smile that made Danny feel a thousand years old. "I'm Ashley. These are my friends, Victoria and Samantha."

"I'm Danny." He filled their cups and nodded to their packs. "Big plans today?"

"Just the usual." The tall blonde shrugged. "We always carry extra provisions. It's important to be prepared."

"You never know what can happen in the wilderness," Ashley added. "We're always equipped to spend at least one night in the open."

"That's smart." Danny smiled. He'd had survival training in the army. He'd learned the basics, but he hadn't liked it. In fact, all those training exercises made camping about as attractive as torture. Sleeping in the open, eating bugs, and freezing your nuts off sucked. "Where are you headed?"

Victoria added cream to her cup. "We're hiking the Klimpton trail today. We already wrote it in the book."

"The book?"

"Uh-huh." Victoria nodded and stirred her coffee. "The inn has a book to log your plans. That way if you get lost, they know where to start looking for you."

"Sounds sensible." And ominous. Just how many people disappeared in Maine? If someone in the city went missing, somebody usually saw something. Not that they'd say, but folks just didn't go *poof*. There were security cameras everywhere.

"Do you hike?" Ashley was eying him up like he was a slice of chocolate cake. "Because you could join us. We're here for the rest of the week."

Danny backed away. Was this what a rabbit felt like when a hawk hovered overhead? "Sorry. I can't. I'm helping out in the kitchen."

"Too bad," Ashley lamented.

"You all have a great day." Danny made his escape. He went back to the kitchen. Mandy was filling glass pitchers with juice. "What else needs to be done?"

His hand trembled, and the familiar pins-and-needles tingle started in his fingers. Dammit. It was early in the morning for his nerves to be pulling their shit. If he were smart, he'd give it a rest. At the very least, he'd better not handle glass.

"You could cut up another melon." She carried the pitchers toward the dining room. The smile she gave him over her shoulder made him forget any ideas of resting.

"Got it." Melons were very durable. He grabbed a cantaloupe from the icebox, scrubbed it in the sink, and set it on the cutting board. With a knife from the block, he halved the melon and went to work slicing it. He paused every few cuts to clench his hand and give it a shake.

Mandy returned and went to check her latest batch of waffles. Danny's gaze was drawn to the fit of her worn jeans below the tie of her apron. Mm, mm, mm.

As if she felt his stare, she glanced back at him. "You're bleeding."

Danny looked down. Blood ran off his left hand. Suddenly lightheaded, he averted his eyes. He put the knife down and went to the sink. A flush of cold water revealed a long slice across his palm. Mandy leaned against him and grabbed hold of his forearm to examine the cut. "That's going to need sutures."

Danny decided that having her soft body pressed to his was worth a few stitches, even if the sight of blood turned him into a wimp. "Sorry. I ruined your melon."

Mandy gave him a short laugh of disbelief. "Doesn't that hurt?"

Danny snagged a paper towel and applied pressure to the wound. "No. I don't have much feeling in this hand."

"Dr. Chandler should be in his office by now." She picked up the phone and dialed. A few sentences later she hung up. "Go right over. Do you know where it is? Do you need me to drive you?"

"Yeah, I know where it is. It's only a few blocks away. I think I can make it."

Mandy opened a drawer and took out a first aid kit. Throwing the blood-soaked paper towel in the trash, she bandaged him up enough to keep him from bleeding all over his car. Enjoying her touch, Danny let her. When she was done, her hand lingered on his arm, and her blue eyes darkened, like she was interested in more than his cut. He leaned in, but Mandy jumped back, nearly tripping over her feet in her haste to put some space between them.

Awkward. "Mandy—"

"You'd better go. You're bleeding through the bandage." She opened the door. "Are you sure you're all right to drive?"

"Don't worry. I'm used to doing things one-handed."

The drive to Doc's office took all of three minutes, most of which was spent at the town's single traffic light. Not much time to contemplate Mandy's skittishness. But one thing was clear. He needed to take whatever might happen between them slower.

The clinic was on a side street just three doors from the main intersection of town. The barn-red two-story was almost nauseatingly quaint, with its fresh white trim and flower boxes spilling over with purple-and-white flowers. The front door opened in to a small waiting room decorated in castoffs. Thirty-year-old chairs and tables too ugly for Goodwill but not old enough to be antiques vied for space. An old wooden teacher's desk in the corner was empty.

A white-coated Dr. Chandler appeared in a doorway. "Come on back." He turned and disappeared.

Danny walked down the short hallway, passing a tiny room with a desk and bookshelves. The doc's office? Danny hesitated. A few thick volumes stacked on the shelf closest to the door caught his attention: *Sleep Disorders, Inherited Prion Diseases, Psychiatry Today, Neurological Disorders that Affect Sleep.* Heavy subjects for a family practitioner. Dr. Chandler had been researching Nathan's disease. Had he known about the family history before December? Had Dr. Chandler treated Nathan's uncle? Did he know who Nathan was sleeping with?

"Mr. Sullivan?"

"Right here." Danny followed the doctor's voice to the next doorway, which led into a small examination room. "Slow morning?"

"I don't officially open for another hour, which is why I'm the only one here." The doctor gestured to the usual padded table. "Let's see it."

Danny sat. Paper crinkled under his ass.

Doc washed his hands and donned gloves. Then he slipped on a pair of half glasses and unwound the tape. Blood started flowing as soon as he lifted the bandage. "Definitely needs stitches. How'd you do this?"

Danny stared at an eye chart on the opposite wall. "Cutting up a melon."

"Hmmph." The doctor hooked a stool with his foot and wheeled a small table closer. Instruments were already lined up on a sterile drape. Perching on the stool, he picked up a syringe. "I'll numb it and stitch you up. Should heal just fine. Luckily, it's in the fleshy part."

"You can skip the shot. I don't have much feeling in that hand." Danny's fingers, obviously unhappy with the fresh wound, twitched like they were having a seizure. "You'll have to be careful, though; I can't do anything about that."

"So, you can't feel your hand and it shakes uncontrollably."
The doctor irrigated the wound.

P, E, Z...Danny concentrated on the bottom row of letters.
"Pretty much."

"And you thought it was a good idea to handle a sharp knife?"

"Probably not one of my best decisions," Danny admitted.

"You think?" Doc picked up his suture needle. He pointed
to the thin scar that ran from Danny's wrist to elbow. "Tell me
about the original injury."

"It was an IED explosion. The hand was crushed under a pile
of debris. Broken bones, shrapnel, lots of nerve damage. For a
while it was iffy that I'd even get to keep it. The surgeon at the
veteran's hospital did a hell of a job putting it back together. I had
a nerve graft about ten months ago, but it didn't take."

Doc was quiet for a few minutes. Danny was keeping his gaze
averted, but in his peripheral vision he could see the doctor sew-
ing. He tied another knot. *Snip.* "That should do it."

Danny glanced down at his palm. Seven neat black knots
closed the cut in his palm.

The doctor bandaged his hand. "Keep it dry. Come back in
five days and I'll remove the stitches."

"Thanks. What do I owe you?" Danny rubbed his forearm.
The cut didn't hurt, but the pins-and-needles sensation had
expanded from his fingers to his wrist. Soon those pins would
turn into bayonets and spread up to his elbow.

"Pain?" Dr. Chandler frowned at the bandage.

"Some. Sometimes I get a stabbing sensation when it's too
cold or too hot or I overuse my hand. I guess the gash is making
it worse."

"Call me if you need pain medication."

"Thanks, but I'm not a fan of drugs." Narcotics aggravated
his PTSD. "Rest usually helps."

The doctor led the way back to the schoolmarm desk. He lowered his tall, lanky body into a cheap office chair. He typed into the computer and printed out a bill. Fluorescent light glinted off silver threads in his dark hair as he bent over the keyboard. "Give me a minute. My receptionist isn't in yet. I'm a lot slower than she is at this."

Danny pulled out his wallet to pay the bill. The total was laughably small. "That's it?"

"Small town, you know."

Danny paid. "While I'm here, I wanted to ask you a couple of questions about Nathan Hall."

Doc's face tightened from friendly into suspicious. "You know I can't talk about a patient."

"Of course not," Danny said. "But you can give me some general information about Campbell's Insomnia."

Scowling, the doctor crossed his arms over his chest and leaned back in the chair. "Lesions form in the thalamus of the brain. That's the area that regulates sleep. Afflicted people develop severe insomnia, gradually losing the ability to sleep at all. Coma and death follow within a year or two."

All textbook information Danny already knew. "How quickly is the person completely incapacitated?"

"Depends on the individual," the doctor said.

"But case studies show that the person's mental state is affected long before the body shuts down. Dementia hits hard during that period. So, an afflicted person could be mobile and potentially dangerous for a long time."

The doctor's lips pursed with annoyance. "The disease is very rare. There aren't enough cases to make generalizations."

"But people with Campbell's can have violent hallucinations that drive them to bizarre behavior."

"It's not my specialty. I really wouldn't know."

"So you have no idea how long Nathan could be dangerous?" Danny pressed.

"No. I really can't say."

"Can't or won't?"

"In this case, it doesn't really matter, does it? I'll see you in five days, Mr. Sullivan, if you're still in town. Don't feel the need to stay, though. Any doctor can remove those stitches." The doctor put his hands flat on the desk and pushed to his feet. The conversation was over.

Danny walked toward the door. He glanced over his shoulder. "I'm not going anywhere."

Anger, cold as his stainless steel instruments, flickered in the doctor's eyes. "Some people in this town have been through hell. There's no need to drag them down to the next level."

"I'm just trying to find a killer."

"Don't forget that those with good and bad intentions often end up in the same place."

With that send-off, Danny made his exit. His injured hand twitched as he started the engine. A compact SUV was parked at the curb behind the Challenger. A woman dressed in scrubs got out and walked into the clinic. Dr. Chandler's nurse?

He turned the wheel to pull out onto the street. Pain shot into his elbow. He clenched his fist and steered through a turn. There was no point rushing back to the inn. He wasn't going to be any more help to Mandy today. Why would she want anything to do with him? Not only was he useless to her at the bed-and-breakfast, he was still doing the one thing she had asked him not to do. He was still trying to find Nathan. But Danny couldn't let it go. If he could just accomplish one thing, meet one goal head on, maybe he could move forward. Quitting definitely wasn't going to help.

Driving aimlessly, Danny headed away from town. He needed some time alone. Thoughts of his prospects filled his head. What did his future hold? What kind of a job was he going to get with only one good hand? Sullivan's Tavern could only support so many family members. His only other marketable skill was fixing cars, but his bum hand slowed him down too much for that to be a viable career. It was probably best that Mandy wasn't interested in him. He didn't even know what he wanted to do with the rest of his life. How could he contemplate a relationship? He glanced at the dashboard clock. More time had passed than he'd intended. Such was the time-sucking nature of a pity party. It was time to meet the insurance adjuster at Reed's house.

As Danny turned onto the interstate, his eyes were drawn to the mountains on the horizon. How could a place so peaceful harbor so much evil and madness?

CHAPTER FOURTEEN

The sound of wood scraping woke Kevin. He opened his eyes to dusty daylight. Lifting his head over his son's body, curled in his arms, Kevin scanned the barn interior. No people in sight. The double doors were ajar. Fresh air flooded the cage. Against his chest, Hunter's rib cage expanded with each reassuring breath. But they'd been without food or water for two days, maybe more. He wasn't sure how much time had passed. Exhaustion and the drugs they'd been given had bent reality like a fun-house mirror.

He recognized that fear should be pounding through his veins, but dehydration had sapped his body's ability to respond. He stretched a leg out. His foot encountered something. He turned his head and squinted. Two meal bars and a liter-size bottle of water had been placed in the cage during the night.

Multiple things occurred to Kevin immediately. One, some-one had been close to them while they slept, completely vulnerable. He curled tighter around his son while panic took a slow spin through his already nauseated gut. Two, there was a good chance that the water was drugged. Three, without water, Hunter wasn't going to survive much longer. Four, there wasn't anything Kevin could do to save his son.

Hunter shivered, and Kevin tried to cover more of his shrinking form with a combination of his own jacket and body. The child's skinny frame didn't have any body fat available for fuel, and his smaller mass left him more susceptible to fluid loss. The damp, cold nights were an added insult. Looking down at his son's pale and sleeping face, Kevin's heart ached more than his water-starved joints. Terror for his son welled in his chest, filled his lungs, and constricted his next few breaths. The pressure threatened to render Kevin useless. He fought back with action. Right now, they were stuck, but who knew what opportunities might crop up. The more Kevin studied his surroundings the better.

He took another inventory of the barn. There was nothing he could reach through the bars of the cage, but potential weapons littered the building: a hammer, pieces of lumber, a couple of other farm tools he didn't recognize but that looked potentially harmful. Of course, all of these things could be used against them, too.

The big tractor hadn't moved. Nothing had changed. Wait. Kevin squeezed his eyes shut and opened them again. Yes. The woodpile in the corner had doubled in size.

What was his captor planning? More cages? Kevin blinked as his eyes adjusted to the light. No. The pieces of wood were thin branches, too flimsy to build another prison.

Kevin sat up. The rough wood beneath his body dug into his bones. He scooted to the other side of the cage, picked up the water bottle, and examined it. It was a refillable sports-type bottle, not a sealed commercial product. Easy to tamper with the contents. What to do?

He opened the bottle, put it to his lips, and sniffed. Smelled like water. He took a small sip, barely enough to wet his chapped lips, and waited. When he felt no adverse effects, he drank more. Cool water soothed his dusty throat, but he put the bottle down after drinking about a quarter cup. Hunter needed the fluid more. Kevin sat and let ten or fifteen minutes pass. He didn't die.

Kevin cupped his son's face. "Hunter, wake up."

His boy's freckled face blanched in fear the second his eyes opened. But his eyes were cloudy. If Hunter didn't get some water, Kevin wasn't going to have to worry about their captor's plans. So plan A: Hunter would get the majority of food and water. With just a little fluid, Kevin's spare tire would keep him going for another day or two. If Kevin was wrong and the supplies were drugged, he could only hope the dose wouldn't be worse than no water at all—and that if the opportunity to fight for their freedom did come, they would be able to respond. Drugged, he couldn't protect his son. But dead, he'd be of even less use. He refused to think about the horrors playing out in his head. Of his son helpless at the hands of a psycho and of Kevin powerless to protect his boy.

Of what the psycho was planning to do to them.

His instincts told him they were being kept alive for something. Something big. Something evil.

At the moment, he really had no choice. Hunter's eyes were sunken, his lips dry and cracked. His skin lacked elasticity. He'd stopped crying sometime the day before. They'd start with a half cup of water and see how Hunter reacted.

Praying he was right, Kevin lifted his son's shoulders and tilted the open bottle to his lips. "Drink this."

Hunter drank. And Kevin prayed.

Just outside the door, boots scraped on dirt. Kevin automatically shielded Hunter with his body. Someone was coming. Their captor walked into the barn, but the blond man barely glanced at them as he crossed to the tractor and started it up.

Where was he going?

⸺

Nathan checked on his captives, then drove the tractor to the edge of the lake, unhitched the boat, and launched it into the smooth water. The process was awkward, but beggars couldn't be too picky. Other than the lack of a dock, the location chosen by his assistant was perfect. His demands hadn't been easy to meet. The property was quiet, out of the way, and had a large enough outbuilding for his very special project.

He tied the boat to a fallen log, then moved the tractor back into the shadows of the trees. Sweat dripped into his eyes. He wiped his brow on his sleeve. So much work still to accomplish. Beltane occurred in just two more days. He'd earmarked today for hunting.

He needed four more sacrifices to fill his effigy.

Nathan rowed along the shoreline. On his last outing, he'd seen evidence that someone else was taking advantage of the isolation of the north end of that lake. A small, semipermanent encampment fashioned from scavenged bits.

Last time, the motor had frightened off his intended prey, but this time Nathan intended to hunt the man down as if he were a wary buck.

The oars dipped. Nathan pulled, and the boat slid smoothly through the water. He was getting close. There. The boulder. He steered to the edge and dragged the boat up onto the bank.

A narrow game trail led toward the rough camp. Nathan crept through the trees, his steps silent on the damp pine needles underfoot. At the edge of the clearing, he stopped and peered around a tree. A tent had been fashioned into an *A* by string-ing a tarp over a rope and staking down the four corners. Food hung from a high branch on the other side of the clearing. Smoke curled from embers inside a circle of rocks.

But the camp's occupant was nowhere to be found.

Disappointment and panic whirled in Nathan's belly. What if he couldn't find enough sacrifices in time?

He would wait. Eventually, whoever lived here would return. Nathan pulled the Taser from his pocket. Best be ready.

Boom. A shotgun blasted through the quiet woods

Nathan dropped to the ground facedown. He hugged the back of his head as leaves and bits of bark rained down on him.

"Who goes there?"

Nathan rolled. A grizzled old man stood on the trail behind him. His hair and beard were gray and long and nearly as dirty as his threadbare military fatigues. Nathan raised the Taser and fired. The old man was more agile than he appeared. He jumped behind a tree. The Taser barbs fell to the forest floor.

The shotgun boomed again. Bark exploded above Nathan's head.

"I'll kill you. Motherfucking aliens. I'll kill you all."

Boom.

Nathan heard the sound of shells being shoved into a shotgun. He scrambled to his feet and ran. Pine needles and branches whipped at his face as he darted through the trees. The next *boom* was farther away. He didn't slow until he reached the lake's shore, then he wasted no time pushing the boat out onto the water.

This time he opted to use the small outboard motor.

Stealth was no longer an issue.

Steering the boat to the south, he took stock. No injuries, but the fact remained that his mission was a failure.

Time was running out.

Tomorrow he'd have to venture south, to the more frequented areas of Lake Walker, where he was sure to find people. There was a chance he'd be seen and possibly recognized, but if he didn't succeed it wouldn't matter.

Risk be damned.

No matter what happened, tomorrow he was filling his cages.

CHAPTER FIFTEEN

Steam poured from the dishwasher vents as Mandy wiped the counters. Breakfast was over hours ago. Where was Danny? All morning, she'd resisted the urge to call Doc and check up on him, but enough was enough. Ignoring the soaking pans in the sink, she picked up the cordless phone. A quick exchange with Dr. Chandler's nurse, Shelly, put Mandy's mind at ease about Danny's injury. But where had he gone?

The door slapped open, and Bill burst through. "I'm hungry. Is there more cinnamon bread?"

"Of course." Mandy wrapped a leftover slice in a napkin and poured him a glass of milk.

"Where's Danny?" Bill took a bite.

"I don't know."

"He didn't leave, did he?"

"I don't think so. He didn't check out." Although that's what she wanted him to do, the thought that he could be gone left an empty space inside her.

Bill looked doubtful. He ripped another chunk off his bread. Mandy chewed her thumbnail. Should she check Danny's room for his things? No, he was free to come and go as he pleased. He hadn't made her any promises. At the most, he would be here for two weeks. But the apprehension in her brother's eyes doubled the hollowness inside. One more reason Danny had to leave immediately. Bill was getting attached to him. When Danny went home, Bill would be devastated.

"After Danny leaves, can I call him?" Was Bill reading her mind?

"Sure. Did you like talking to Reed yesterday?"

"Uh-huh." He finished the slice and took a long swallow of milk.

"I'm glad." She should have thought of letting Bill call. Maybe she'd been wrong about a clean break being the best way to handle the situation. Everything she did for Bill seemed to be wrong.

Bill downed the rest of his milk and wiped his mouth with the back of his hand. Mandy handed him a napkin.

"I thought he forgot about me."

Ugh. Mandy rubbed her forehead. She'd definitely made the wrong call on that. Exhaustion pulled at her. The dirty pans beckoned. Danny's words echoed in her mind: *everyone needs to be useful.*

She pushed up a sleeve. "I could use some help. Want to dry the dishes?"

Bill's face brightened. "Sure."

Mandy tossed him a dish towel. She scrubbed her way through the stack of pans. Bill carefully dried each one and put it away.

"Thanks."

"I like helping you, Mandy." Bill tilted his head.

"I know. I've been really busy. Sometimes I forget to ask."

"If you ask me for help, you won't be so busy. Can I do anything else?" Bill asked.

She almost asked him to bring in the mail but changed her mind. "The porches need to be swept."

"OK." Bill grabbed the broom from the pantry and went out onto the back porch. Mandy filled a watering can and joined him. She gave both pots of pansies a thorough drink. "Thank you for the flowers."

Bill paused midsweep, his face crinkling in confusion. "You already thanked me when I gave them to you."

"For the first ones, but not these." Mandy tilted the can over the new container.

Bill shook his head. "I wouldn't give you anything like that. The flowers are pretty, but the pot is ugly and kind of scary."

Mandy pointed to the branch tied over the door. "Have you ever seen that?"

"Nope." Bill imitated Danny's voice. The broom whisked across the floorboards.

Mandy scanned the yard. The bright sunshine contrasted with the darkness of her thoughts. Who had been on her porch last night? She set the watering can on the painted gray boards and squatted to examine the flowerpot. It was about a foot high and maybe a foot and a half across. The metal was dull silver in color. In addition to the repeated image of a man's face in circle of flames, the pot was adorned with spirals and horses and interlocking triangles. The overall effect was primitive—and intimidating. It didn't look like anything available at a garden center.

Mandy leaned closer. A small tag on a green stem nestled amid the blossoms. A floral arrangement gift tag? She reached for it, turning the cardboard around to read the front. Tiny roses and hearts decorated the face. In the center, a message was typed in fancy script. A leftover Valentine's Day card?

Be Mine.

Mandy flinched away from it. Straightening wobbly knees, she backed away. Her heartbeat amplified until the echo of blood rushing in her ears drowned out the tweeting of birds and the faint scrape of straw sweeping across wood. She scanned the yard, her gaze burrowing into every shadow. No one was there.

The other threats had been direct, point-blank instructions. The flowers that had been pretty two minutes ago now gave her the creeps. This was different. This wasn't blackmail. This had a whole different feel. This was personal. Someone who knew her favorite flowers. Could she have more than one stalker?

You're mine, Nathan had said, but it couldn't be him.

Bill's broom stopped moving. "What's wrong?"

"Nothing." She gave her brother a fake smile. "Let's go inside. It's almost lunchtime."

"But I'm not done," he protested.

"You can finish later."

Bill's jaw clenched. "Danny says it's important to finish what you start."

Mandy caved. "All right. You finish up the sweeping, then I'll make us both lunch. How's that sound?"

"Great."

Reason told her that whoever had left the pot was long gone. But Mandy kept her eyes on the perimeter of the property and her thoughts on her revolver while her brother finished his task at an agonizingly deliberate pace. Bill did not leave one speck of dirt behind. Fifteen minutes later, he nodded at her. "I'm done. We can eat now."

"That looks great. Thanks." She hustled him into the kitchen. He beamed with pride as he followed her. Relief swept through Mandy as she locked the back door. "Can you ask Mom if she wants a sandwich?"

"Sure." Bill ducked into their apartment.

Mandy wiped her sweaty palms on her thighs. Bill returned in less than a minute with their mother right behind him.

"What's going on, Mandy?" Her mom fisted a hand on a padded hip. Even with the weight she'd lost, her midsection remained lumpy as an old down pillow. "Bill said someone left a strange present on the porch?"

"It's just some flowers."

Her mother went out onto the porch for a minute. "I don't like this." She picked up the phone.

"What are you doing?" Panic raced through Mandy.

Her mother gestured with the cordless. "Calling the police."

"Why are you calling the police?" Worry tinted Bill's voice.

Mae patted his hand. "It's not a big deal, but someone was on our porch last night without our permission. Considering everything that's happened, I want Doug to come out here and take a look around."

"But all they did was leave some flowers." Bill propped his elbows on the counter and rested his chin in his hands.

"Bill's right, Mom," Mandy reasoned. "Calling Doug is pointless." And potentially dangerous. What if her stalker was watching? Would he think Mandy wasn't keeping up her end of the deal? "You know he'll just blow it off."

"Our taxes pay his salary, and he can damn well get his butt out here when I call." Her mother's face reddened with her temper. "I'll do it if you're not willing to—"

"No, you're right." Alarmed by her mother's color, Mandy jumped in.

"You're damn straight I'm right." Mae dialed the phone and spoke to the dispatcher.

"Why don't you sit down and have some lunch?" Mandy took her mother's elbow.

Breathless, Mae pressed a hand to her chest. "I'm not hungry. If you'll handle Doug when he gets here, I'll go lie down."

"Of course I will." Mandy would have promised anything to get her mother to rest.

"I'm hungry." Bill lifted his head.

"OK, Bill." Mandy made tuna salad and spread it on rye. She gave Bill two sandwiches, and they ate at the kitchen island in silence. When was the last time she'd *enjoyed* time with her brother? But the strange things on the back porch and the police lieutenant's imminent arrival intruded on their companionship. Mandy's appetite dimmed. She put her sandwich on her plate. "Stay right here, all right?"

Chewing, Bill nodded. Mandy walked through the house and out the front door. The mailbox sat at the end of the brick walk. White with a black flag to mirror the house's colors and some daffodils peeking through the dirt around its whitewashed post, it was quaint, innocuous. But Mandy knew with complete certainty it held something dangerous. Call it premonition, women's intuition, or survival instinct, sometimes one just knew trouble was waiting. There was no avoiding it, though.

She scanned the street. Empty in both directions. No one skulking behind the shrubs. She shoved her shaking hands into her front pockets as she went down the steps. In the flower beds that lined the front walk, more tiny green heads of spring bulbs, hyacinths here, poked through the soil. The mailbox opened with a creak. Mandy pulled out a stack of letters. Her eye fell on a familiar white envelope. No return address. No stamp. Her name printed neatly in the center.

She ripped it open and pulled out an eight-by-ten glossy. Bill and Danny standing over the lawn mower in the backyard. Mandy held the photo up. Light came though cuts in the image. Someone had cut the picture right across her brother's neck, decapitating his image. Fear curled in Mandy's belly. Bold red print spelled out the new message on Bill's chest.

DON'T FORGET.

———

Danny parked behind the inn. He glanced at the back of the house. He was contemplating whether to knock on the back door or go around to the front. Just where did he stand with Mandy? Bill waved through the kitchen window, then opened the door.

Danny walked into the kitchen. "Hey, Bill. What's going on?"

"Dunno." Bill shoved his hand into a bag of potato chips. "Mandy's upset about something."

Guilt sandbagged Danny. Was she worried about him? He should have called to let her know he was fine.

The door opened. Mandy came through. "Bill, would you—" Spying Danny, she stopped short. "Oh, you're back."

"Yeah. I'm sorry I didn't call."

"It's all right. You didn't make any promises." But she kept her distance, moving to the counter to clean up some dirty dishes. "Bill, would you check on Mom?"

"Sure, Mandy." Bill tucked a bag of chips under his arm. "Maybe she'll watch *Star Wars* with me."

Mandy smiled, but her eyes were sad. She glanced at the bandage on Danny's hand. "How's your cut?"

"Fine. Just a few stitches."

She nodded, and Danny wondered how to address the awkwardness that had sprung up between them. Was she upset that he'd wanted to kiss her? Or had she remembered she wanted him to leave because he reminded her of a terrible incident? Or was something else bothering her? He'd been careful not to mention Nathan.

Tires crunched on gravel. Mandy startled. Danny went to the window. A police cruiser pulled into the lot. Doug Lang got out.

"What's he doing here?"

Mandy crossed her arms over her chest. "Mom called him."

Alarm buzzed through Danny. "Why? What happened?"

Mandy looked away. Her pretty mouth tightened in a way that made Danny want to fix everything for her, right after he kissed it. "Bill didn't put the flowers on the porch. He didn't tie that branch over the door either."

Danny shoved a hand through his hair. "I'm sorry I wasn't here earlier."

"I told you. It's OK." But her voice was chilly enough to keep cocktail shrimp fresh.

"No, it's not. I had to meet the insurance guy at Reed's house, but I had plenty of time to stop back here. I just…" *don't feel like much of a man anymore.* "Needed time to think." Christ. He'd almost spilled his girly guts. That would really make him feel more manly. Tune in at six to watch an Iraq war veteran spontaneously grow a vagina.

Danny followed her outside. Together they watched Lieutenant Lang strut across the back lawn. He climbed the three wooden steps onto the porch and stopped a few feet away from them. "OK, what's the problem?"

Mandy pointed at the flowers and the branch over the door. "Someone left those here during the night."

Hands on hips, the cop stared at the container of flowers. "And you think a pot of pansies is threatening?"

"My mother was concerned," she said.

"They're flowers," the lieutenant scoffed. "It was probably your brother. He does weird shit all the time."

Mandy shook her head. "He says he didn't."

The cop's eyes narrowed on the kitchen window. Bill's figure was moving around in the kitchen. "Bill!"

"Don't yell at him," Mandy snapped.

Bill shuffled out the door. His head hung in a way that put Danny's protective instincts on edge. He put a hand on Bill's shoulder and gave it a gentle squeeze. Bill focused on the floorboards.

"Are you sure you didn't put these flowers here for your sister?" The cop had lowered his voice, but his tone was short on patience.

"N-no." Bill backed away from the cop until he was flat against the closed door. "I'd never give Mandy anything like that. It's scary."

The cop rolled his eyes. Bill studied his gigantic sneakers and dug a toe into the doormat.

Mandy stepped in front of her brother. "Lieutenant, I don't appreciate—"

"Hey, Bill?" Danny cut her off. Making a major production out of the cop's assholeness wasn't going to help her brother. Bill's gaze lifted to Danny's knees. "My hand really hurts. Could you get me a bag of ice?"

"Sure, Danny." Bill slunk through the door like a kicked puppy.

The door closed behind Bill. Mandy glared at Lang. "You could be nicer."

"I don't have time to coddle your retarded brother," the cop shot back.

"Do not use that word in my house." Mandy's tone was blast-chiller cold. "It's an insult."

Danny's good hand clenched into a fist, and he itched to plow it straight into the cop's face. But Danny wasn't a teenage trouble-maker anymore, and he wouldn't be much use from a jail cell. He had no doubt the cop would *love* to arrest him. Power-hungry Lang would enjoy arresting anybody.

"Sorry, handicapped. No, mentally challenged. Is that the politically correct term these days? It is what it is, whatever you call it," Lang shot back.

Mandy's eyes narrowed to tiny, furious slits. "You have no right—"

"No right to do what?" Lang interrupted. "Come here when someone calls the police?"

Mandy looked as pissed off as Danny felt. Her glare was a freaking dagger, sharp, pointy, and ready to disembowel the cop standing in front of her.

Lang inflated his chest like a rooster. "Have you asked all your neighbors if they left this for you or if they saw anyone around the inn?"

"Well, no," Mandy admitted. "But none of them would leave me something like this."

"You neighbors never give you anything?" The cop lifted his sunglasses from his nose. Unnaturally large biceps threatened to burst the seams of his too-tight uniform shirt's sleeves.

Mandy sighed. "Mr. Kane gives me cucumbers and tomatoes if he has too many, but nothing like this."

Doug emitted a long-suffering sigh. "Look, Mandy. Everybody knows you like flowers. Maybe one of your neighbors bought too many. In any case, flowers," he glanced at the door, "or a twig are hardly dangerous." He snapped his notebook closed. "I'm busy. I spent the morning hauling a crazy homeless dude into county for a psych evaluation. Claimed an alien with a ray gun tried to abduct him. Please tell your mother not to call the police again unless there's been an actual crime." He pivoted on a heel and strode back to his car.

Mandy put a hand to her forehead. "As much as I hate to admit it, Doug's right. I should have checked with my neighbors." She walked off the porch and around the house. Danny followed. He stood in the background, watching, as she knocked on the houses on either side and talked with the homeowners. The house on the left was owned by an elderly couple, the Kanes, who were too old to be a threat to anyone. Nor had they seen anything or anyone skulking around the inn. On the right, a frazzled young woman opened the door. She jiggled a sleepy toddler on one hip. A baby wailed in the background. Her husband was in Florida on business, and she hadn't slept since he left. There was no way she'd been delivering flowers in the middle of the night. Strike two. The neighbors weren't stalking Mandy.

They returned to the inn. Mandy stomped across the lawn between the houses. In the backyard, she whirled. "I swear, one of these days if Doug Lang ever calls my brother that…that name again, I'm going to punch him right in the nose."

"Whoa." He reached out and rested his hand on her shoulder. "You need to calm down. Bill is upset enough already."

Mandy jerked away. She climbed the steps and sat on the porch swing. "You're right. Doug is such a jerk."

Danny sat next to her. "Lang's a dick. No doubt about it. If it makes you feel better, I wanted to hit him, too. But he would've enjoyed arresting me too much."

Mandy huffed. "You have that right. It would have made his day."

"You can't let people like Doug Lang get to you."

"I hate how he bullies Bill."

"He bullies everybody he can." Danny wrapped an arm around her. He pulled her head to his shoulder. She resisted for a minute, then relaxed with a sigh.

Danny's eyes drifted to the pot of purple blooms. Where else had he seen flowers like that?

"There's something else I never considered." Mandy sat up. "You know who was really close to Nathan?"

"Let me guess," Danny answered. "Lieutenant Doug Lang."

CHAPTER SIXTEEN

"Doug followed Nathan like a loyal dog."

Why hadn't Danny thought of it before? Doug was the perfect person to help Nathan. He would have information about the manhunt and would know where to hide.

"It'd be pretty tough to investigate a cop." Danny rubbed his chin. "Maybe Reed can help us out on this." As a former policeman, Reed would at least know where to start.

"Good idea," Mandy said.

"I'll call him today." Danny tucked her back onto his shoulder.

"Why do you understand my brother better than I do?"

"Because you're too close," Danny said. "I have the advantage of not growing up with him. For example, I think my brothers are giant pains in the ass, but you would probably like them. Most people do."

Mandy laughed. "That makes a lot of sense in a weird way."

"Yep. Weird. That's my family." Danny laughed. "Look, I have no business giving you psychological advice. It's not like I have my shit together." His tone sobered. "I came home from Iraq with a side dish of post-traumatic stress to accompany my injury." He raised his hand and stared at it. "I still seem to be having trouble admitting how bad the damage is."

The door opened. Bill stuck his head out. "Danny? I made that ice pack for you."

"Thanks, man. I appreciate it." Danny gave Mandy's shoulder a pat and got to his feet. They went into the kitchen. A ziplock bag of ice lay on the counter. Danny dutifully put the ice on his hand. He glanced at Bill. Mandy's brother sat on a stool at the island and rocked back and forth in a quick rhythm.

"How about a snack, Bill?" Mandy asked.

"I'm not hungry." Bill shook his head and continued to rock.

Danny tried. "How about we go watch *Star Wars* together?"

Bill hugged himself. "I don't wanna."

With a silent curse at the cop, Danny looked to Mandy. She had the phone in her hand and was punching numbers. "Jed, could you bring Honey over for a while?" She glanced back at Bill. "I'll tell you later." Pause. "Pretty bad." She put the phone back in its charging cradle and spoke to her brother. "Honey's coming over, Bill."

He paused for a second before picking up his rhythm again. Helplessness filled Danny's chest.

The fifteen minutes that followed while they waited felt much longer. At the sound of tires on gravel, Bill's head turned a few inches. A minute later, Jed knocked on the back door. Mandy let him in. Honey raced to Bill. The dog butted her head against his knee until he slid from the chair to the floor. She leaned her body against his chest and rested her head on his shoulder. He hugged her close and went still.

Finally. Danny let out the breath dammed in his lungs. The pressure in his chest abated.

"Thanks." Mandy wiped a tear from her eye.

Danny didn't blame her. The sight of the dog calming Bill threatened to make Danny's eyes misty.

"Works every time." Jed nodded with satisfaction. "Want me to leave her here for the night?"

"That would be really helpful." Mandy's voice cracked.

Jed's eyes softened. "OK, then. I'll come back for her in the morning." He jingled his keys in his hand.

"Thanks, Jed. I don't know what I'd do without you and Honey." Mandy opened the door for him.

Jed slipped out of the house, but not before Danny caught the wounded look in his eyes.

Something was off with him. Murmuring brought Danny's attention back to Bill and the dog. It almost seemed as if Honey was holding him still.

"That's a terrific dog," Danny said.

"She's special." Bill hugged her close. Honey licked his face.

While Bill communed with the dog, Mandy started the breakfast prep. She kneaded dough and mixed batter, but she kept one eye on her brother until he seemed to be back to normal. Danny hoped the company and conversation eased her workload. He wished he could do more.

Bill glanced at the oven clock. "Oh, it's time for *Phineas and Ferb*." He rushed from the room, the dog plastered to his side.

"Honey's uncanny." Mandy went to the fridge and pulled out a pitcher of iced tea. "I don't understand how she knows what to do." She poured two glasses and set one in front of Danny. Mandy took the sandwich bag, now just full of cold water, from Danny. "Did you really need ice?"

"Not really. It was all I could think of on the spot." He flexed his fingers and grimaced.

"Does it hurt?"

"Just stiff." He winced. "I don't have much feeling from the elbow down. In fact, I had no business handling a knife this morning. I have permanent nerve damage from the explosion. My fingers get shaky. I've had trouble accepting that isn't going to change."

"That's understandable." Mandy loaded the last pan of muffins into the oven and set the timer. "Thanks for being nice to my brother."

Danny's brow creased. "Why wouldn't I be nice to him?"

"Lots of people aren't."

"Yeah. Assholes." He stood up and rounded the island to stand in front of her.

"I've even had guys fake being nice to Bill to get close to me," Mandy said. Even years later, the memories were a shocking stab of reality. "Then once they realized it wouldn't work, they'd never bother with him again. It was hard on him."

"Is that what you think I'm doing?" Danny brushed a hand across her cheek. "You had flour on your face."

"I'm not the neatest baker." She looked up at him. *Hold your ground.* But the sincerity in his eyes was too much to resist. Danny was too much to resist. Her shoulders fell forward as her resolve crumbled. "No. I don't. But it's not fair to him to make him like you. You'll leave, and he'll be heartbroken again, like he was when Reed moved.

"Bill can come and visit Reed anytime." His fingers trailed along her jaw.

Mandy shook her head. "Bill has anxiety attacks when he leaves Huntsville. As soon as he doesn't recognize where he is, he loses it."

Danny inched closer. "I've seen the scar. What happened to him?"

"When he was a baby, he and my father were in a bad car accident. Bill almost died. He was left with a traumatic brain injury that affected everything from his mental development to his coordination. Physically, he's a large man, like my father, but Bill didn't progress much beyond a cognitive age of seven. No, that's not fair. He's more complicated than that; for example, his language skills are pretty good, but the whole concept of math doesn't make sense to him. His emotions aren't easy to pin down either. For instance, he seemed to understand my mom's heart attack, and he was a big help taking care of her. I expected him to freak out. He didn't. He even went to the hospital to see her, even though he hates strangers and prefers everything to be routine."

"What happened to your father?"

"He walked out one night and never came back. Just like that." She snapped her fingers. The memory of that night was as clear as the conversation she and Danny were having right now. She could hear her mother's pleas and her father's excuses. She could see the door close behind him and feel the stab of betrayal and loss. The pain of his abandonment was a permanent splinter lodged in her soul. It was part of her. Could she let it go the way Danny had put his parents' deaths behind him?

"I'm sorry." Danny stepped closer.

"I don't know how my mom managed. It's hard enough now, taking care of her and Bill and keeping the inn going."

"She's a strong woman." Danny wrapped his arms around her. He pulled her close. She didn't resist. Leaning against his chest felt right. Like the strain of the past twenty years since her father left was bearable. "And so are you."

Danny stroked her back. She arched under his touch.

"Geez, you're tense. You need a massage."

"Good luck finding a spa around here. We live in the middle of nowhere, if you hadn't noticed." Though Danny's hands would suit nicely. Mandy had never been so tired. Every part of her body ached. His fingers rubbed a knot between her shoulder blades. She nearly purred.

Danny laughed. "Believe me. I noticed."

And there it was. Danny would never stay in Huntsville. Her mother was right. She pushed out of his arms, her muscles coiling tight as springs.

"I can't do this." She left the kitchen.

"Do what?" Danny called as the door to the apartment closed.

In her room, Mandy locked the door. What was she thinking? He'd almost kissed her. She'd wanted him to kiss her.

Nothing could happen between her and Danny. To remind herself why, she lifted the corner of her mattress and stared at the threatening pictures.

She briefly contemplated calling the state police. No doubt Detective Rossi would come to the same conclusion as Lang. A pot of flowers was hardly a threat. Many people knew that pansies were her favorite spring flower. If she hadn't been so busy, the inn's front walk would be lined with them already.

She couldn't risk telling anyone about the threats, not with potentially two stalkers moving freely about town. The state police were too far away to protect her family, and Huntsville's own Doug Lang was useless. Danny would tire of Huntsville in a week or so and go back to Philadelphia. Mandy was on her own.

She needed to be prepared to protect what was hers.

Mandy did what she always did when she needed help. She called Jed, the one man she knew she could depend on. "I know you just left, but can you come back and stay with Bill and my mom for an hour or two?"

"Sure. What's up?"

She unlocked the gun safe in her closet and took out a box of bullets. "I need to run a few errands."

"Um. OK."

By the time Mandy was ready fifteen minutes later, Jed had returned. Danny was nowhere in sight.

Damn. Damn. Damn. How did he fuck that up?

By pushing too hard, too fast, stupid.

But all he'd been offering was a hug. What kind of shit would make a move on a woman who was that upset?

Danny rubbed his forehead. He unlocked the back door and went out onto the porch. His eyes locked on the flowerpot. Guess it wasn't evidence. He contemplated putting it in his trunk and dropping it in the nearest dumpster. But something stopped him. Maybe they weren't evidence right now, but if something else were to hit the fan, who knew?

He hefted the pot first. Damn thing was heavy. He put his bad forearm under the bottom for support. Pain shot up his arm. Bad idea. The container plopped to the ground. Danny dragged it across the back lawn to the concrete apron in front of the garage. He pulled on the overhead door. It wasn't locked and gave way to his tug. He shoved the pot of flowers against the wall. He jogged back to the porch and removed the branch from over the back door. He returned to the garage and tucked it behind the container. Just in case something else happened and the authorities suddenly decided the seemingly harmless items were important clues.

Now what? His arm twitched like a puppet, and the needles of pain had become nails. As much as he hated to admit it, he needed a break. He went through the empty inn. All the other guests were out pursuing their chosen outdoor adventures.

In his room, Danny stretched out on the bed. He elevated his arm on a pillow and dialed Reed's number on his cell.

Reed picked up on the first ring. "Are you OK?"

"I'm fine. I just wanted to ask you a question."

"Shoot."

"What do you think the chances are that Nathan had an accomplice here in town?"

"Besides his uncle?"

"Yeah." Danny adjusted his arm on the pillow. "I was thinking the local cop, Lang, was awfully obnoxious."

"That's Doug." Reed sounded disgusted. "He's a total jerk, but I can't see him helping Nathan. He was pretty shook up when he found out what Nathan had done."

"Still, they were close, right?"

"Yes, they were." Reed was quiet for a few seconds. "Do you want me to call Detective Rossi and run it by him?"

"Do you think that's the right move? Rossi didn't seem too helpful."

"Rossi's a good cop." Confidence projected through Reed's voice. "Sometimes you just can't get a break on a case."

"I'll take your word for it."

"In fact, why don't you come home and let Rossi handle this?" Reed asked. "Jayne's worried about you."

"Not yet. I want to check a few more things."

"OK. I'll call Rossi and ask him to check Doug out. Take care of yourself, Danny, for Jayne."

"I will. Thanks." Danny punched END.

A car door slammed. He got up and went to the window. Jed was walking from his truck to the house. A second later, Mandy crossed the lawn and got into an old Subaru wagon. She pulled out of the lot. Alone.

CHAPTER SEVENTEEN

Danny rushed down the stairs and into the kitchen.

Jed was sitting at the island eating a fresh muffin. He looked up at Danny. "What?"

"Where's she going?"

"The range."

"The range?"

"The shooting club." Jed got up and pulled a coffee mug from the cabinet over the coffeepot. "When you carry a gun, it's important to practice regularly."

"Mandy carries a gun?"

"Of course." Jed's already prominent brow dropped. "I wouldn't let her run around alone without one."

Danny digested that tidbit for a few seconds. He knew plenty of people who had guns in their homes, but not very many carried a firearm. "Why didn't you go with her?"

"Because she asked me to stay with her mother and brother." Jed poured coffee. "Look, I don't like it any more than you do. But do you really think it's possible for her to not go anywhere alone for four months, while at the same time making sure her family is looked after?"

"I guess not," Danny said.

"Mandy might be small and pretty, but as much as I hate to admit it, she *can* handle herself." Pride tinted Jed's voice.

"How do I get to the range?" After Jed gave him general directions, Danny went out the back door, jogged to his car, and drove out onto the street. A few turns later, he spotted Mandy's green Subaru. He followed her. She took a side street and drove through a section of residential homes that declined in value and upkeep as they left the main business section. Glossy shutters and wide lawns gave way to narrow lots and peeling paint. Deep green grass shifted to clover. She came to a stop sign. He saw her glance in her rearview mirror.

Snagged.

Danny waved. Mandy ignored him and continued out of the town proper. A couple of miles later she turned onto a dirt lane. A sign read Huntsville Gun Club. Danny parked next to her in a dry but rutted lot. "What are you doing?"

"Making sure I'm able to protect my family." She grabbed a nylon bag from the passenger seat, closed the car door, and walked away from him. Danny hurried to catch up.

It was an outdoor shooting range. No store. Just a shack with a soda machine under the overhang. A long wooden roof on posts angled away from the rough building. Underneath, picnic tables were spaced end to end. Targets dotted the expanse of meadow that stretched away from the tables. Big grass berms rose at the rear of the range to catch stray bullets.

Two men were popping off shots with handguns. Mandy gave them an absent wave and set her nylon bag on a center table. She pulled out ear protection, both foam plugs and over-the-ear muffs, and safety glasses. "If you're going to stand there, put these on." Without looking at him, she handed Danny the muffs. She rummaged around in her bag, dug out a spare pair of protective glasses, and handed them over. She looked all business. He did what he was told. When Danny's sister eyeballed him like that, he knew better than to argue.

Mandy pulled a revolver out from under her sweatshirt. What the fuck?

"Where did you get that?" he yelled.

With a sigh, Mandy pulled the foam plugs out of her ears. "I've had a concealed carry permit for years, but I admit, until this winter, I didn't carry that often."

"But you do now?"

"Every minute of every day." She put the plugs back in and turned back to the range. Danny noticed the two other guys had stopped shooting. They were watching Mandy.

She took her stance, brought the gun to level with both hands, and squeezed off five rounds at the twenty-foot target, hitting it smack center each time. She reloaded and put the next five into the next target with equally impressive aim.

Well, damn. She could outshoot Danny any day. He'd been a decent shot before his injury, but he hadn't won any awards for marksmanship. From the disgusted expressions of the other two dudes, they sucked even more. They packed up and cleared out before she could reload.

Mandy looked back at him. "Have you tried shooting since you got hurt?"

He shook his head.

"Do you want to?"

Danny took the gun and stepped up to the table. He popped off a couple of rounds one-handed and missed with every freaking one. Not unexpected. His military sidearm had been a 9mm, which had a whole different feel than Mandy's .38 revolver. Plus, he was sadly out of practice. He loaded the gun and raised his arm, confident that with a little practice, his aim would return.

"Wait." Mandy stepped up behind him. Her arm came around his body. She lifted the forearm of his wounded hand, her fingers sliding along his skin. "I know you can't use this hand, but if you can hold this arm across your body and tighten your chest, it'll give you more stability."

His chest? Yeah, like *that* was what had gone tight.

She put his arm into position, wrapping around him in the process. Damn. How long could they stand like this? He'd gladly fire all his rounds into the dirt if she'd hug him a little tighter.

"Try again."

Danny sighed. He sighted on the twenty-foot target and squeezed. *Pop, pop, pop.*

His first two shots went wide. The third smacked into the left edge of the target with a quiet *whoomp.*

"That's better." Mandy snuggled up closer. Her thighs cradled his. Her head tilted toward him. Danny inhaled. The faint scent of flowers drifted over the smells of dirt, grass, and forest.

"Mmm. Much better." Oh, yeah. This shooting lesson could go on all day. He put his next two shots exactly where he wanted them, two feet short of the target. The bullets hit the ground with little puffs of dust. "How did you learn to do that?"

Mandy's hand gripped his shoulder. "Jed's daddy showed me. I broke my left wrist in high school. Couldn't use it to shoot for months."

"You and Jed have always been close?"

"Best friends since grade school." Mandy slid her hand to his elbow. Danny squeezed off another shot to keep her interested. His bullet hit the base of the target. For a woman who worked so hard, her fingers were soft. Strong, though, too. And that was Mandy, an intriguing combination of soft and strong. "My father left us. Jed's daddy reluctantly let me tag along. I'm not sure why. He had very strict guidelines about women's roles, but for some reason, he didn't apply them to me. Maybe because he felt sorry for me, or maybe it was because I was just a kid. I was a scrawny tomboy until I hit sixteen."

Enough about Jed and his daddy. Danny took another shot, sending a bullet into the middle of the target.

"Oh, look." The pitch in Mandy's voice rose to girly excited, which was funny considering they were at possibly the most masculine place on earth this side of a strip bar. "You hit it, dead center."

Satisfied that he could shoot where he aimed, Danny lowered the weapon. "You're a good teacher." He unloaded the gun and placed the safety gear on the table. A quick scan of the range and parking lot assured him they were alone. He turned to face Mandy. Empty and quiet, the range was peaceful. He lifted the glasses from her face.

"You already knew how to shoot." She tossed her earplugs into her bag.

"Haven't touched a gun in more than a year, though." Despite all his time in the military, Danny wasn't a firearm enthusiast. But he appreciated a gun's ability to keep a person alive.

Mandy shifted her weight to move away from him. Danny stopped her with a hand on her hip. He leaned down to get another whiff of her hair. Her blue eyes went dark and wide. Danny brushed his lips against hers. She stiffened for a split second, then sighed against his mouth, as if she didn't have the energy to fight their attraction anymore. Her eyes closed as he tasted. Just a sip.

He slid his hand around to the small of her back and eased her closer. Her hips nestled into his. A perfect fit. But Danny held back, remembering her skittishness in the kitchen. He kept his kisses light and strictly outside the mouth.

Until she pressed against him. Her lips parted, but it was the feminine moan that challenged his control.

Mandy wanted him.

Danny angled his mouth to take more. He deepened the kiss. Her mouth was hot and sweeter than her cinnamon bread. A groan worked its way out of his chest. Raw and powerful, it echoed what was going on in the rest of his body. Need. Fire. Everywhere.

Mandy tilted her head away. She blinked up at him, her eyes showing equal amounts of desire and confusion. Yeah. That about summed it up.

When she moved away, he let her go. "We shouldn't have done that."

That was so not what Danny was going to say. A lot of thoughts were flying though his head. *Wow. Holy shit. Incredible.* But Danny didn't have a single ounce of regret.

Unfortunately, Mandy had enough for both of them.

"I have to get back." She brushed past him to pack up her supplies.

"Mandy." Danny caught her bicep. "What's wrong? Talk to me."

With her eyes firmly fixed on her bag, she shook her head.

"There isn't anything you can't tell me."

Her gaze lifted to his. There were many things swirling around in the beautiful blue of her eyes. Regret. Sadness. Determination. "You have to go."

But the lust was gone.

Sometimes retreat was the best option. The object was to win the war, not necessarily every single battle. "OK. We'll go."

He reached for the nylon straps of her bag.

Mandy stopped him with a hand on his forearm. "No, you have to go back to Philadelphia. All you're doing here is stirring up things best left settled."

"Nothing feels settled to me." Danny crossed his arms over his chest. "I'm not going anywhere."

Danny cruised down the main drag past dark shop after dark shop. Most of the local businesses closed at six. He pulled into a strip mall and parked in front of a pizza joint. He ordered a large pie with mushrooms and a Coke.

Hours had passed, and Mandy's rebuff still stung as badly as if she'd slapped him across the face. When they were alone next, she wasn't getting away so easily. Of course, he seriously doubted she'd ever let them be alone again. She'd successfully hidden from him all afternoon. He'd even skipped lunch in hopes of seeing her, but she hadn't ventured into the public areas of the inn all afternoon.

She wanted to forget their kiss along with the case. Danny couldn't get either out of his head.

The waitress brought his pizza. The aroma of hot cheese and spices wafted to his nose. Danny's stomach rumbled, and he wolfed down slices in rapid succession. He took the remaining few to go.

He started the engine and rested his left wrist on the wheel. His fingers trembled, but they weren't dancing like this morning when the doctor had stitched him up. Apparently, that rest thing really worked.

Since Mandy wasn't talking, Danny had to find another information source. Who else knew stuff about Nathan? Like the identity of the secret girlfriend, for instance.

The Challenger drove past the clinic all by itself. Smart car. Danny did a double take. The flowers from the doctor's window boxes looked like the same kind that had been left on the inn's back porch. Bingo. He knew he'd seen them somewhere. Wishing he drove something less noticeable, Danny found an alley to park in a block away. The streets were deserted, but he strolled back to the doc's office in the shadows just in case anyone was looking out a window.

Danny stopped in the shadow of a thick shrub. Lights still glowed in the clinic windows. Dr. Chandler had said his office closed at five. Was the good doctor working late? Or was he up to deeds best done in the dark?

The front door opened. Someone hurried out. A woman, from the shape and movement of her shadow. She passed under a streetlight. Carolyn Fitzgerald. She was stuffing a small package into her purse. Interesting. She didn't look terribly ill or injured or anything else that would cause the doctor to keep his office open late to see her. The real estate agent strode to her car, parked at the curb fifty yards down the street. The engine turned over, and the car pulled out into the street and headed away from town. Red taillights faded into the dark.

The clinic went dark room by room, starting at the front. A few minutes later, Danny watched an SUV pull out of the alley that ran next to the clinic.

Nothing moved, not even Danny. Patience was, if not a virtue, a necessity when casing an establishment. A cool night breeze shifted Danny's evergreen screen. A car passed, the headlights sweeping within five feet of his feet. The street went silent and dark, and Danny emerged.

He opted for the back door. Did the doctor have a security system? Danny popped the locks, opened the door, and waited. The building remained quiet. Guess not.

He slipped through the door into the darkness of the hall. His eyes had already adjusted to the night. Danny borrowed a handful of latex gloves from the first exam room. Handy, with the breaking and entering and all. Snapping a pair on, he stuffed the extras in his pocket. Inside the doc's office, Danny used his flashlight to illuminate the hanging files inside the cabinets. He searched three drawers before finding files for Nathan and his uncle.

Read them or steal them?

He did a quick perusal. Lots of info.

The overhead light snapped on. "What the fuck?"

Uh-oh.

CHAPTER EIGHTEEN

"What part of patient confidentiality do you not understand?" Dr. Chandler glared from the doorway.

Danny closed the file and stood. "The part that might keep me from finding a killer."

"Don't you think that if I knew anything that might lead to Nathan's arrest, I'd have told the police?"

"Well, I'd hope."

"Dammit." The doctor threw up his hands. "You know they subpoenaed copies of all his medical records, right?"

"Um. No." *My bad*, Danny thought.

"Well, they did, and I'll bet the cops read through them pretty carefully. But what do they know, right?"

Well, didn't Danny feel like an idiot. "Just because they're cops doesn't mean they're perfect."

The doc gave him a you've-got-to-be-kidding-me look. "It doesn't matter. I can't give anybody access to my clients' records without a court order. It's illegal and against my oath."

Shit. Danny hated when people brought superior morals into a discussion. He'd always seen things in shades of gray, specifically when things like breaking the law for the greater good were concerned. "Did you know a man and his son are missing?"

"What?" Dr. Chandler ran a hand through his hair.

"A fisherman and his kid just vanished on a family camping trip. There's been no sign of them despite an extensive search."

"I read about that. Sadly, they probably drowned." The doctor waved a hand. "Doesn't excuse you for breaking into my office."

"Remember what really happened the last time a couple of outdoorsmen went missing?"

The doctor's eyes narrowed. "You think this disappearance is related to the hikers Nathan and his uncle kidnapped last December?"

"Seems odd to have them occur back-to-back in the same area."

"Maybe. Or it could be a giant coincidence. Huntsville is in the middle of the woods. People get lost out there every year." The doctor scratched his head. "What does any of this have to do with Nathan's medical records? All they show is that the man has a brain disease. He isn't sane anymore. What more do you need to know?"

"Who filled your window boxes?"

"What?"

"The flowers out front. Who planted them?"

"I have no idea." The doctor scratched his head. "My receptionist maybe, or the town business chamber. I don't have time for flowers."

"I think someone has been helping Nathan."

"Well, shit." The doctor dropped into a chair in front of his desk. "What makes you think that?"

"This whole area was searched multiple times. If he's in the area, somebody has been keeping him under the radar." Danny told him about the flowers on the inn's porch and the branch nailed over the back door.

"That's crazy. Nathan's probably dead." Doc sighed. "But even if your wild theory is correct, you can't think I had anything to do with it?"

"I don't know you, and you were evasive when I asked about Nathan."

"Of course I was evasive," the doctor snapped. "Doctors don't talk about patients. Mandy doesn't think I'm in collusion with Nathan, does she?"

Danny shook his head. "Mandy doesn't know I'm here." Doubt flickered in Danny's gut. He probably shouldn't have told the doctor that no one knew he'd come here.

The doctor gave him a thoughtful stare. "I should call Doug and have you arrested."

Danny stared back. "You could do that."

Dr. Chandler's mouth tightened. "I'm giving you a second chance, based on your altruistic motives." The doctor stood. His fingers moved in a give-it-here gesture. "But I'll take my file back."

Danny handed it over.

"Honestly, there's nothing in there of any use." The doctor shook the file at Danny. "Now get the hell out of here."

The hair on the back of Danny's neck was going haywire. Had that been a threat? Was the doctor hiding something, or was he merely adhering to his medical oath?

Danny did not wait for the doc to change his mind. But that didn't mean the doctor was off his suspect list. Nathan's file had been awfully thick, and the volumes of specialized medical books told Danny that Dr. Chandler knew a lot more about Campbell's Insomnia than he was willing to share. Plus, there was the late-night business between the doctor and the real estate agent to consider.

For a small town, Huntsville held a lot of secrets.

⁂

The sound of female chatter carried over the running faucet. With one eye on the clock, Mandy rinsed a baking pan. She shut off the water with her elbow, then dried the pan and stowed it in the cabinet. On the opposite side of the kitchen island, Danny glared at her. At least he'd waited until she finished with breakfast.

There was only so long she could avoid him. This morning he hadn't come down to offer any help with breakfast. Unfortunately, she'd missed his company more than she wanted to admit. After the kiss, she'd hidden—yes, hidden—in the apartment, only venturing into the kitchen to do the breakfast prep after she'd seen his car pull out of the lot in the evening.

But now that he was here, full of questions, she didn't want to talk to him.

"Were you serious yesterday? Do you really want me to leave?"

No. Mandy pictured her brother with his throat slit like bleeding game, like the boy Nathan's uncle had killed last fall. The boy who'd been decapitated. "Yes."

He glared at her from the other side of the kitchen island. "I can't leave until I have some answers." The sexy warmth in his voice was gone. Damn, she really missed it. Almost as much as she missed the contact with his lean body and his masculine scent in her nose. She could pretend that she didn't need a man, but Danny was a constant reminder of what she was missing. It went beyond physical contact. Being with a man made her feel like a woman, not a sister or a daughter or an innkeeper. A woman. Desirable. An individual who didn't exist solely to take care of others.

It was a feeling no one in her hometown evoked. Just Danny.

Unfortunately, her first loyalty was to her family's needs, not her own. Speaking of which…

Mandy ducked into the family apartment. The buzzing and whooshing of a lightsaber battle sounded from behind her brother's closed door. Her mother and two friends were sitting on the living-room sofa, drinking coffee and munching on fresh blueberry muffins. "Mom, do you all need anything before I go?"

Her mother waved her off. "We're fine. You go right ahead, dear."

Mandy returned to the kitchen. Leaning a hip on the counter, arms crossed over his chest, Danny hadn't budged. He would not be so easy to dissuade. Once again, she considered trusting him with everything. What would he do if she simply told him the truth? Would he go away if she asked him? She looked at him. His expression was tight and angry, with an undercurrent of aggression in his posture. He was a soldier. A fighter. Unlike her, he wasn't a person who would roll over for a blackmailer. But what choice did she have? How did one fight an unknown enemy?

No, she couldn't take the chance. Danny had to leave. "What if there aren't any answers?"

"Then I don't know." Danny paced two steps, pivoted, and strode back. "But I can't go until I've taken care of Reed's house. Plus, I have this...this feeling that something very bad is coming. I can't explain it."

The dishwasher emitted a hiss of steam. He was right. There was a real *Something Wicked This Way Comes* vibe to the air, minus the carnival fun.

"Then don't you want to get out of its path?"

"And leave you to face it alone?" Danny stopped pacing. The glance he fired at her was full of possession that Mandy wished didn't make her feminine heart thump. Damn her sentimental heart. "No."

She didn't have a response. She flipped the keys around in her hand. "Look, I have a short window of time this morning while the ladies from my mother's church are here. I have to attend the chamber meeting and run some errands on my way back." Grabbing her handbag and keys, she started toward the door. "We'll talk about it later." And she'd think of some way to make him go home.

She went out into the backyard. Danny followed and fell into step beside her. "I'll come with you."

"That's not necessary." She rested her hand on the gun at the back of her hip. The weapon was well concealed by her bulky sweater. The sun, unusually warm for April, hit her back. Sweat broke out between her shoulder blades. "As you know, I can protect myself."

"Against a deadly sack of sand, yeah." Danny spun around. "Shooting a person is a much different experience. For instance, people move. They shoot back. And sometimes they look you right in the eye and remind you they're human. If you can't kill them, you're dead." Danny's voice cracked.

Mandy stopped, remembering he'd been to war. How many people had he killed? Did their deaths haunt him at night? "I'm sorry."

Danny kept walking. There was no cowardice in his strides, just pent-up fury and determination. No. Danny would never walk away from a challenge. He'd meet it head-on. No matter what it cost him. Or her.

He had to go.

Mandy got into her car and started the engine. She did not invite him to ride with her. On the way to the meeting, she pictured the chamber members. Other than her, they were probably the people closest to Nathan.

Was one of the chamber members blackmailing her? She hoped so. The thought of insane Nathan freely running around her backyard sent paralyzing fear into her bones. She doubted he was dead. Nathan was a survivor. It was in his bones. Even if he wanted to give up, he wouldn't be able to. Persistence was a genetic flaw. Nathan couldn't help himself.

She heard Danny's car start up.

Just as Danny couldn't leave until he'd exhausted all his opportunities to free his sister from fear.

Nathan was a gregarious and charismatic man, but he didn't have close personal friendships. As far as she knew, he had family and business associates and Mandy. She couldn't even remember him dating anyone, ever. Huntsville was a small town. Rumors spread like crabgrass in a pristine lawn. If Nathan had had any other affairs, he'd ventured to another town or he'd concealed them as well as he'd kept their relationship secret. Had he chatted up another lonely woman? Charmed her with his sad story? Told her how beautiful she was and made her feel special?

Could he have had another secret affair? Discomfort tempted her to brush the idea away. It was bad enough he'd charmed her and lied to her. To think she was just one of many was somehow worse.

Mandy turned onto Main Street, drove a few blocks, and made a left. Since the diner had closed and the municipal building burned down, the coffee shop/bookstore had taken over as the gossip hub of Huntsville. The chamber of commerce met there every week for coffee. Usually she let her mom handle town politics, but Mandy had taken over that aspect of their business as well. She'd blown off the last few meetings, but today she was going to change her ways. As the former mayor and owner of the town diner, Nathan had dealt with the town business committee on a constant basis. What did his associates know about him?

It was just ten o'clock when she rushed into Ray's Books 'N Brew and took the stairs to the second floor. The smell of Ray's signature freshly ground dark roast hit her hard. She splurged on a latte and a cinnamon bun. As much as she enjoyed cooking, sometimes food she didn't have to prepare tasted all the sweeter.

"Mandy! Over here." The shop owner, Ray, waved from a small table. He gestured to the empty chair across from him.

Empty because no one wanted to sit with the annoying little man, including Mandy. But dorky Ray knew everything that went on in town. With a sigh, Mandy wove her way through more than twenty people gathered in a space meant for twelve. Folks leaned on walls and perched on the wooden railing around the eatery.

She hung her purse on the back of the chair and sat. "Hi, Ray."

Ray flushed from the base of his crewneck sweater to the top of his completely bald head. "Hi, Mandy."

Ugh.

Dr. Chandler crossed the landing. He ordered a black coffee, turned around, and leaned against the counter. Lines around his eyes suggested he seriously needed the brew. Real estate agent Carolyn Fitzgerald looked like she'd rather be anywhere but the meeting. As usual, the older woman was decked out in a flashy suit, full makeup, and modern haircut. Her war paint, Mandy thought. Carolyn was no wimp. Despite her problems, she suited up and took on each day as it came.

Ray unwrapped a lollipop and pulled his reading glasses off the neck of his sweater before bringing the meeting to order with a rap of his knuckles on the table. "The first item on the agenda today is that we still don't have a single candidate for someone to replace Nathan as mayor." Ray lifted the glasses from his face and scanned the now-silent room.

Someone coughed. Shoes scraped on the wood floor. There was a pointed lack of eye contact. Mandy sipped her latte.

"Ian, how about you?" Ray suggested. "You'd make an excellent mayor."

The doctor lowered his coffee from his mouth. "You mean in my spare time?"

A round of chuckles met his sarcasm.

"Regardless, the town needs leadership." Ray turned both palms up in plea. "Surely one of our esteemed business leaders will step up, unless you want some outsider to take office. Someone who wouldn't understand what we need to do to stay afloat."

"Face it, Ray. No one wants the job," Carolyn said. "You could always run yourself."

"I already run the chamber. There's only so much one man can do." Ray's forefinger moved on his notes. "OK. We'll shelve that discussion at present. Moving on to the new municipal building. The town council approved the plans. Construction should begin in the next month. Hopefully, we'll have our regular meeting place back before next winter."

"What about the diner? How long will it take for the town to take it over?" someone asked.

Good question. The boarded-up restaurant was a blight on the town's image and echoed Mandy's depression.

Carolyn raised her hand. "I can answer this, Ray. If things stay as is, the town will have to wait for taxes to go into arrears. They'll file a tax lien. Eventually, if Nathan doesn't come back, the property will go up for auction. It will take time."

"Couldn't someone run his business for him until he comes back?" Ray asked.

"Who cares?" Steve, the gift shop proprietor, raised a flannel-shirted arm. "He's a murderer."

"And probably dead," added Ralph, the taxidermist, also dressed in the latest lumberjack attire.

Ray banged his mug on the table. Coffee sloshed over the rim. "We don't know any of that is true."

"Give it up, Ray. Nathan went nutso. No need to suck up to him anymore." Steve laughed.

Ralph snickered. "The real reason Ray can't run for mayor is because he's not flexible enough to kiss his own ass."

While hilarity ensued, Mandy pondered Ray's concern. How close was he to Nathan? Ray's business had picked up considerably without the diner as competition. He should be glad the diner was closed.

Ray stood and pointed at Steve. "What happened to innocent until proven guilty? Doesn't Nathan deserve our support?"

Steve got to his feet and towered over Ray. "He gave up the rights to our support when he killed that kid and our police chief. Hugh was a good man."

"Innocent people don't run away." Ralph nodded. "Nathan's business is the least of his worries. If he shows up in town, we'll issue a bounty on his head."

Steve huffed. "You won't need to."

No love lost there.

Ray knocked on the table. "Let's get back to business and let the police handle the case."

Steve sank back into his chair and crossed his arms over his chest. "What happens if somebody stumbles across Nathan's decomposing body?"

Ray crunched his lollipop between his molars, no doubt yearning for the cigarettes he'd given up the prior year. "Then it becomes an estate issue. Let's move on to the next item on our agenda."

Mandy scanned the other faces. No one else seemed to be bothered by the thought of Nathan's death. Was she reading motives into Ray's behavior?

The next fifteen minutes were spent arguing about the spring beautification campaign. Business owners on Main Street squabbled for position. Carolyn looked like she wanted to stick a fork in her eye, and Mandy remembered why she let her mother be the inn's representative at these meetings whenever possible.

With another impatient and annoying tap of his knuckles, Ray brought the meeting to a close. People started milling about. Mandy stood, bumping into Carolyn as the real estate agent hurried down the aisle.

"Oh, excuse me." Mandy wiped a few drops of spilled coffee from the table. "Any idea how long it will take for the diner to go into arrears?"

"No." Carolyn snapped. Her eyes sharpened. "Why do you care? Are you thinking of buying it?"

"No, but vacant buildings aren't good for the town's image." Or her peace of mind.

"True." Carolyn's whole face sagged with a frown. "But who would buy it? This place isn't exactly Manhattan." She stared at her pumps and toyed with her necklace, sliding it back and forth on its chain.

Steve butted into the conversation. "Mandy's right. A boarded-up restaurant on Main Street is an eyesore. It's only three doors from my gift shop. Can't the town declare eminent domain or something? We could bulldoze it and do something else with the space."

"The situation is what it is, Steve. There's nothing anyone can do to rush due process of law." Sounding defeated, Carolyn waved off any more discussion. "I have to get back to work."

"Me, too. Nice to see you," Mandy said to Carolyn's back. Steve rejoined the larger group. The real estate agent exited without her usual round of good-byes. Mandy looked around for Ray. He was arguing with Steve and Ralph.

Danny was ordering from the barista. His back was to her.

Mandy headed for the steps. She glanced back at the group. No one was looking at her. They were all still engaged.

At the bottom of the stairway, she turned down a hallway toward the restrooms. Without giving herself a chance to chicken out, she opened the door marked OFFICE. Light streamed through the tilted miniblinds. Ray's office was clean and neat. A computer monitor occupied the corner of a utilitarian metal desk. The center of the desktop was clear, except for paperwork neatly piled in the IN and OUT bins. Mandy skimmed through the papers. Invoices, inventory, employee time cards. Nothing unusual. She opened the desk drawers and perused the contents. Boring.

Mandy stooped in front of the credenza and skimmed through the hanging files. In the last drawer she found a folder full of newspaper articles about December's crimes and the subsequent search for Nathan. Was Ray simply keeping up with news?

Something scuffed in the hallway.

CHAPTER NINETEEN

Boston, June 22, 1975

Nathan shivered in the early morning damp.

"You cannot tell your dad about this day, Nathan." Uncle Aaron's oars cut through a layer of swirling predawn fog and dipped into the glassy surface of the lake. The old wooden rowboat creaked as his uncle shifted his weight back and pulled on the long handles. Muscles rippled. The boat glided forward into the quiet morning. "He won't understand."

Uncle Aaron paused, forearms resting on his thighs, waiting for Nathan's response. Water dripped from the blade of an oar into the smooth, dark water. Tiny waves rippled away from the hull. Nathan dipped the tips of his fingers into the silky liquid. The lake was deep here. If he slipped over the side, he could just sink into cool nothing.

What was death like? A painless fade of consciousness? Or could a person feel the soul being ripped from his body?

"Nathan? Swear."

"OK." He felt like he was cheating. The promise was too easy. Dad didn't have the time or energy to talk anyway. His whole life was taking care of Mom, who didn't do much except pace and twitch and ramble. Nathan wasn't sure she even recognized him. He tried to picture her smiling but couldn't. Overwhelming sadness rose, scratchy and salty in his throat. He reached for the small cooler Uncle Aaron had stashed between their seats and pulled out a Coke. The bubbles burned on their way down, but he welcomed the discomfort. At least it made him feel alive.

Uncle Aaron stopped rowing and rested the oars across the peeling paint of the seats. Water lapped against the side of the boat. He scanned the shoreline all around. They were in the dead center of the lake. Dawn edged over the horizon, and the eastern sky brightened to watercolor pink.

"But what are we doing out here?" Nathan watched his uncle's sweating face. Uncle Aaron preferred the cold of winter to a Boston summer's heat and humidity. He said his blood was thick from his Scottish highlands boyhood. Nathan's head was full of his uncle's stories: living in the shadow of mountains that held on to their white caps year-round, wind whipping across the high plateaus, sleeping in the cold loft of a tiny cottage, burning peat, whatever that was, in an iron stove for heat.

"We're asking the gods to cure your ma."

"Dad took me to church yesterday. The priest said a blessing, and we lit a candle for her." He'd been praying as hard as he could, but it didn't seem to be helping.

"Ah. That's good," Uncle Aaron said.

"Then why are we here?"

"Because you cannot have too many blessings."

Uncle Aaron made a good point. Nathan wanted his mother to get better more than anything. He missed meatloaf and mashed potatoes. He missed the way his school uniform was always stiff and smooth, the way his mom fussed over his hair as he went out the door. His life was divided into two distinct chapters, before and after.

He'd do anything to return to before.

Uncle Aaron reached into the box behind the seat. He pulled out a black iron pot. "See this, Nathan?" He lifted the lid. Inside, gold chains and silver coins glistened as the first rays of the sun cut *through the morning mist. "Before you can ask something of the gods, first you have to make an offering. Nothing's free, lad."*

His uncle hefted the pot to the side and shoved it out of the boat. It disappeared with a trail of bubbles. Nathan nearly reached for it. Dad would flip if he saw what Uncle Aaron just did. Mom's doctor bills were draining them dry. "How much was that stuff worth?"

"Aye. That's the point, Nathan. A worthless offering isn't a sacrifice." Instead of getting mad at his question, as Dad would, Uncle Aaron met Nathan's gaze with patience. "Tell me, lad. What hangs in the front of your church?"

"A crucifix." Sometimes when he was supposed to be listening to the Mass, Nathan stared at the gory statue, finely detailed down to the drops of blood running from Christ's hands and feet.

"And what does that stand for?"

Nathan repeated what he'd been taught. "Jesus died on the cross so we could go to heaven even though we're all sinners."

"Ah." Uncle Aaron shrugged. "So why didn't God just save his son?"

"I don't know." The nuns at school weren't big on answering questions. They pretty much liked the kids to sit still and keep a lid on it during Mass.

"Because mankind's salvation is attained through God's sacrifice, Nathan. To keep the world in balance, there has to be payment for everything gained." Uncle Aaron pulled a long wooden statue from under his seat. It was a woman. Huge eyes, lidless and wide-open in a permanent state of wakefulness, took up most of the face.

"What's that?"

"A statue of your ma's sickness. I carved it myself out of good oak hardwood. My labor adds value to the offering." Uncle Aaron floated the statue on the water. It bobbed on the surface. "Water

has power. It heals. It gives life. I'm asking the gods of this lake to cure your ma. The Celts worshipped the earth long before anyone even thought about Christianity. The principles aren't that different, though. Salvation through sacrifice. That's your ancestry, Nathan. And your legacy."

Uncle Aaron dipped his hand in the water. He brought a palm full to Nathan's face and wiped the cool liquid across his forehead, down his cheeks and neck, like a baptism.

"Doesn't the water need to be blessed?" Nathan asked.

"Take a good look around, Nathan. The gods already blessed this place." Uncle Aaron doused his own face and set a huge, wet hand on the top of Nathan's head. "Thy faith make thee whole."

The warmth of his uncle's love spread through Nathan's chest.

"There's one more thing you need to know about sacrifices, Nathan. They have to come from the heart, the cost offered willingly and without regret. That's the key to true salvation."

Nathan raised the posthole digger in both hands and slammed it into the earth. He turned the tool and clamped the jaws closed and withdrew the tool, dumping the dirt in a pile to the side. He repeated the act until sweat dripped down his chest, and his back muscles ached.

Physical pain was a welcome relief from the agony in his head.

If only he could close his eyes. Sleep, just for a couple of hours. But it was not to be. Over the last few weeks, he'd lost the ability to do anything but doze for minutes at a time. His thoughts grew more muddled each day. His time was running out. Beltane was truly his last chance.

Satisfied that the hole was deep enough, he set the tool aside. He'd selected the maypole himself, a narrow, young oak with the straightest trunk. He'd felled and stripped it of branch and bark with his own hands. His labor, his direct connection with the sacred object, would enhance the power of the sacrament. He hefted it to the hole and let the end fall in, then packed dirt around the base. Ropes from the top secured the pole on four sides to anchors in the earth. Picking up a length of rope, he tested its strength between his hands. Definitely substantial enough to hold Mandy. As much as he hated the thought of shackling her, or risking any injury to her delicate skin, she mustn't be able to break free. She wasn't going to come to him willingly. He knew that. He'd made too many mistakes to expect her immediate forgiveness. But by the end of the ritual he would have proved his devotion. Then she would be his forever. He slipped a hand into his pocket and withdrew the ancient silver ring. Once it went on her finger, their eternal bond would be sealed.

He walked into the barn, past the woodpile and the offerings his assistant had provided. The chest of ancient coins gleamed dully in a sunbeam. Nathan scooped up a handful of the golden discs then let them fall through his fingers. They landed on the pile with a soft *clink*. He stroked a dent in the muted bronze of a warrior's shield. An ancient Celt had gone to war with this shield. Perhaps the soldier had fought the Roman invasion of his land, thus defending his people against the eradication of their way of life. Belenos would be pleased. The objects of this offering had value beyond their monetary worth. They represented the history and tradition of his faith, the very same culture that Nathan was calling upon for salvation.

But his material offering wasn't enough payment for the salvation Nathan was seeking. The price for the lives of Nathan, his son, and all future generations was greater than the symbolism. A request of this magnitude required direct and equal payment.

Nathan needed to make the gods an offer they couldn't refuse. Six deaths, threefold the number of lives he was seeking, surely would convince Belenos to lift the curse from the family. Three was the holy number, the Druid trifecta. One sacrifice each for past, present, and future. Maiden, mother, and crone.

He moved his gaze to the structure he'd painstakingly constructed. Two sacrifices slept deeply on the bottom level. The upper cages sat waiting to be filled. Four more.

Time was running out. Tomorrow night was Beltane Eve.

He went into the storeroom in the corner of the barn. Opening his backpack, he checked his supplies. Taser with extra cartridges. Syringes. Plastic ties. Check. He slid the pack's straps over his shoulders. Two bottles of water and a few protein bars went into the bottom cage. Sacrifices had to be alive.

Before he left, he checked on Evan. The food Nathan had left out remained untouched. Refusing to eat was Evan's latest protest. Fortunately, the ceremony would be over before he starved. Four months of imprisonment were taking their toll on his son's physical and mental health. But everything Nathan did was for Evan's benefit, whether he knew it or not.

Nathan strode out of the barn and around to the rear of the building. There he started the tractor and towed the boat along the track to the water's edge. The boat wasn't big, but launching it took some effort. Tying the bow line to a tree, he moved the tractor and trailer to dry ground and returned to the boat. He said a quick prayer for a day of good hunting.

He paddled to deeper water, then switched to the small outboard motor, grateful for the assistance. He tired quickly these days. The summer solstice was seven weeks off. At his current rate of decline, he wouldn't be much use by then. He leaned over the side and scooped a handful of water. Cool and dark, the lake water invited him to slip over the side, bypass the torture of his disease, and skip right to his inevitable demise. Tempting. So tempting. A few minutes of submersion would allow his mind to escape, to surrender, to seek the eternal rest his body craved.

With exhaustion pounding in his temples like an incessant bongo, death sounded like a vacation.

If it weren't for Evan. Thought of his son brought Nathan back to the moment. Water lapped against the sides of the boat, and feminine voices drifted over the whisper of air through leaves.

Could it be that easy?

Three figures appeared, strung out single file along the rim of the lake. Triple luck indeed. Nathan watched them hike up the slope toward a trail. The tall blonde in the lead moved like a gazelle.

Belenos liked prime offerings.

Nathan steered toward the bank. Could he subdue all three? He pulled his Taser from his bag and stuffed plastic zip ties in his pocket. It would be best to catch them on the narrow path, when they were single file. He scanned the lake's shores. Empty and desolate. Perfect.

His chances were better if no one could hear them scream.

"Will you slow down?" Victoria stopped and drank from her water bottle. Twenty feet to her right, the trail dropped off a steep embankment. The Long River flowed past. Sunlight sparkled on the rippled, dark surface, like light reflected off the cuts of a gemstone in a jeweler's case. On the left side of the trail, a rock outcropping jutted out of the earth and angled away from the river.

The midday sun had turned unexpectedly warm. Under her nylon jacket, sweat soaked her gray University of Boston T-shirt between her shoulder blades. She didn't know which burned more, her thighs or her lungs. There might not be any mountains in the area, but this trail had been an uphill hike all morning. "Not all of us are cross-country runners."

Ashley caught up and wheezed. "Seriously."

"Sorry." From twenty feet up the trail, Samantha spun around and bounced back to her friends. "The lake is just over the rise." Despite her skin-tight black leggings, the collegiate runner didn't have an ounce of jiggle on her ridiculously long legs.

Victoria bent double and touched her toes. Her hamstrings tightened, then gave. *Ahhh.*

They trudged over the summit and out of the woods. Waves on the lake sparkled. Fifty yards away, a man piloted an old fishing boat across the water.

"Oh. Pretty." Victoria let the slope carry her down to the water's edge. "Look, there's a nice beach on the other side. Who's up for renting kayaks tomorrow?"

Beside her, Ashley eased her butt onto the weedy bank. She unzipped her yellow windbreaker. Red splotches colored her face.

"Are you OK?" Victoria asked.

"Yeah." Ashley held up a hand and sucked air. "I just need a minute."

With a conspiratorial glance at Victoria, Samantha glanced at her watch. "You know what? It's time to head back anyway."

"No, you guys wanted to go farther. We don't have to stop because of me," Ashley protested.

"It's not because of you. It's because I want cookies." Samantha grinned. She adjusted the blonde ponytail looped through the back of her Red Sox cap.

"And lemonade," added Victoria. Her stomach rumbled. She let her pack slide down her arms to the ground and dug a protein bar out of the front pocket. "Anyone else hungry?" She gestured to her remaining food stores: trail mix, energy gel, more protein bars.

"Nah, I just ate a PowerBar." Samantha bent a leg, caught her boot behind her with her hand, and stretched the front of her thigh. Her mouth stretched in a mischievous grin. "Besides, we can drive to the beach tomorrow. If we go back to the inn early enough, maybe we'll get to see Mr. Super Hot."

Victoria fanned herself. "Could he get any more tall, dark, and handsome?"

"Mmm. Mmm." Ashley pulled her inhaler out of the pocket of her cargo pants. She squeezed the pump and huffed the medication into her lungs. "He is the definition of tall, dark, and handsome," she said in a breathy voice.

"Too bad he's all hung up on our innkeeper." Victoria watched her friend's breathing ease. But Ashley's color didn't improve, and her mouth was still gaping for air like a fish in a cooler. Victoria broke a small piece of protein bar off and popped it into her mouth. Chewing slowly, she recapped her water bottle. Maybe a few more minutes of rest would help.

Dry foliage crunched from the nearby woods. She glanced around, looking for an animal. Nothing. The shimmering water pulled her gaze back. What happened to the guy in the boat?

"Did you hear that?" Samantha whispered.

"Shhh." Ashley chastised. "Maybe it's a deer." She pulled her camera out of her fleece vest. None of them moved for several long minutes. The only sound on the windless air was the gentle rush of the river. "Guess it wasn't anything." She stood and brushed some dirt off the seat of her khaki pants.

They turned around then started walking single file. As usual, Samantha took the lead. They trudged up the steep slope to the trail. After they mounted the summit, the downward slope was a relief to Victoria's tired legs. "Maybe next year we could mix it up and go somewhere warm. Not Florida, though." She shuddered. "The whole girls-gone-wild deal just doesn't appeal."

"How about Mexico?" Ashley suggested. "Or the Bahamas."

The trail narrowed. Leaves and twigs brushed their legs as they walked. Bringing up the rear, Victoria couldn't see the trail ahead.

"Spring break at a tropical beach is so cliché," Samantha chimed in. "And think of it this way. We'll be the only girls to come back from spring break in better condition."

Something snapped in the underbrush.

Ashley slowed. "What was that?"

Victoria bumped into her. "Probably just an animal. Move on. There's nothing to see here." She gave her friend a playful tap on the shoulder.

Zap. In front of them, Samantha froze, then dropped to the ground.

Ashley screamed, and Victoria tried to see past her friend on the narrow path. A man blocked the trail. Tall. Blond. Scruffy-looking. He could have been handsome, except for the Unabomber haircut and beard. He held a black-and-yellow gun in his hand. He snapped something into the front of it and pointed it at Ashley. *Zzzap.* Her body went rigid, and she went down like a tipped domino.

Victoria turned to run. *Click. Zzzap.* Something slapped her back. A *zing* snapped through her body as if she'd touched a hot outlet. Every muscle in her body flexed and locked in place. Unable to break her fall, she pitched face-first to the ground. Her chin struck a rock. Pain lanced through her head.

She heard him approach, his footsteps cracking through dead leaves. Her body tingled, but she couldn't move anything except her head. She turned it to focus up the trail. Ashley sprawled motionless three feet away. Ten feet ahead, the blond creep was squatting next to Samantha and binding her twitching hands and feet with plastic ties. Samantha groaned. Her eyes were open wide enough to show the whites all the way around. She opened her mouth and inhaled.

He slid a knife from his pocket. "If you scream, I will cut out your tongue." Impersonal, cold, and steady as the river, the voice held no malice or anger. Its just-the-facts lack of emotion sent Victoria's racing heart into a fresh sprint.

Samantha stilled. He stuffed something in her mouth, wrapped a bandana around her face, and threaded it through her mouth. A tight knot secured it behind her head.

He moved to Ashley. Kneeling next to her, he touched her face, frowned, and continued to Victoria's side.

Ashley was too still.

Victoria commanded her body to rise, told her hands to lever her body to her feet, instructed her legs to run. But nothing happened. Her body's connection to her brain had shorted out. Rough hands closed around her ankles and brought them together. He bound them just above her low boot tops. The plastic tie cut into her skin. He maneuvered her hands behind her back. Her face ground into the dirt.

Just as he finished binding her, tiny pinpricks signaled the return of her muscle control. She wiggled her toes and flexed her feet. Her body responded, the epitome of too little, too late. Pulling another bandana from his pocket, he shoved the fabric into her mouth and fastened it tightly. It tasted of dirt and sweat and pulled painfully at the corners of her mouth. Victoria gagged. He dragged her by the feet through the dirt past Ashley. Her friend's body remained motionless.

He left Victoria and Samantha on the bank and ducked back into the brush. Victoria turned her head. Fear and hopelessness clouded Samantha's eyes. Tears glistened on her cheeks. Victoria couldn't cry. Numbness spread through her, a self-defense reaction against what her brain knew was coming. Though they were bound, she felt the connection as their eyes met. Mentally, they were holding hands.

They were thinking the same thing. Serial killer.

He returned empty-handed, and clambered down the bank. Victoria couldn't see what he was doing, but she heard him moving around. Metal banged on rock. Velcro ripped open. When he climbed back up to stand next to them, he held a syringe in his hand. He drew clear liquid from a bottle into the needle.

Samantha tried to worm away. He jabbed the shot into her leg. She stopped squirming. He refilled and moved to Victoria. She braced herself. The needle bit into her leg through her pants.

He pulled her toward the water. Her sight dimmed as the drugged lethargy took command, but she raised her head to look back up at the trail. It was empty. Darkness rolled over her like a blackout shade.

What had he done with Ashley?

CHAPTER TWENTY

Mandy ducked behind the desk.

"Hey, Ray." Danny's voice boomed through the closed door. "Can I ask you a few questions?"

Mandy couldn't hear Ray's response. She slid the folder into her purse and quietly closed the drawer. She cracked the door a half inch and peeked through the opening. Danny had snagged Ray at the entrance to the hallway. She slipped out, closed the door silently behind her, and ducked into the ladies' room.

She waited for the door to Ray's office to click open and closed before walking out into the hallway. Danny was leaning on the wall. A fresh cup of coffee steamed in his nonbandaged hand. He smiled. "Find anything interesting?"

"Shhh." She hurried down the tiled corridor.

Danny fell into step behind her and whispered over her shoulder. "Well?"

She shook her head. "Not much."

"Let's go search his house. He probably keeps the good stuff there."

"Breaking and entering is illegal."

"What did you just do?" Danny asked.

"The door wasn't locked. I just entered."

"Nice. Getting off on a technicality." Danny grinned. "Except for the file you stole." His gaze flickered to her purse and back.

Mandy looked down. The edge of the manila folder was peeking out. She zipped her bag completely closed and walked away.

Danny was right on her heels. "Is the Realtor always so weird?"

"Carolyn has a lot on her plate."

"Does she?" Danny drank his coffee.

"Her husband isn't well." Mandy skirted the chin-high bookshelves and headed toward the front door.

Danny opened the glass door and stepped aside. "Ray seems to have a man crush on Nathan."

Mandy blinked at the late morning sunshine and skirted a few pedestrians. "You noticed? Most of the town is ready to order Nathan's tombstone and bulldoze the diner, but Ray is still entrenched in his bromance. Kind of ironic, don't you think? His business has probably picked up since the diner closed. Why would he want it to reopen?" Why was she talking to Danny about this? She was supposed to get rid of him, not conspire.

"Strange." Danny's eyes sparkled with mischief. "Going to share what you lifted from Ray's office?"

Mandy raised her chin. God help her. She wasn't just attracted to his physical attributes, though they were plentiful. She glanced sideways. Worn jeans and a sweatshirt showcased his lean-as-sin body. She liked the whole man, from his courage to his wicked sense of humor. "Maybe."

"Promising." Danny's quick grin turned thoughtful. "So the diner that Nathan owned is still sitting just the way he left it?"

"Other than the things the police took, yes."

"What about his house?"

"The same, I guess."

He was quiet for a minute. Thinking, no doubt. "Do you have his home address?"

"I know where he lives, sure." Though she'd never been inside Nathan's house, a fact that still pricked her conscience. Father abandonment issues aside, how had she let him charm her? She glanced at Danny. What would he think? How would he respect her if he knew she was the most naive woman in the state?

"Is it far?"

"No. Two miles outside town. Big cedar and stone house on Route Twelve. You can't miss it. It's the nicest place for miles. Kind of stands out."

Danny turned and walked briskly across the entryway. Mandy jogged to catch up. "Where are you going?"

Key in hand, he paused at the curb. "You should probably go back to the inn."

"No way."

His gaze pierced. "Go home, Mandy."

She propped a hand on her hip. "No. I know what you're going to do." She winced. She hadn't intended to sound like a petulant teenager.

Danny glared, but Mandy didn't back down. She had to know what he discovered, what he was planning to do, so she could react.

"Suit yourself." He got into his car and drove off, but she'd caught the quirk of his mouth. She scrambled to start her little wagon. Pulling out onto the street, she followed him through town and out onto Route Twelve. He stopped at the circular driveway. Nathan's house was modern with a stone facade and landscape that was still ornate despite the lack of maintenance. Another month of spring growth and the property was going to go downhill fast.

Danny parked behind a clump of ornamental evergreens. She pulled in behind him, making sure her car wasn't visible from the road either, and joined him on the walk.

He glanced up the road in both directions. "How busy is this street?"

"Not very." Was he going to break in? "What are you doing?"

He shrugged and went up to the front door. A ribbon of torn yellow tape dangled from the doorframe. With a subtle movement, Danny produced a pair of gloves and a small tool from his pockets. A few deft twists and turns unlocked the door. It swung inward with a creak of unused hinges and swollen wood.

"That was fast." Alarmingly so.

"Like stealing a bike." Danny tucked her behind him as he walked into the house.

"You can't do this." Panic pulsed through Mandy's veins. Clammy sweat gathered between her breasts as she stepped into Nathan's foyer. This felt creepy and wrong in a hundred different ways.

"Why not? You just searched Ray's office."

"This is illegal, big-time." Though it wasn't the law that Mandy feared. What would her blackmailer think of them snooping through the house? She was supposed to be getting rid of Danny, not aiding and abetting him in illegal entry, and certainly not helping him find Nathan.

Danny closed the door behind them and faced her. His glare was a mix of challenge and disbelief. "Are you going to call a cop?"

She should. Doug could arrest him and then boot him out of town. Mandy's problems would be solved.

"Well, are you?" Danny tried to read Mandy's expression, but she dropped her eyes to the stone floor. Guilt gave him a quick jab in the ribs. *Here we go again, corrupting an otherwise good girl.* His sister had a juvie record because he'd talked her into stealing a car with him. Slippery as usual, he hadn't even been caught, but someone had ID'd Jaynie by her bright-red hair.

"No."

"Then let's see what's here." He told his conscience to suck it and checked out the house. Despite the warm spring day outside, the chill in the house seeped through the soles of his shoes. No heat. No surprise. As Danny and his siblings knew firsthand, it didn't take long for utility companies to act on unpaid bills.

"The police have already taken everything connected with the case." Mandy's eyes skittered around the room as if she was afraid of what she might see.

"I'm looking for more general information." Danny wanted to know what made Nathan tick. In the few days he'd been here, all he'd learned was that the family was close-knit, something he didn't particularly want to dwell on. Danny understood how tightly tragedy and suffering could cement a family bond.

He'd do anything for his sister.

The interior was bachelor spiffy, heavy on overstuffed leather furniture, light on knickknacks. They did a slow tour of the formal living and dining rooms. Under the dust, the furniture had an unused look to it. He followed the hall to the back of the house. A kitchen opened into a family room. Danny paused at the mantle. Empty frames lined up like soldiers. The police must have taken the photos. Oddly empty shelves indicated they'd taken other things as well. "What happened to Nathan's wife?"

"She died a week after Evan was born. Pulmonary embolism."

"So he was a widower for over twenty years?"

"Uh-huh."

"Did he ever date anyone in town?" A girlfriend, past or present, might know personal details about Nathan.

"I never saw him date anyone." Mandy tucked a strand of hair behind her ear.

"Twenty years is a long time for a man to go without a woman," Danny said.

"I wouldn't know." Mandy's eyes flitted toward the window overlooking the tree-ringed backyard.

If he didn't have a local woman, did Nathan have one-night stands or rendezvous with women in other towns? Prostitutes? All questions Danny wasn't going to ask sweet, small-town Mandy, who was clearly uncomfortable talking about her ex-boss's sex life.

Just how sheltered was she? Danny shook his mind from the thought of Mandy and her sexual innocence. This was not the time.

Danny walked to a door between the kitchen and family room. He opened it. A stairwell led down. There was nothing down there. He knew it. But the darkness was intimidating. On the way down, he flipped a switch on the wall. Nothing, which was exactly what happened when electric bills didn't get paid. Danny pulled the small flashlight he'd taken from his glove box out of his pocket. He swept the beam around the dusty room. Scant light filtered through a few dirty, narrow windows at ceiling height.

The basement looked ordinary. Raw concrete floor, white-washed cinder block walls, unfinished ceiling. Empty shelves lined the walls. A long workbench spanned the far wall. Had Nathan prepared the props of his religion on its scarred wooden surface? There were no signs of the evil that had been planned here. Until Danny looked closer. A circle in the center of the room was dotted with globs of hardened wax in different colors. Danny squatted next to it. Under the dust, faint symbols drawn in chalk decorated the concrete around the space. Spirals. Interlocking triangles and rings. Pentagrams. Afraid of indoor lightning strikes, he avoided church unless someone was getting married, baptized, or buried. But the Catholic boy inside him cringed. He could practically hear his mother saying the rosary from heaven.

This was where it happened. A human sacrifice had been planned right here.

He looked over at Mandy, who was hugging herself at the bottom of the steps. She took a step backward, up onto the last wooden step, as if she were also repulsed by the remnants of pagan rituals on the concrete.

He pulled out his phone and snapped pictures of the circle. The flash illuminated more symbols painted on the rough walls. Stick figures and bonfires galore. Danny photographed everything.

What had he hoped to accomplish by coming here? The police had taken everything that could possibly be considered evidence. But nothing could clear the dusty air of the desperation that clung to the space, or eliminate the taint of ruthlessness that drove a man to kidnap and slaughter innocents to save his own family.

Brutality lingered because the events that were put into play here weren't over yet. Evil was sticking around.

"What about all the artifacts that were down here? Did anyone know about them?" Danny asked.

Mandy lifted a shoulder and moved up two more steps. "Sure, everybody knew about Aaron's collection. He had a degree of some sort in Celtic history. Collecting artifacts from Scotland was his hobby. That's where he was born."

In that light, Danny supposed it didn't seem strange at all.

"I'm getting out of here." She tripped up the stairs.

Danny swept his light over the space one last time. The beam settled on a dark discoloration on the floor beneath the far window. He walked over. The window was cracked an eighth of an inch open. The lock was busted. Water had dripped onto the cement, and mold had grown over the winter.

Was the window jimmied before or after Nathan disappeared? If it happened over the winter, who had broken in and why? The answer could be as simple as a vagrant looking for a dry place to weather a storm. Or Nathan could have returned.

Danny went upstairs at a jog. He couldn't get out of the cold, dank cellar fast enough. The patio door caught his eye. He walked out back to the broken basement window and shone his flashlight on the shaded frame. Definitely jimmied from the outside. He swept the beam over the surrounding area. Something was crushed between the cinder block foundation and the weeds that grew around the building. Danny stuck his finger in the mud and pulled it out. He put it in the palm of his hand. A faded white lollipop wrapper.

Ray?

He remembered a flash of his first night in town. He'd seen someone in the alley next to the diner. Could that have been Ray? What would he be doing in the vacant restaurant?

CHAPTER TWENTY-ONE

Feeling trapped, Mandy scurried out of the basement. Above ground, she rubbed at a tight spot in the center of her chest. Under her sweater, her skin was clammy and damp. She could barely draw a full breath.

Just a few more minutes, then she could get out of here. What else needed to be searched? The steps leading to the second floor pulled at her gaze. Mandy crept upstairs alone. She stuck her head in the first room. Dirty clothes and used plates vied for surface space, and the air smelled of many, many things gone sour. Evan's room, no doubt.

The next door led to a spartan space. Nathan's uncle's room? Shelves and surfaces were bizarrely bare. The police had taken most of Aaron's personal possessions. Small picture frames lay on their backs, the photos removed. Mandy walked to the dresser and opened a drawer. Sweaters. She looked in the other drawers. More clothing. The closet held pants and jackets. Nothing unusual. A few boxes sat on the floor, the tops off-kilter, summer clothes hanging over the sides.

Nathan's room was orderly but not insanely so. Most of his personal items were missing from the medicine chest and dresser tops. Mandy wandered into the closet. Traces of his cologne sent nausea ripping through her stomach.

She'd slept with a killer. He'd lied to her, but she'd been honest. Foolishly, she'd thought they were in love. She'd confessed her private thoughts, and now he knew many personal things about her. Things he could use to hurt those she loved. As he'd proved in getting threats to her, Nathan might be crazy, but he was smart. She wrapped her shaking hands around her middle. If he wanted to kill her brother, he'd do it.

"Anything in here?"

She jumped.

"Sorry." Danny put a hand on her shoulder.

"It's just creepy being in here." Mandy put a hand to her chest. Her heart pounded against her palm.

"I know. Relax."

Mandy sucked in a deep breath. Not helping. "No, I didn't find anything in here. How about the basement?"

"Nah. Looks like the cops got everything interesting." Danny shook his head

Small lights twinkled in Mandy's vision. Her knees buckled.

"Whoa." A strong hand supported her elbow.

"I need to go outside."

"Yeah. Sure, of course." Danny steered her from the room, down the stairs, and out the front door.

"You OK?"

She gulped pine-scented air until her head cleared. "I don't know what happened."

"Looked like a panic attack." Danny's hand was still under her elbow.

"I don't have panic attacks," she protested.

"OK." But his expression and tone made it clear he didn't believe her.

"But no more breaking and entering."

"No argument from me. Good girls aren't cut out for criminal activity." Was he holding back a grin? If he knew why she was so upset, she doubted he'd be amused.

"I need to go." She pulled away from his support. Nothing wobbled. She was good to go.

"You're sure you're all right to drive?"

"Fine."

"I'm going to make a stop on the way back."

Distracted, Mandy closed the door and started the car. The upbeat music of Maroon 5 thumping from the speakers sounded obscene after viewing Nathan's home. Misery lingered in that cellar like black mold after a flood. She clicked off the radio in her car and drove back to the inn in silence.

Danny filled up his tank and drove through town. As he passed the doctor's office, Carolyn Fitzgerald was getting out of her red sedan. Her beige suit was spotted with blood. Danny pulled over. He got out of his car. "Do you need help?"

"No, thank you." Tension added ten years to her face since he'd seen her. She opened the passenger door for a frail-looking man in his sixties.

The man shook his head. "No."

"Please, Walt," she begged. "We'll go right home afterward. I promise."

A teenager emerged from the back of the sedan and stood at her side. Danny recognized the sullen slouch and moody eyes of an angry adolescent. It was like looking in a mirror during his own youth. "Come on, Dad. Dr. Chandler needs to look at your head. You fell, remember?"

Danny had been better at covering the pain in his voice with insolence. Practice makes perfect and all that.

The old man sawed his jaw back and forth. His eyes were wide and had a confused sheen. He turned his head to look at Danny. Stubbornness and hostility lingered behind the fear, much like his son's expression. Blood was dripping from a long cut on his forehead, but he seemed oblivious to the injury.

Keys in hand, Danny hesitated. Carolyn didn't seem to want assistance, but he hated to just leave her in obvious distress. "Are you sure I can't help?"

Carolyn moved closer to Danny and lowered her voice. "I don't know. He gets confused. Sometimes strangers are good. Sometimes not. My husband is hard to predict. It's so hard to see him like this. He used to be a colonel in the army."

Danny looked over at her husband. A vague, opaque film clouded his eyes. The colonel squinted, as if he knew the truth was in front of him but he couldn't focus on it. Frustration tightened the age-slackened muscles of his face. Alzheimer's? If not, something similar.

"Let me try." Danny pocketed his keys and strode to the car. "Colonel." Danny snapped a salute. "Sergeant Daniel Sullivan. We're ready for you, sir."

The colonel blinked and straightened in what appeared to be a reflex to Danny's formal address. Purpose filled his movements as he reached for the door handle. Danny itched to help him but restrained himself. Carolyn stepped forward. Danny shook his head, and she backed off. With great effort, her husband climbed out of the car. Danny hustled to the doctor's office door and opened it wide. He stood tall, gaze straight ahead, and saluted again as the frail old man shuffled through.

Carolyn wiped a teardrop from her cheek. "Thank you. Sometimes I forget he still needs respect."

"Anytime." Danny closed the door behind the family. Now that he knew the extent of the old man's illness, Danny agreed with Mandy. The relationship between Carolyn and Dr. Chandler was normal.

He considered the parallels between Nathan's disease and Alzheimer's. Danny imagined the heart-wrench of watching a loved one succumb to dementia. Had seeing his uncle descend into darkness pushed Nathan into madness? The colonel's son looked to be about fifteen. How would watching his father's decline into dementia and death affect him? And what had become of Nathan's son?

He jogged back to his car. Back at the inn, he parked his car next to Jed's truck. Not good. Danny wanted some privacy with Mandy. Whether she liked it or not, they had things to discuss.

Mandy wasn't sure how long she sat in her car, waiting for her stomach and her nerves to settle. When she was able to plaster a benign look on her face, she opened the car door and walked across the grass.

She took a minute to listen to the wind rustling though the tree branches. She used to wish something would happen out of the ordinary in this trap of a town. Now she just hoped life could return to the normal, boring routine she hadn't known to appreciate until it was whisked away.

The throaty rumble of Danny's engine stopped her. Tires crunched on gravel. She turned to watch him get out of his purple convertible. He stopped to wipe something from the fender with the hem of his T-shirt. The gesture brought a bubble of giddiness up into her throat. Like shiny paint was going to help him catch a homicidal maniac. God, she was losing it.

"You all right?" he asked.

"Yes." She led the way into the kitchen. Forget the lemonade. She needed a glass of wine. A big one. Danny closed the door behind them. Too bad it was so early, and she had too much work ahead in her day to indulge.

Jed was drinking coffee at the island. "Mrs. Stone just left. The rooms are clean. Your mother's friends picked her up a few minutes ago. They took her to get something done to her hair. Said they'd be all afternoon."

"OK." Mandy dropped her duffel by the door so she wouldn't forget to clean the weapon later.

Honey sat at Jed's feet, ears pricked forward. Despite their entry, the dog's focus didn't waver from her master's face. Behind her, the door to the family quarters was propped open with a stool.

"Find Bill," Jed commanded. The dog spun around and dashed into the apartment.

Mandy plunked her purse on the counter. "What are you doing?"

"Just a game we've been working on." Jed got to his feet, rinsed his mug, and put it in the dishwasher. "Keeps the dog and your brother busy."

With the thud of heavy footsteps and the clatter of dog nails on hardwood, Bill and Honey rushed into the kitchen.

"She found me again! That's five times in a row." Bill dropped to one knee and threw his arms around the dog's neck. She licked his face. "Honey is the smartest dog ever."

Mandy gave Jed a what's-going-on look.

He shrugged off her stare. "It's good to keep her nose in practice."

"But she's a retriever, not a scent hound," Mandy pointed out.

"What's the difference?" Danny asked.

"Honey doesn't find the birds. Her job is to remember where the ducks fall and bring them back," Mandy explained.

"Whatever. I have to go." Jed patted his thigh.

"I'm hungry." Bill looked hopefully at Jed. "Can we get burgers for lunch again, Jed? Please. Then I could help you train Bear. He's almost as smart as Honey."

Jed's face looked pained, but to Mandy's surprise, he nodded. "Sure."

"Yay." Bill loped out the door. Mandy watched the trio cross the yard. Jed was acting differently lately. More patient, less work-oriented. Had his injury changed him, or was he up to something?

Danny stepped up beside her and looked over her shoulder out the window. "Some dog."

"Jed's the best dog trainer around, but Honey was special from day one. Field trial champion two years in a row. Jed was supposed to breed her this spring, but he changed his mind."

"Because of his injury?"

Looking for unfinished chores, Mandy turned back to the kitchen. A quick scan of the counters and sink showed everything to be neat and tidy. "That's what he said. But he could use the income with his hunting guide business on hold. He sold four dogs over the winter. He only has a few left."

Jed hadn't bred any dogs or taken any retrievers in for training since the stabbing. Was he depressed by his physical limitations or weaker than he'd admit?

The inn was strangely quiet. Behind her, Danny shuffled his feet. Uh-oh. They were alone. No guests, no Mom, no Bill. When was the last time she'd been alone at home? She picked up a sponge and wiped an imaginary spot from the stainless faucet. Now what?

"Now that we're alone, how about showing me what you found in Ray's office?"

"I didn't get much of a chance to look at it." Mandy unzipped her purse and pulled out the file. Staying on the opposite side of the center island from Danny, she opened the cover. Inside were newspaper clippings and printed Internet articles, all detailing Nathan's case. She laid a few out on the counter. *Maine Mayor Organizes Ritual Murder, Sadistic Killer Disappears, Manhunt Continues in Maine, Killer Vanishes Without a Trace.*

Danny thumbed through the pile. "He must have every article printed on the case."

Mandy scanned the clippings. Everything she wanted to forget was laid out in front of her. A cold ache formed inside her belly, as if she'd swallowed ice water too quickly. The chill rose into her chest and froze her throat, choking off her next breath. Tiny white spots danced in front of her eyes.

"Hey, are you all right?" Danny's hand on her arm startled her.

She inhaled, a sharp and audible gasp that flooded her brain with oxygen. Her knees weakened. Danny was beside her in an instant. His body pressed against her, supported her, and thawed the mass of frozen panic that threatened to shut down her body.

"I'm fine."

"You're not fine." Danny pulled a stool closer and guided her onto it. "Sit down for a minute."

He filled a glass of water from the dispenser on the refrigerator and handed it to her. She took a sip, but stopped when the first swallow of cold water hit her stomach. Sitting still let her mind roam. Never a good thing. She had to move. She had to *do* something.

She checked the clock on the microwave. It was barely noon. She had hours before it was time to put out an afternoon snack for her guests. She could start prep for tomorrow's breakfast or she could throw in a load of wash. Physical labor was the best thing to work off the excess of nervous energy. She slid off the stool. "I have some work to do."

Danny grabbed her hand. "When was the last time you took an afternoon off?"

"I don't remember."

"Well, what do you like to do to relax?"

"I don't have much time for relaxing." Sunlight pulled Mandy's gaze to the window. She imagined the heat of its rays on her skin. Outside, budding trees and greening grass tempted her. When was the last time she'd spent a day outdoors? A crazy idea popped into her head. "Do you like to fish?"

"I've never been fishing."

"Never?"

"Nope." Danny shrugged. "I grew up in the city."

"There are plenty of bodies of water in Philadelphia."

"True, but we spent most of our time keeping the business afloat. There wasn't much time for leisure activities."

"I know what you mean." They had more in common than she would have expected.

"Besides, I don't think I'd want to eat anything that came out of the Schuylkill River." He shot her a grin. "You could teach me."

Memories of his hard body under her hands at the gun range flushed a welcome heat through her veins. Who was she kidding? It wasn't just the promise of a few quiet hours in the woods that enticed her. Since Danny's arrival, she'd realized how much male companionship was lacking in her life. Other than Jed, she didn't have many friends. Her goal of going to school and getting out of Huntsville had consumed her life for the past few years. She'd let her few friendships lapse. "I'll pack some sandwiches. Then I'll get the equipment together."

Danny stopped her. "I'll pack lunch. You take care of the rods and stuff."

"OK. There's a small cooler in the pantry."

"I'll dig for what I need. Is anything off limits?"

Was that a loaded question? "No."

Excitement building, Mandy went out to the garage and entered through the side door. The two-car space was crowded with sporting equipment stored for guest use. Snowshoes, cross-country skis, and croquet sets were stored in tubs along the wall. Fly rods and reels hung above them. Mandy tripped. She righted herself with a hand on a wooden shelf and glanced down. The ugly pot of flowers and odd branch huddled behind a horseshoe set. Goosebumps rose on her biceps. Who had put those in the garage?

Danny. Had to be. She hadn't told Jed about the flowers.

She rubbed her arms and turned away. One afternoon. That's all she was asking. One afternoon to recharge. Maybe if she cleared her head for the next few hours, she'd think of other options to deal with the mess her life had become.

And figure out how to identify her blackmailer.

The tall cabinet that held her personal outdoor gear stood in the rear corner. Mandy twirled the combination lock and opened the doors. She selected two rods, grabbed her fly box and a few other odds and ends, and loaded it all into the back of her wagon. By the time she'd finished, Danny came out the back door, cooler in hand. With a wistful glance at his convertible, he climbed into the passenger seat.

Mandy started the engine. "No offense, but your car doesn't look like it would handle going off-road."

"I'm sure it wouldn't. The car is more sentimental than practical. My brother Conor and I rebuilt it together when I was in high school."

"Sounds like you two are close."

"We are. He and Pat, he's the oldest, tried to fill in for my parents as best they could."

Danny's life had been filled with hardship, too. No easy road for him or his siblings. But the Sullivans seemed determined to bask in whatever sunlight they could find during the lulls in the darkness. She envied their strength and their bond.

Could Mandy learn to squeeze lemonade out of the rotten fruit life threw at her?

She drove out of town. With all the work that waited and all the happenings, was she crazy to be taking a day off? And spending it with Danny, no less. The one man she should be avoiding. But instead of doing what she should, she was driving off into the woods alone with him.

CHAPTER TWENTY-TWO

Danny got out of the car. Mandy had parked at the end of a rutted lane of weeds and dirt. The rush of water dominated the soundscape, with a backdrop of chirps, tweets, and rustles. Twenty yards in front of the car, the river swept through the forest. Clumps of boulders ranging in size from basketball to Buick broke up the flow. Water eddied around them in frothy swirls.

He grabbed the picnic basket from the backseat and followed Mandy to the riverbank. She carried the fishing gear to the water's edge.

"Which waterway is this?" The river turned forty-five degrees and created a dog-legged V in front of them. He spread a blanket on the soft grass where the woods curved around the small clearing.

"The Long River." She dropped a small box and a net in the tall weeds next to the fly rods.

The trees blocked the breeze, and the sun warmed Danny's skin. Scanning the trees and river, he peeled off his sweatshirt and pulled his Hard Rock T-shirt back down over his stomach. Something pulled him back to Mandy. She flushed and turned her attention to her gear. Had she been checking out his abs? Nice. "Popular spot?"

"Not here. This is my special fishing hole." Mandy fiddled around with the rods and reels and line and other things he couldn't identify.

"What are you doing?"

"Just getting the lines ready." She tied a fuzzy fake insect to a section of fishing line, then walked to the riverbank. Holding the line in one hand and the rod in the other, she whisked the tip back and forth. The line whipped smoothly through the air and soared across the water. It landed with a light *plop* on the moving water. She let it sink for a few seconds, tugged it a bit, let it sink some more. Then she reeled it in and repeated the motions. He watched her cast for a while. As she got into the flow and rhythm of her task, her face and posture relaxed. She smiled at him, her eyes lighting up. "Want to give it a try?"

"Sure." Remembering the shooting lesson and all the touching involved, he sprang to his feet and joined her. The river flowed past with a quiet, peaceful rush. Mandy handed him the rod. His bandaged hand was limited to guiding the line, but his fingers weren't trembling today. She gave him basic instructions and adjusted his grip, her fingers soft on his bare forearms.

Then she backed away. "Go ahead."

Bummer. Fishing just got less fun, but he supposed standing next to a beginner flailing around with a sharp object wasn't smart.

He managed a few weak attempts, but his bandaged hand got in the way. Not wanting a repeat of yesterday's spasms, Danny lowered the rod. He was going to give this rest thing a fair trial. Maybe he needed to let his stubbornness go as well as his past anger. "Here, you take it back. I'll try again after my hand is all healed up." He turned.

Mandy was shrugging out of her bulky sweater. Oh, yeah. The gray T-shirt she wore underneath was snug, showcasing her tight little body. Her handgun was in its holster behind her right hip.

He put the rod down and joined her on the blanket in two strides. "I'm starving. How about we eat?"

"Good idea." She knelt and opened the cooler. She pulled out a couple of bottles of water. "What did you pack?"

"Ham sandwiches, apples, some cheese." Danny sat next to her and leaned over her shoulder. The scent of flowers wafting from her hair blended with the outdoor smells of grass and pine. Mandy fit in with the natural scene. She belonged here. They ate in silence. Danny didn't taste any of his food. All of his attention was focused on the woman next to him.

Mandy gathered her trash and stuffed it back in the cooler. A wistful half smile tugged at her mouth—and Danny's heart. He wanted to see her relaxed and happy all the time, not just for a single hour. "It's such a beautiful day. I hate to go back."

"There's no rush." He tugged on her hand, pulling her closer until their faces were only inches apart. Her eyes darkened, and everything inside Danny tightened. Need and longing filled him. She was so perfect. Wholesome and pure as the forest around them. Just being with her refreshed him. Yup. Axl Rose had it all right. Green grass and a pretty girl was all a man really needed.

He dipped his head and took her mouth, firmly this time, pouring his desire for her into the kiss. Instead of pulling away as he expected, she leaned in. Her weight toppled him. He fell backward. Laughing, she tumbled onto his chest.

"Oops. Sorry." She smiled down at him.

Danny wrapped his arms around her and rolled until she was on her back. Her hair spread out behind her in a dark halo. "God, you're beautiful."

Her shy blush was a total turn-on.

He dipped his head and kissed her again. She opened her mouth to him, and his tongue plunged past her lips. The hot sweetness of her mouth made him want to taste other parts of her. And thinking of *that* threatened to short-circuit his brain.

Danny's hand was on her breast before he could stop himself. Her soft moan surprised and delighted him. He slid his palm down to her waist and up under her shirt. More soft skin met his touch. He stroked up her back and released the catch on her bra. His hand swept around. Yes. Her breast filled his palm. She was perfect. Everywhere.

The next groan was his. "Let me see you."

He tugged her shirt over her head and tossed the bra aside. Lying back on green plaid cotton, her nipples peaked for him. Sunlight played over her smooth, creamy skin.

"Don't stop, please." Her plea was breathless, excited, urgent.

No worries. Stopping was the last thing on his mind. He started his tour of her body with his lips on her neck, paying attention to her soft, sexy moans to find all her most sensitive spots. Her pulse thrummed under his mouth on the delicate column just under her jaw.

Her hands pulled restlessly at his shirt. "I want to see you, too."

"Yes, ma'am." Danny peeled off his T-shirt. Her seeing and touching him was a fantastic idea. Her fingers were greedy on his chest. They roamed down his stomach. He sucked wind as she toyed with the waistband of his jeans. His erection practically jumped out of his pants toward her hand.

Need roared through him like a subway train, and his brain promptly shut down the whole thinking section.

He closed his mouth over her nipple. She arched toward him. He moved lower, hand skimming over her skin, mouth following. His tongue on her rib cage elicited a deep groan. Danny made a mental note. He unfastened her jeans. The quick catch of her breath urged him on. His hand delved inside to find her soft and slick and, God help him, totally ready.

A deep groan burst from her lips as he stroked her softest flesh.

Desire consumed him. He needed more. Her jeans slid off her hips. Danny pressed his face to her panties and breathed her in.

Still not enough.

His thumbs hooked her panties and drew them down her legs. He kissed his way back up her leg. Her body writhed as he licked the inside of her thigh to where he really wanted to be.

The taste of her nearly drove him over the edge.

"Danny..."

She didn't have to say anything else. Danny was out of his pants and yanking a condom from his wallet in two seconds. He rolled onto her. The way she opened for him filled him with solid and steady warmth. Sliding inside her was like nothing he'd ever experienced. It was beyond sex. It was all-encompassing. Nothing existed in the world beyond the woman clinging to his body.

Danny moved back and pushed forward again. Mandy tightened around him. Pleasure pounded at the base of his spine.

This moment—with Mandy's soft body under him, her passion-dark eyes locked on his, the sun warm on his back, the scents of the woods in his nose—was the closest thing to a religious experience he'd ever had. Everything but the choir of angels. He slowed his movements. He wanted this to last. Hell, he wanted this to last forever.

But nothing lasted forever. As he well knew, the best things in life were especially fleeting.

He made the attempt anyway. He slowed his thrusts, drawing out the pleasure in long waves that swirled and ebbed like the rushing river. But Mandy's body was having none of it. She bowed back. Shuddering around him, she wrapped her legs around his waist and pulled him even deeper. Bliss shimmered like sunlight. And that was it for him. He followed her over, helpless in the wake of her pleasure.

He fell forward, supporting his greater weight on his elbows. Her eyes were closed, her expression contented. A healthy flush colored her skin. Joy coursed through his heart. For the first time since he'd returned from Iraq, he felt healed, whole. No more ruined man.

Mandy's eyes opened wide and turned horrified in one blink.

"I can't believe we just did that." Mandy looked around. The treetops waved at her. They were outside. Naked and outside. Naked and in a more-than-compromising position outside. She thought of the other things Danny had done to her in the great wide open.

"We're outside." She squirmed, but he pressed his hips against hers, pinning her down.

"Mmm. I know." Danny pressed his lips to her collarbone. "It's beautiful."

"Someone could see." She gripped the firm muscles of his shoulders with tense fingers.

He grinned down at her. "Like who?"

"Like anybody."

"Honey, I doubt there's another soul for miles. Relax. Enjoy." Danny brought his mouth to her shoulder. The rasp of his chin brought a fresh round of delicious shivers to her belly. "You just made the great outdoors a whole lot more appealing."

She craned her head over his shoulder. No one in sight. Probably no one anywhere nearby. Probably. "We have to get up and put clothes on."

He traced the underside of her jaw with his tongue, bringing to mind other things he'd done with it. "Are you sure? Because I'd rather do it all over again."

Something fluttered inside her. *Not now.* She tapped him on the back. "Danny."

A sigh rolled through his body.

"All right, but I was really getting into this back-to-nature thing." Danny levered his body off of her. She instantly missed the contact with his warm skin. Without the weight of him anchoring her, she felt adrift.

Clearly comfortable with his nudity, he stood and stretched. Muscles shifted. Mandy's gaze swept up his strong legs to narrow hips and—oh—he wasn't kidding. He was ready to make love again. Desire gathered fresh.

She lifted her eyes, past the broad chest and equally delicious shoulders to his face. His sparkling turquoise eyes and wicked grin said he knew what she was thinking.

"Are you sure you want to go back?" He lowered his voice and waggled his eyebrows. "I have another condom."

At this moment, she wanted nothing more than to spend a week naked with him, preferably in some tropical location, but that wasn't her reality. "I have to. I have responsibilities." Mandy averted her eyes before she was tempted to give in to his obvious desires.

"OK." But regret tinted his voice as he stepped into his jeans.

Mandy scrambled into her clothes. They gathered the fishing gear and hauled it back to the car. She closed the hatch. Danny's hands grabbed her hips. He spun her around and pinned her to the rear of the car. "How about a little something for the road?"

But Danny didn't do anything in a small way. He kissed her until she was breathless. When he raised his head, he gazed down at her with more than sexual desire in his eyes.

Mandy's heart skipped. A pang of fear shut down her internal happy dance. Would Danny still look at her that way if he knew about her and Nathan? How naive she'd been, how she'd let him play her. She pulled away. The passion and pleasure of the afternoon faded away. Instead, guilt and dread vied for space in her chest. The resulting shoving match brought those cold bubbles of panic welling back into her throat, like giddiness's nauseating cousin.

So much for recharging.

She gently pushed him away. His brows knitted, but he moved back without comment. The sun dimmed, and a breeze ruffled Mandy's hair. She glanced up. Clouds blotted out the warm rays.

Her time with Danny was as short-lived as the day's warmth. He might understand why she'd slept with Nathan. After all, the man hadn't been a crazy killer at the time. But Danny would never forgive her for lying about the affair.

No. What happened on the riverbank could never be repeated. As much as the thought of never being with him again made her shrink inside, it simply wasn't fair. Mandy covered her sadness with movement. Tugging her oversize sweater back over her torso, she climbed behind the wheel and started the car.

Danny was right. It had been beautiful—too beautiful to soil with dishonesty.

"How far are we from where that angler and his son disappeared?" Danny shut the passenger door.

"A few miles."

"Is the river deeper or swifter there?"

"Not really. It's closer to Lake Walker and a bit wider, but the current is about the same. Why?"

"Because I don't see how two people could fall in and just disappear."

"The water's very cold," Mandy said without conviction. "It doesn't take long for the body to shut down."

Danny didn't look any more convinced than she was. "Wouldn't the body get caught on rocks or something?"

"Maybe." She glanced back at the river, swirling past boulders that, yes, should snag two bodies floating downriver. "Stranger things have happened out here."

"But not all of them have been nature's fault."

CHAPTER TWENTY-THREE

Mandy loaded coffee cups and small plates into the dishwasher. The last hour had rushed by in a flurry of chores.

Danny carried the empty cookie tray into the kitchen. He stepped on the foot pedal of the garbage can and brushed the crumbs inside. "Have you seen the girls from Boston?"

Mandy recalled the small crowd in the dining room. She mentally ran through her guest list. Between what had happened on the riverbank and getting back to the inn late, she'd been flustered through the refreshment hour. "No, but I think I saw everyone else." She squinted out the window. Dark clouds had steamrolled over the sunny day. "I don't see their car." Apprehension coiled in her belly. "And I don't like the looks of that sky."

"There's still two hours of daylight," Danny said.

"They've been back by this time every other day." Mandy dried her hands on a dish towel. "I'm going to check their room. Maybe they came back, changed, and went out for pizza or something. Would you please check the weather report?"

"Sure." He was already moving toward the little-used countertop TV.

She grabbed her master key and jogged up the steps. Staring at the door, her stomach crunched tighter. She knew as she put her knuckles to the wood that no one would answer her knock. The lock yielded to her key, and the door opened with the soft squeak of old hinges crying for oil. The room was empty. Inside, three suitcases appeared to have exploded. Clothing was strewn across chairs. Toiletries covered the dressers. The three twins beds were neatly made, but the inn had a policy of not touching the guests' belongings.

No backpacks. Mandy scanned a pile of shoes in the corner. No hiking boots.

The girls hadn't returned.

The Winston Museum of Art and Archeology was a big-ass brick house on a side street in Bangor. Conor parked his latest POS, a twenty-year-old Porsche 911 still in the restoration stage, at the curb. Unlike his brother Danny, who treated his convertible like the high school sweetheart he married, Conor restored a new car every year or so. He fed the meter and jogged up the steps onto a wide porch. According to the plaque by the door, the place was open. The door wasn't locked, and he walked into a tiled lobby big enough for a half-court game of basketball. The old house was a center hall design. A dark wooden staircase bisected the foyer, and a hallway led to the rear of the house. An archway on each side of the huge entryway led to exhibit rooms.

There was no sign of the curator, Louisa M. Hancock, PhD, or anybody else, for that matter.

Not a lot of security for a place that had just been robbed. Feeling like he was casing the place, Conor walked through the arches and checked out the front rooms. Tall ceilings, ornate molding, and thick wallpaper gave the space an old-as-the-Mayflower-money feel. Glass cases held an assortment of broken pots, bits of metal, and other stuff that looked like it had been buried in the dirt for a thousand years. Descriptions of each item were typed neatly on ivory-colored cards. Conor stopped to examine a four-foot-long tusk.

Mammoth tusk, Siberia, 2007. There was a list of people responsible for digging up the discovery and several paragraphs describing the find. Conor skimmed the details. Global warming. Shrinking permafrost. Bones popping up all over the tundra. Interesting. He moved to the next case.

Floorboards creaked overhead.

Conor walked to the bottom of the steps. "Hello?" The narrow staircase hampered his view of the top.

"Just a moment, please." The voice was female, the footsteps on the wooden treads light. The first things Conor saw were old-fashioned pumps, then legs. Slim but shapely calves. The skirt fell just past her knees. Too bad. But it was snug, which was a bonus.

A tall, willowy figure in a conservative gray suit descended. She was sleek as a deer and blonde, with silky hair bound in a fancy, prudish knot, the kind of do a man couldn't wait to undo, one pin at a time, while he tasted every inch of that slender neck.

He raised his eyes and nearly flinched. The look she scanned him with was cold as Siberian permafrost. It chilled him from his leather jacket to his motorcycle boots. Being a hopelessly perverse man, all Conor could think of were the various ways to melt her icy veneer.

She raised her chin and looked through dark-rimmed glasses perched on the end of her nose. "Can I help you?"

Oh, yeah. No. He was here for information, not to thaw the frigid curator. But God, it was tempting. Loosen the hair. Flick a few of those buttons open. Hike that skirt up. Toss the glasses. Yup. She had the hot librarian thing going on.

Was it getting warm in here?

Her stare narrowed. Unfortunately, Conor found disapproval to be a turn-on.

Conor unzipped his jacket. "Yes. My name is Conor Sullivan. I'm looking for Dr. Louisa M. Hancock."

"I'm Dr. Hancock."

No shit? Conor covered his shock with a cough. He held out a hand.

She glanced down as if it were infected with MRSA before resigning herself to touch it. Once she made the decision, though, he had to give her credit; she treated him to a firm, professional shake. "What can I do for you?"

Conor almost laughed at the images rolling through his head. "I'd like to ask you about the robbery."

"Oh, you're a policeman." Something clicked in her eyes, as if being a cop was the reason he was dressed in Levi's instead of Armani. Come to think of it, some of Conor's friends were cops, and they *were* strictly off-the-rack guys.

"No. I'm not a cop."

"Are you a reporter?" Suspicion laced her voice.

Conor shook his head. "No."

Her perfectly arched brows pinched tightly. If she kept that up, she was going to have a Mariana Trench between her eyes. "I don't understand."

"This is going to seem a little odd."

She took a step back, as if strange were contagious.

"Not that odd." He hooked his thumbs in the front pockets of his jeans and tried to appear harmless, not a look he usually went for.

She put one hand to the single strand of pearls at her throat and the other around her waist. The vulnerable gesture roused guilt in Conor. He took a step back. They were alone in an empty building. He was a pretty big guy. He wasn't an ink man, but he was wearing a lot of leather. The shadow on his jaw had passed five o'clock two days ago. She was slender and feminine and probably not used to disreputable-looking types perusing her exhibits. She might be more comfortable in a public place, with a guy in a tie and loafers. A public locale he could offer her. The tie and loafers were a no-go. A man had limits. "Can I buy you dinner or a cup of coffee?"

"I'd really just like to know what this is all about, Mr. Sullivan."

"OK." He sighed at the persistent coolness in her voice. Best to get to the point. "I'd like to know what was stolen from your museum. Did you read about the guy that tried to commit a Celtic ritual murder upstate last December?"

"Yes." She paled. Not an easy feat when her skin was already the color of fresh cream. "You don't think the theft is related, do you?"

"Honestly, I don't know, but I want to find out. He tried to kill my sister."

Cool green eyes considered his candor.

"Do you want me to lock up, Dr. Hancock?"

Conor turned his head. A young woman in a miniskirt and flats stood in the archway. How had he not heard her walk in?

"Yes, please." Dr. Hancock nodded seriously. "Thank you, Lindsay."

"Should I check all the windows?" Lindsay asked with a snotty sneer she tried to cover with innocence.

"No. I'll take care of it." Dr. Hancock's jaw clenched hard enough to grind coffee beans. She turned back to Conor, all traces of consideration wiped clean. "I'm sorry, Mr. Sullivan. I can't help you. Museum records are private."

Bouncing on her toes, Lindsay gave Conor a flirty wave and smile, but he wasn't buying the sweet act.

"They're trying to hang the theft on you, aren't they?"

"The museum is closing, Mr. Sullivan." Dr. Hancock pivoted and walked to the hall. "I'll see you out."

Great. His brother had asked him to do one simple thing, and Conor had blown it by pissing off the one person who could help him.

Guess he was spending the night in Bangor. He certainly wasn't leaving without that list of stolen artifacts.

CHAPTER TWENTY-FOUR

Danny crossed his arms over his chest and leaned on the counter. Outside the window, thanks to the approaching storm, the darkness that dropped on the yard was more blackout than twilight.

Lieutenant Lang stood by the kitchen island taking notes from the Boston girls' registration cards. His lips were clamped in a grim frown. "Do you know where they were headed?"

Mandy opened the inn's logbook on the countertop. "They were hiking the river trail today."

Danny wondered how far that trail was from the spot where Mandy and he had been. Had it really just been a few hours since he'd made love to her in the sunshine? Seemed like much, much longer.

Doug held up a card. "Did you try the cell numbers listed here?"

"I did." Mandy sighed. "The calls wouldn't go through."

"If they took the river trail, they're way out of cell range. Did they have provisions?" Lang asked. Maybe Reed was right, and Lang had nothing to do with Nathan's activities.

Mandy shook her head. Exhaustion and worry deepened the circles under her eyes. "I don't know. I didn't see them leave this morning."

"When they went out the other day, they had full packs," Danny offered. "They told me they always carried enough for an overnight."

"Good." Lang shut his notebook. "Most likely, they either got lost or one of them is injured. I'll contact the rescue squad and put them on notice. I'll drive out to the trailhead now and verify their vehicle is parked there. If the girls don't show up in the next two hours, we'll start a preliminary search. At least we know where to start looking for them."

Danny's gut clenched. This felt wrong. "I don't like this."

"None of us like this, but hundreds of hikers go missing every year." Lang frowned. "Temperature's dropping, and the weather's going to get nasty. Hope they find a place to hole up and stay dry."

As much as it pained Danny to agree with the cop, he couldn't argue with his logic. Lang seemed genuinely concerned and was acting like less of an asshole than usual.

"I don't understand. What makes three chicks want to go out in the woods alone?" Lang tucked his notebook into his pocket. "Why can't they stick to spa days?"

And the asshole was back.

Mandy let it go but didn't waste any time ushering the cop to the door. "You'll let me know what's going on."

"Yes. And you'll call me if the girls turn up."

"Of course." Mandy closed the door on Lang.

"So what do we do while we wait for Lang to call?"

Mandy went into a closet by the back door and pulled out a large backpack. "We don't do anything. I'm going to get ready to search."

"Do you have an extra pack?"

"Jed will probably come with me." She pulled an ultralight tent and a sleeping bag out of the pack. "Or someone from town."

"Anybody but me?"

"I didn't say that."

"Look, I'm not Mr. Outdoorsman, but the army did teach me a couple of things about survival in the wilderness. I assure you that I can hold my own out there." He nodded toward the window. "I'm sure you can."

"If you don't have a pack, I'll borrow one from someone else," Danny said. "If you're going out there, where Nathan just might be running around abducting unsuspecting hikers, I'm following you."

"The girls are probably just lost." With a distracted and worried frown, she returned to her task. "But you can use Bill's pack. I'll pull it out for you."

The faint rumble of distant thunder punctuated her offer. Perfect. Just fucking perfect.

"We could use some light, dense calories. Nuts, candy bars, stuff like that."

Mandy opened the pantry. "I have some trail mix. I don't keep candy in the house. It makes Bill hyper."

"I'll be right back." Danny grabbed his keys and headed outside. A stiff, cool wind hit him, an about-face from the afternoon's perfect weather. Mandy might not think he was much of an outdoor guy, but the army had taught him to scrounge food in the wild. In his opinion, eating bugs and squirrel kebobs was highly overrated. He drove to the convenience store and filled a basket with Peanut M&Ms and Slim Jims. If they were going to spend the night traipsing around the wilderness in the frigging rain, he and Mandy were going to need serious calories to stay ahead of the storm and find those girls in time.

A half hour later, Mandy was checking the contents of her first-aid kit when Danny returned. She stowed the red box in her pack. Jed paced the kitchen. Her mom and Bill sat at the island with Honey stretched out at their feet.

"Your pack is there." She nodded toward the backpack lying on the table. "Doug called. We're meeting at the trailhead in twenty minutes."

"OK." Danny opened the backpack and checked its contents, then added the beef jerky and candy. He tested the bag's weight. "We have enough water?"

"Yes. And iodine tablets just in case," she said.

Danny went to the pantry and pulled out a loaf of bread and a jar of peanut butter. "Want a sandwich?"

"No. I'm not hungry. Thanks." Mandy put a hand to her nervous stomach. She glanced out the window. Tree branches swayed in the wind. The temperature was dropping. Could the girls find shelter? "You'd better get some extra clothes. We have to leave soon."

Danny downed one sandwich in a few bites, washed it down with milk, and made another. He strode out of the room still chewing. "I'll be five minutes."

"Mom, are you going to be all right here alone?" Mandy stepped into her worn hiking boots. She'd changed into cargo pants earlier and sincerely hoped Danny had something to wear other than jeans. Wet denim wasn't much fun.

"Mandy, I'm hardly alone. We have a house full of guests," her mother pointed out. "Bill's here, and I have my shotgun in case of emergency."

Mandy doubted her mother could lift and fire it. "Don't tire yourself out. I told the guests that breakfast would be cold food only, and that they should feel free to help themselves if I'm not back by then. They were fine with that."

Mae put a hand on Mandy's forearm. "Go find those girls. You and Danny are the ones walking into danger. Be careful. I love you."

"Love you, too." Mandy hugged her mother and brother.

"Bill, can you look after Honey for me?" Jed asked.

"I sure will." Bill put a hand on the dog's head. Honey panted up at him, her brown eyes filled with complete adoration.

"Can't the dog help find the hikers?" Danny asked. He'd changed out of his jeans into tan camouflage army fatigues tucked into military-type boots. A snug T-shirt outlined the lean muscles of his chest and shoulders, reminding her that for all his easygoing nature, Danny had been a soldier until very recently. All decked out in his military gear, he looked more badass than bad boy.

Jed shook his head. "Honey's a retriever. She isn't trained to follow a scent."

"She can find Bill." Danny shoved a few items into his pack.

"She knows Bill. That's different." Jed faced Mandy. "You ready?"

"Yes. Let's move." Mandy led the way out into the yard. "Jed's going to drive us to the trailhead and set up a base camp for the searchers."

Jed's strained expression and tight-as-a-raw-clam mouth said he wasn't happy with staying behind. But Mandy knew he'd do what was best for her—and for the missing girls. As much as she wanted to push him away, Danny had already proved back in December that she could trust him with her life. Other than Jed, every other man in town was a possible blackmailer.

"We're about the same size. I have a spare waterproof jacket in my truck." Jed opened the pickup and rummaged behind the driver's seat, coming up with a green nylon jacket. "Weather looks like it might get rough."

"Thanks, man." Danny took the jacket, tossed his pack into the extended cab, and climbed in behind the driver's seat. "How about a sidearm?"

Mandy handed Danny her pack. He stowed it next to him. She got into the passenger seat.

"Got you covered on that, too." Jed handed his 9mm, a holster, and several clips over the seat. Danny checked the weapon and secured it to his belt. They drove out of town. By the time they'd reached the turnoff, he'd secured the weapon and shrugged into Jed's jacket.

The truck bounced along the dirt lane. The trailhead was a clearing with space for parking and a sign with crisscrossed wooden arrows marking the trails. Three weather-beaten cedar picnic tables occupied the open area to one side. A police cruiser was angled behind the hikers' Ford Edge. Mandy got out of the truck. Though a cold front had chilled the night air, the shiver that zoomed through her wasn't temperature related. Nor was it a result of the electric snap of the coming storm in the air. Thunder rumbled in the dark.

Doug Lang got out of the police car. "You're sure you want to go tonight? The storm headed this way is going to be a bad one."

"All the more reason for us to find those girls." Mandy secured her pack and adjusted the straps. Though Bill often went into the woods with Jed, responsibilities had kept Mandy out of the woods for the past year or so. Had her pack always been this heavy? "They were only planning for a day hike. They shouldn't have gotten much farther than the lake. If we're lucky, we'll find them in a few hours."

"I have more volunteers coming." Doug opened a map on the closest picnic table. "There are actually three trails that leave from this spot."

"Did they leave a trail plan in their car?" Jed clicked on a flashlight and illuminated the map.

"I wish." Doug glanced at Mandy. "You're the first team here. You get first dibs. Which trail do you want?"

Mandy stared at the map. Which path had the girls taken? The most scenic route pointed north. It angled toward the river and continued along the water. With an uphill grade and rocky footing, it was the most difficult choice. She thought of the ultra-fit blonde who acted like the leader of the group. She'd want the challenge. "We'll take the north trail."

Jed handed her a walkie-talkie. "You be careful. Check in every thirty minutes."

"I will." She took the handset and zipped it into a pocket of her jacket.

Jed gave Danny a pained look. "You look out for her."

"Of course," Danny answered.

Mandy didn't bother to insist she could take care of herself. She switched on her powerful flashlight and shone it on the ground in front of her. Danny followed close behind her as they started up the trail. As Mandy's thighs burned, she realized she wasn't in the best shape of her life.

"How long does it take to reach the end?" Danny asked.

"This trail leads to Lake Walker. We'll hit the river in about a mile. Then it's another four before it ends at the lake. The girls probably hiked it in a morning, but with the dark, it'll take us longer."

On the other side of the river, lightning snaked across the deep-purple sky.

"We'd better move," Danny said. "It's getting closer."

Four check-ins later, Danny trudged uphill. He kept close behind Mandy. The woods bordered the path to the right. To the left, the ground dropped off sharply. Twenty feet below, the river undulated.

"Careful here," she said over her shoulder.

Danny tripped over a tree root. Rocks and loose dirt shifted underfoot and cascaded down the packed earth behind him. A dislodged stone tumbled over the lip of the trail. A second passed before it plunked into the river below. Danny glanced over the edge. With no moonlight, the water was black as an oil flow. "How much farther is the lake?"

Mandy stopped at a level patch of ground and looked around. She checked her watch. "We're not even halfway."

Mandy's voice was strained. Her breaths sounded labored. Danny lifted the beam of his flashlight to her face. Her cheeks were flushed, but not in a healthy way. He'd been pushing her hard the last half hour. Running had kept him in decent shape. He suspected Mandy didn't have much time for exercise. Though she hadn't complained once, the steep grade and heavy pack were taking their toll. Plus, the temperature had dropped as the storm barreled toward them.

The first raindrops pinged off the hood of his borrowed jacket. He reached into his pocket and pulled out one of the latex gloves he'd lifted from Dr. Chandler's office. He tugged it over his left hand to keep the bandage dry.

Camping, hiking, the woods. It all sucked in the rain.

Static blasted. "Mandy."

She removed the bright-yellow handset from her pocket. "Here."

"That storm is about fifteen minutes away from you. Find some cover." Jed's voice squawked from the receiver. "Now."

"Will do." She put the walkie-talkie back in her pocket. Another bolt of lightning sprinted overhead. "That was closer."

Much closer.

Danny squinted ahead in the darkness. Wind whipped off the river and dampened his face. "We should move away from the water. Does this trail open up anytime soon?"

"Not really, but if I remember correctly, there's a rock overhang we can take shelter under coming up. It's hard to get my bearings in the dark," Mandy shouted over the howl of the wind.

"Let's move, then," Danny yelled back. Solid rock would be preferable to the flimsy emergency tent they'd packed. He glanced down at the river to his right. They were high enough above the water that he doubted flash flooding would be an issue.

Mandy slipped. Danny caught her by the bicep until she righted herself. "Let me take your pack."

The last three times he'd suggested it, she'd waved him off, but urgency supplanted pride as the rain turned the incline from unstable to treacherous. She let him pull the straps from her shoulders. Lightened from her load, her pace recovered. She pushed onward. Danny followed her lead. She was better at finding decent footing.

The rain turned into a downpour, slashing into Danny's face. Lightning lit the woods in a few quick, strobe-like flashes. Thunder crashed. A few feet ahead, Mandy jumped. Her foot slipped on the muddy incline. She fell to her butt and slid toward the drop-off.

Danny lunged forward. "Mandy!" His hand swiped air, and Mandy's orange jacket disappeared over the edge.

CHAPTER TWENTY-FIVE

A clap of thunder woke Kevin. A breath hitched in the dark. He looked down at his son, cradled in his arms. Hunter's eyes were closed, his breathing even in deep sleep. Someone else was in the barn with them.

Was that sobbing?

Kevin sat up slowly, carefully sliding away from his son so he didn't wake the sleeping boy. He surveyed the interior of the barn. Rain pounded on the roof. Water dripped through the holes and puddled on the dirt floor. Lightning flashed. His ears strained for noise not related to the storm.

Hiccup.

Kevin looked up at the solid wood ceiling of his cage. There was someone above them. Except for the crying person, the barn seemed empty. Thunder boomed. Hunter jolted. Another soft cry sounded above them.

Hunter pressed his lips to Kevin's ear. "Dad?"

His son's weak voice chiseled another crack into Kevin's heart, threatening to splinter it into pieces. Their captor had been supplying them daily with water and food. Yesterday there'd been some sort of charred meat and a pile of weeds. Not enough to give them real strength, but sufficient to keep them alive. The fact that they both tended to sleep heavily after drinking confirmed the presence of drugs in their rations. But they had little choice. Several days had passed. At this point, dehydration and starvation were as threatening as their captor.

Kevin whispered back, "I think there's someone else here."

Her cries echoed in the lofty space.

Hunter trembled. "It sounds like a girl." His breath passed over the side of Kevin's face.

"It does."

"She sounds scared," Hunter said. "We should call out to her."

His son's brave comment fractured Kevin's heart anew. Through the agony of helplessness, his boy wanted to reach out to another in need. Chivalrous despite his own terror.

What did they have to lose?

"Hello?" Kevin cringed. His voice rang out louder than he'd intended.

The crying cut off suddenly.

Kevin tried again, with a softer voice. "Is someone there?"

"Here." Wood scraped above them. "We're here. I can't see you."

We?

"We're under you. How many of you are up there?"

Something tapped at the top of his cage. Kevin crawled to the edge and reached up through the bars. His fingers closed around a slim, feminine hand.

"Two. There are two of us." Her skin was ice-cold. "My name is Samantha. My friend Victoria is still unconscious. She won't wake up."

Kevin squeezed her hand. "Hi, Samantha. I'm Kevin."

Hunter crawled into his lap. He stuck his bony arm through the slats and followed Kevin's forearm up to Samantha's hand. "I'm Hunter."

Samantha's breath hitched. She switched her grip to give Hunter an awkward shake. "Where are we?"

"I don't know, Samantha," Kevin answered.

"What's he going to do with us?" Her voice dropped.

"I don't know that either." He was trying to be optimistic for Hunter's sake, but their captor hadn't protected his identity. One of the deepest fissures in Kevin's heart was the certainty that the blond man didn't care if they knew who he was.

No fear of police lineups, mug books, or sketch artists.

Their captor fed and watered them like a farmer treated the cattle intended for slaughter.

Where was she? Stretched out on his belly, shoulders hanging over the precipice, rain ran into his eyes. "Mandy!"

He strained his ears but heard only the rush of water and wind.

"Where are you?" he shouted.

"Here." Her voice was strained.

Danny batted the underbrush aside. He caught a flash of bright orange. Her jacket? Lightning flashed. And he saw her, hanging onto a tree root five feet below him. Her feet dangled a few yards above the river.

"Hold on." He slid back. Where the hell was her backpack? There. He spotted the yellow-and-black nylon on the trail where he'd dropped it to try and catch her. He dug out a coil of rope, tied one end around his waist, and made a loop at the other end. Returning to the trail edge, he tossed the loop toward her. "Grab this."

Her free hand swiped through the air and missed. The base of the root, loosened by her movement, jerked partially out of the dirt.

"Oh!" Mandy slid another foot down the nearly vertical slope. One hand clutched the loosening root while the other clawed at the dirt for another purchase, but there wasn't anything else for her to grab. Pebbles and dirt cascaded into the river below.

"Stop moving." Danny coiled the rope and threw it again. It bounced on the slimy slope beside Mandy's head. She inched a hand toward the rope ring until she gripped it in a tight fist. Slowly, she pulled it to her body and worked it over her head and one shoulder. The root sprang free.

"Ah!" She let go and caught the rope in both hands. Danny shifted back on his haunches and pulled on the rope. He dragged her up over the edge and back onto the trail.

She lay still in the mud for a minute.

Danny crawled over to her. He put his hand on her back. "Are you all right?"

She nodded and sat up. Her hood had fallen back. Rain plastered her hair to her head, and her sodden ponytail dripped. Mud splattered her face. "We have to get moving."

That's my girl. Danny stood and helped her to her feet. He picked up her pack and stuffed the wet rope inside. She led the way up the trail while the rain, driven sideways by the wind, lashed their faces. A hundred yards farther, she stopped and pointed to the left. "There!"

Danny looked where she pointed. Between the sheeting rain and the dark, he didn't see shit.

She led him away from the river. The trail widened around an outcropping of boulders. Thirty feet of sheer rock rose from the earth. Danny put a hand to the wall, which was already blocking some of the deluge. They continued, circling to the side opposite the river. Millennia of rock movement had resulted in a five-foot-deep, ten-foot-wide overhang that looked as inviting as a five-star hotel.

Mandy shone her light into the space. "Empty." She sounded disappointed, as if maybe the girls could've found this tiny hole. Danny was just glad there weren't any bears inside.

She scuttled into the space. Danny followed. He couldn't stand without hunching his shoulders and ducking his head, but the tiny shelter was blissfully dry.

The tent and a fire wouldn't both fit in the tiny space. Since the overhang was blocking the rain, the warmth from a fire won the mental coin toss. "Let's see if we can start a fire."

"OK." Mandy's voice trembled, and her teeth chattered. "Our chances of finding dry wood aren't good, but I have fire starters, which should help." She set her pack on the packed earth. Her hands were shaking from cold or effort or both. "I'll scrounge up some mostly dry wood."

He was not sending her out in the rain. Danny emptied one of the packs. "I'll do it."

She didn't argue. With her can-do attitude, she must be in worse shape than he thought.

He tightened the cord around his hood and stepped out of the shelter. The rocks blocked most of the rain. Danny rooted around until he found some nearly dry pinecones and twigs under a fallen tree. Using the knife blade of his Leatherman tool, he scraped dry timber from the underside of the tree and stuffed everything into the backpack to keep it dry. He scouted under rocks and logs for moderately dry wood and gathered an arm-load before heading back to the overhang.

When he was shipped off to Iraq, he'd thought the training exercises in the woods had been a waste of time. Finding dry stuff and keeping warm hadn't been an issue over there. Now he was grateful the army had prepared him for survival in multiple environments.

Danny dumped the dry bits from the pack in the rear of the shelter. "We'll start with some of that. Make the fire small so we can keep it going. Build it at the edge in case the damp stuff smokes."

"I got it." Mandy knew what she was doing. She rummaged in her pack for matches and fire-starter sticks. Danny left her to it while he scraped the wet bark from the wood he'd gathered and stacked it out of the rain. By the time he'd finished, a tiny flame was dancing in the center of her timber pile.

Mandy rubbed her hands over the small fire. Her teeth chattered loudly enough to carry over the sounds of wind and rain lashing through the surrounding woods.

"How wet are you?"

"Not very. J-just cold."

Danny pulled out their sleeping bags and unzipped both. There was just enough room between the fire and the back wall to squeeze them in. He spread one out and laid the other on top. The rock around and above them was trapping the heat from the fire nicely. He stripped off his wet jacket and tossed it over a boulder to dry. Underneath, his T-shirt was damp around the neck where rain had leaked in. Danny removed his shoulder holster, then pulled the shirt over his head and spread it on a warm rock. The thighs of his fatigue pants were wet, but they were made to dry quickly.

He fished in his pack and came up with another shirt. Next to him, Mandy was fumbling with her jacket.

"Let me help you." He unzipped her nylon shell and tugged it off. Her fleece sweater, like her pants, was made of synthetic material that didn't hold water. He put a hand to her neck. Her skin was freezing. "Why didn't you tell me you were this cold?"

He tugged off both their wet boots and pulled her toward the sleeping bags.

"Didn't want to s-slow us down."

Danny lifted the top cover and pushed Mandy under it. He climbed in with her and wrapped the down snugly around them both. Her shivering body clung to his bare chest.

Really, she probably could have warmed up all by herself, but after her tumble-and-dangle act over the water, he needed to hold her. He wrapped his arms around Mandy's body. Her softness fit his hard angles just right. Breasts squished against his ribs. Maybe the wilderness didn't suck as badly as he'd thought, even in the rain.

Her shivers faded. Danny remembered her turning down peanut butter sandwiches. "Did you eat dinner?"

"No. I was too worried." She sat up. Too bad.

Keeping the blanket around their shoulders, Danny reached into his pack and pulled out the M&Ms. "Quick carbs first."

"I brought plenty of trail mix." She opened two packs of candy while Danny cracked out the beef jerky and a bottle of water. Slim Jims and chocolate were surprisingly good together.

"Your cut is bleeding."

Danny held up his hand. The thin latex glove hung in shreds around his hand. Blood seeped through the soaked bandage. "Must have torn the stitches."

"Let's get it cleaned up. Hand me the first aid kit."

Miraculously, only two of the stitches were ripped free. Mandy did her best to close the wound with butterfly strips. She covered his hand with fresh gauze and tape. Watching her, it occurred to Danny that if he hadn't rested his hand all day, he might not have been able to save Mandy.

The radio crackled. "Mandy? Are you OK?"

Mandy picked up the receiver. "We're fine, Jed. Just holing up under some rocks until the storm passes."

"The weatherman says this front will take a couple of hours of clear out."

"Got it. Thanks. We'll hang tight."

She tossed the receiver back into her pack and finished off a handful of candy. Her eyes were bright, her color back to normal, but her expression was still tight.

"What's wrong?" Danny added a few skinny branches to the fire. Damp wood popped and crackled.

"I'm worried about the girls."

"We're doing all we can to find them."

"I know." A tear trickled down her cheek.

"Come here." Danny tugged her back into his arms. "We'll find them."

Thunder boomed. Mandy jumped. "I hope they're not out in this storm. They could be hungry and cold—"

"Shhh." Danny tilted her chin up and silenced her with a kiss.

His mouth was hot and tasted of chocolate. Mandy wanted more. Heat sprinted through her veins to her core, fueled by adrenaline overload from her near plunge into the river. The turmoil of the past four months had intensified from fear to terror with the disappearance of the girls. Were they lost or was Danny right? Was Nathan out there, gathering a fresh crop of victims?

Her brain rejected the debate, electing to yield control to her body.

Danny's mouth angled. His tongue slipped into her mouth, and all she could think was how much she wanted more. Desire swept aside all the self-control she'd practiced over the winter. She couldn't hold her emotions back anymore. She had to have him again. This afternoon by the river had been beautiful. This was desperate.

Danny pulled back. "Whoa. Um, you're getting a little ahead here."

"Please." Begging didn't feel as humiliating as it should. She grabbed the back of his head and pulled his lips back to hers. He took her mouth again.

The man kissed like a pro, the perfect balance of demand and restraint. His hand remained at her bicep. For all his bad-boy talk, Danny was a gentleman. He had no intention of this turning into anything but a kiss.

But desire hummed under Mandy's skin. Held in check all winter, her emotions churned for release. His palm on her arm was hot as a brand. She wanted him to touch her everywhere. She pressed her hands against his bare shoulders. The muscles were gloriously hard under her touch, the skin smooth. Hair dusted the center of his broad chest. She pushed him down on his back.

"Are you sure?" Danny's voice had gone husky. His eyes darkened in the firelight. "You didn't like the outside bit last time."

She met his gaze head-on. "I need you."

The noise that rose from his throat was half surprise and half groan. He rolled to one side. For a man with only one good hand, he had her sweater over her head and her bra tossed aside in seconds. He filled his palm with the weight of her breast. His thumb gently circled her nipple. He bent his head to draw it into his mouth. Desire pooled between her legs. His hand slid down her rib cage to her belly. A finger slipped under her waistband.

Her body arched toward him. Her limbs were on fire. "Touch me already."

A choking sound leaked out of his chest. His hand slipped into her pants. "Jesus."

That about summed it up.

"Danny. Now." Mandy couldn't get her hand on enough of him fast enough. Smooth muscles were sleek under her palms. She unfastened his pants.

"Wait a second." He shucked them, reaching into the cargo pocket for his wallet.

"Condoms are part of your hiking gear?"

"I don't have hiking gear." He wiggled out of his pants, then helped her do the same.

Mandy took a minute to appreciate the ridged muscles of his abdomen, the strong planes of his chest, the powerful hips that were pressing into hers. There wasn't much room to maneuver in their makeshift bed. Good thing Danny knew how to make every movement count.

He stroked her hip while he kissed a path from her neck to her collarbone, nipping playfully at her shoulder. The hand on her hip squeezed, and he moved it to stroke the inside of her thigh. He cupped her center. She pressed against his palm. His fingers went to work in a gentle circle. The momentum built. Mandy's body tightened. Pleasure built in a tidal wave. Her body arched as all her muscles contracted until the release spiraled from her core through her limbs.

She just lay still for a minute until her heartbeat slowed and she could feel her toes.

Danny's hand slipped between her legs again. "How about an encore?"

Before he could work any magic, she wrapped her hand around his impressive erection.

His body bucked. His face burrowed into her hair. He breathed into her ear. "Easy does it. I'm a little too turned on by watching you come right now. You're so freaking perfect."

And flattery will get you anything...

Mandy grabbed the condom and opened the package. She rolled it over him. Danny shifted her under him. She wrapped her legs around him and guided him home. The fit was perfect, as if he'd been made just for her.

He moved, sliding back and forth, stroking a response from the inside of her just as he'd coaxed an orgasm from her a few minutes ago.

"My God, you feel too good." His face strained with the effort of holding back.

Mandy felt the pressure rise again. Her core tightened almost unbearably.

"Come on, baby. Ladies first." Danny shifted higher, increasing the friction.

She closed her eyes. And her body imploded in a haze of sparkling lights.

He spasmed and sprawled, limp, on top of her. She lay still under his body, his skin damp with sweat, his heart thundering in her ear. His shoulder blocked her nose, and his weight on her rib cage kept her lungs from inflating.

She tapped his shoulder and wheezed, "I can't breathe."

He slid off of her. "Oh, sorry."

"God, you're gorgeous." He plucked a wet twig from her hair. A leaf followed.

The chuckle in her throat nearly choked her.

"I'm serious." His eyes brightened, and his mouth shifted into the wicked grin that had first melted her bones.

"Shut up and kiss me."

"Yes, ma'am."

As he did, it dawned on her that, though he wasn't the first man she'd ever desired, he was the only one she also enjoyed all the time. She wanted him, sure. But she also really, really liked him. She wanted to do more than sleep with him again. She wanted to eat and talk and hang out with him, too. Waking up in the morning next to that sexy grin would be a nice bonus.

A gust of wind sneaked under the rock and whipped up embers in the fire. Raindrops hit her skin, the cold a sharp contrast to the heat of Danny's skin. He pulled the cover higher up on her shoulders.

"We have another hour. Do you have another condom?"

"I do." Danny nuzzled her neck. "I like to be prepared."

"Like a good boy scout."

"Honey, I was never a boy scout."

Mandy chuckled, but guilt intruded on the moment. What would happen if he discovered the truth about her and Nathan?

CHAPTER TWENTY-SIX

Boston, December 1975

"Can you eat something, Nathan?" Dad asked from the doorway. His face had thinned since Mom had gotten sick. The skin on his cheeks was slack as melting wax sliding toward the floor.

Nathan shook his head. His empty belly protested with a painful squeeze, but he couldn't eat.

Dad nodded. He understood. "Do you want me to stay?"

Yes. His throat closed off the words. He didn't want either. He wanted it all to go away. His eyes were wet and a tear rolled down his cheek.

"It's OK." Dad blew out a breath. Helplessness lingered, palpable in the air along with the foul odor that filled the hospital's halls.

Nathan's face heated as the tears flowed. Men didn't cry, so why couldn't he stop?

"I'll give you some time alone with her." Dad stuffed his hands in his pockets. "I'll be just outside if you need me." He ducked into the hall.

The room was gray and dreary, from the speckled floor to the plastic chairs. Nathan pulled his knees to his chest to relieve the stiffness in his back. He turned sideways and rested his forehead on the cool sheets of his mother's bed. His eyelids were heavy as bricks, but he couldn't let them close.

For the first time in nearly a year, his mother's body was still. The doctor said she was in a coma, but Nathan thought she looked peaceful, like she was finally resting.

Nathan squeezed her hand. She didn't respond. There was no sign she was even aware he was there.

Fear balled up in his empty belly. She was hanging on just for him. He was sure of it. If he fell asleep, she'd die.

Dad wouldn't say it, but Nathan knew that was what was going to happen. It was on the doctor's face. Every time he stepped into the room it was like he was surprised she was still breathing.

"It's the only hope." Uncle Aaron's whisper carried from the hallway.

"Aaron, stop talking like this. Gwen would be appalled. You should be horrified at what you're suggesting." His dad's voice shook.

"Without it, she won't last the night."

"She won't last the night with or without your barbaric ritual. I won't let you do it. Gwen would never forgive herself."

"You don't understand, Robert." His uncle's voice thickened with anger.

"Oh, I understand perfectly. Get out, Aaron."

There was a thud, and the wooden crucifix on the wall over the bed trembled. "She's my sister. You can't stop me from saving her."

"Take your hands off me. You're crazy. I should report you to the police." Dad's voice was thin and strained.

Nathan's heart zoomed. He tightened his grip on his mother's limp hand, then eased off, afraid he'd hurt her.

"Don't make threats like that, Robert. Your God may ask you to sit back and accept what he's dished out. But mine—and your wife's—they call for action. That's Celtic blood that runs through Gwen's veins. It demands to be heard."

Dad didn't respond, and Uncle Aaron's voice dropped.

"You'll pay for your decision to let my sister die. Her death is on your head. I will not forget it, Robert."

Thunder rumbled in the distance. Nathan killed the headlights and drove into the parking area behind the old inn. He parked next to the detached garage. Mandy's car wasn't in the lot. A blanket of unease settled on his shoulders.

Getting out of the vehicle, he scanned the rear of the house. All the windows were dark and quiet, as they should be an hour before dawn. He stole across the backyard and rounded the corner. Mandy's window was on the side of the house. Standing on his toes, he peered in. The blinds weren't drawn. The bed was directly across from the window, the white sheets and comforter undisturbed. No dark head rested upon the pillow.

Mandy wasn't there. Where could she be?

Who could she be with?

Anger hazed his vision red. He raised his hand, ready to smash the window in search of his May Queen. Wait. Think. He clenched a trembling fist.

What should he do?

He raised his fingers to his temples, where the constant ache in his head blurred his thoughts. He needed a new plan.

He'd come here to collect his queen, to prepare her for their new life together. He had to have her. No one else would do.

So he needed another way to get her.

His gaze shifted to the next window. Was that Mandy's beloved brother's room?

Enthusiasm for his new idea propelled him to the back porch. He stopped. His gifts. They were missing. He suppressed his rage and stalked back across the lawn to the garage. On the side of the little building, he lifted the lids to the garbage cans. Not there. At least she didn't throw them away.

He tried the side door to the garage. Unlocked. A sign for sure. He found his offerings against the wall. Perhaps she'd put them there to shelter them from the storm. The thought warmed him. Mandy cared. She'd protected the items he'd given her. Nothing else mattered. The details of their future together could be worked out later.

He picked up the heavy cauldron and carried it back to the porch, then secured the rowan branch above the door once again. Better.

As in his original plan, he cut a circle of glass from the door. Reaching inside, he flipped the dead bolt and slipped into the kitchen. His ears strained for sound. A second of silence was followed by a soft *woof* on the other side of a wooden door.

Since when did Mandy have a dog?

Nails scratched on wood, the sound boring into his brain. No. No. No. He pressed his palms to his ears. Tonight's mission depended upon quiet. The dog must be silenced.

He lunged for the knob and shoved the door inward. A yellow lab burst through, hackles raised. Was that Jed's prize bitch, Honey? The dog stood splay-legged in front of him, tail low, growling but unsure of what to do.

Nathan reached into his pocket and withdrew a piece of last night's supper, skewered rabbit and fresh dandelion greens. He'd been prepared to take shelter in case another storm arrived. He held out a bit of meat.

The dog shuffled forward, sniffing. Her tail swayed in a faint wag as she licked the treat from his fingers. Labradors were retrievers, not guard dogs. Relief coursed through him. Thank the gods! Plan B could continue. He was far too tired to come up with a plan C.

The door opened again. Nathan's hopes rose. Mandy! Perhaps she'd fallen asleep on the sofa.

A shadow fell across the tile floor. No. It wasn't Mandy. Even in the dark, he could see the shape was much too large. Mandy's brother, Bill, shuffled in. His hand swiped the wall, turning on the overhead lights. Dressed in gray sweatpants and an oversize hoodie, he rubbed sleep-heavy eyes with both fists like a child. When he lowered his hands, surprise registered. "What are you doing here?"

"I've come to get you." Because there was no better way to ensure Mandy's cooperation.

"Why?" Bill stepped back. "Mandy said I'm supposed to stay here."

"I know. She sent me to get you." Nathan smiled. His facial muscles strained with the effort, as if they had atrophied from little use.

"Mandy said you did something bad." Bill's jaw jutted. His eyes narrowed in suspicion. "And Jed said you hurt her."

"I did." Nathan tried to look ashamed. "And I'm very sorry. We all make mistakes. But I'm going to make it up to her by helping her now."

"Where is she?"

Ah, love was such an easy emotion to manipulate.

"She fell and hurt her ankle. She needs you, Bill."

"She fell? In the woods?" Bill shuffled his feet. His blond brows furrowed with concentration.

Rushing Bill wouldn't swing his decision in Nathan's favor, but guests slept upstairs, and Bill's mother could hear them at any moment. Even ill, she was not a person to be crossed, particularly when it came to protecting her children. Nathan wondered if she was strong enough to lift and fire her shotgun.

"OK, but I have to tell Mom where I'm going."

"Mandy told me your mother has been sick," Nathan lied. His assistant had told him about Mae's heart attack. "This would probably upset her. That wouldn't be good for her recovery, would it?"

"I guess not." Bill gave the dog a pat on the head. "You stay here, Honey. Take care of Mom."

Bill dropped into a kitchen chair to tie his sneakers. Nathan waited, anxiety roiling into white water in his head. His heartbeat thudded, simultaneously loud and thin. His mind wasn't the only part of his body degenerating.

Tomorrow night it would all be over.

Nathan led Bill out the door like Willy Wonka, but he'd do what was necessary to make his plan work. No one was as important as Evan. Following his uncle's example, Nathan would save him or die trying.

He opened the sedan's passenger door for Bill.

Mandy would be upset that her brother had been chosen, but it was her punishment from the gods for not being ready for Nathan when he came for her.

Everyone had to pay a price.

Everyone had to make sacrifices.

Danny stared out into the still-dark forest. Behind him, Mandy slept in their sleeping bag nest. A cool breeze stirred the fire, and trees dripped with fresh rain. He checked his watch. The rain had stopped, and the last rumble of thunder had passed thirty minutes ago. He hadn't seen lightning in an hour.

He leaned back and nudged Mandy's shoulder. She jumped.

"Sorry." He stroked the smooth skin of her back. "The storm passed. I thought you'd want to get moving."

She sat up. The cover slipped down around her waist. Mmm. Her skin flushed. All of it, and Danny wanted to lick every inch. But it wasn't going to happen tonight. The forced break was over. Duty called.

"You're already dressed." With an exasperated glance, she quickly tugged on her clothes. Pity.

"I didn't see any point in waking you."

"How long did I sleep?"

"Couple hours. The storm hung around longer than expected."

She tugged on her jacket and boots, then grabbed a few things from her pack. "I'll be right back."

"Where are you going?"

"Just behind that tree over there, and no, you cannot come with me." She secured her holster behind her hip.

"You have to talk to me the whole time, and if you take longer than five minutes, I'm coming after you."

"You show up behind that tree, I'll shoot you in the foot."

"Have I told you how sexy that temper of yours is?" He grinned back at her.

She stalked out of the shelter, but her shoulders were shaking. "We should be serious."

"Why?"

"Because there are three girls missing." She disappeared from sight, but her boots rustled in the underbrush.

"Those girls are going to be missing whether or not we're freaking out. Staying calm will help us find them faster." Under the constant threat of attack in Iraq, Danny had learned that humor, as inappropriate as it sometimes seemed, could help him keep his shit together.

"I guess."

He packed up the stuff they'd used, redistributing their supplies so he carried the bulk of the weight. Mandy's pack got the two-pound tent and featherlight sleeping bags.

Mandy walked back into the cave. Droplets clung to her yellow jacket. "You really think we'll find them?"

He handed her the lighter backpack. "I don't do odds."

She swung the straps over her shoulders. "This feels awfully light."

"We drank a bunch of the water." He shrugged.

She raised a brow. She wasn't buying it.

"OK, I can carry more weight than you. We'll move faster this way. That's what's important, right?"

"Right." She nodded. "And thank you. Let's get moving."

They headed back to the trail. Though the rain had stopped, the air carried enough moisture to dampen Danny's face. Patches of mist drifted through the forest. An hour later, just as dawn brightened the sky to pale gray, they emerged from the woods. The path summited and dropped into a steep decline. Beyond, a huge lake sprawled. Fog hovered over the glassy surface and clung to the tall reeds of the shoreline.

"Look!" Mandy pointed to something in the weeds on the slope. She shifted the beam of her flashlight to illuminate a silver rectangle. "Cell phone? No, it's a camera."

While Mandy retrieved the device, Danny scouted the area. Dawn broke over the lake. Golden sunlight gleamed off the rippled surface. The scent of organic matter and decay drifted off the vegetation near the water's edge.

"Damn. It doesn't work." Mandy turned the compact camera over in her hands.

"Could have water inside."

"Or the battery died." She put it in her pocket. She dropped her pack and marked the spot where she'd found the camera by tying a yellow ribbon around a twig. "Maybe the memory card is still good."

"It might not even be their camera."

"True." Mandy's gaze drifted out over the lake. "I was so hoping we'd find them here."

Danny rubbed her shoulder. "I know."

"Where are they?"

In the dim predawn light, Nathan parked his assistant's car in front of the barn. In the passenger seat, Bill's leg jiggled. They got out of the vehicle.

"Where is she?"

"Just inside." Nathan pointed at the double doors. "Go on in."

Bill hesitated. "It's dark in there. I don't like the dark."

"There's a light switch next to the door. I'll turn it on for you." Nathan prodded Bill's back.

"No." Bill balked. "This doesn't feel good. I don't want to go in there."

"Run!" The feminine shout came from within the barn.

Bill's big blue eyes went wide. He backed up, stumbling backward and tripping on his over-sized feet. "Mandy!"

Nathan fired the Taser.

The barbs shot out and struck Bill in the thigh. His huge body jerked. Twitching, he fell on the closed trunk with a *clunk*. A wild spasm drove his elbow through the cover of the brake light. Bits of red and clear plastic fell to the dirt. Bill rolled off the vehicle and crashed to the ground like a felled giant redwood.

Nathan stared down at the twitching man. Mandy's brother was quite large and could potentially be a serious problem. Nathan hastily retreated to the barn's small office, filling a syringe with tranquilizer and jogging back. Tears flowed down Bill's face as he wild-eyed the needle. Nathan jabbed it into Bill's still-spasming leg.

Bill quieted. Crisis averted.

The barn door rolled open. A camp light, raised lawn-jockey style, illuminated the barnyard.

"How are you going to get him up there?" His assistant pointed through the open door to the stack of wooden cages. The uppermost layer was above Nathan's head. The man in the bottom cage was shielding his son from Nathan's sight. The young blonde woman above him did likewise with her prone companion.

She was the one who'd shouted. Deep in her tear-swollen eyes, rebellion lurked. He'd have to watch that one.

Nathan gazed down at Bill again. He weighed more than two hundred pounds. Nathan's muscles had suffered as much as his brain these last few days. Weakness prevailed over his entire system. There was no way he could lift even a small person over his head, let alone Bill.

Confusion nearly overwhelmed Nathan. His gaze pinged around the space. Surely, he'd planned for this. He wiped sweat from his brow with a grimy hand.

His eyes stopped on a series of ropes and pulleys hanging from the rafters. Relief flooded him. He'd set up a system just for this purpose when his brain had been functioning at its peak. The ropes slid along the beam to the side of his cage structure. A leather harness once used for horses had been adapted to fit around a person. He strapped Bill in. Rusted pulley wheels squeaked as the apparatus dragged him into the barn. Nathan made some adjustments. Hauling on the ropes, the pulleys lifted Bill from the ground. Securing the rope to a support beam, Nathan pushed Bill through the opening in the front of the cage and removed the harness. The remaining cage side was secured with long screws.

Bill wasn't getting out.

"Time to call Mandy." He jumped down and walked out of the barn. His assistant followed.

"There's no cell service out here."

"That's why we're driving toward town."

"In daylight?"

"I'll wear a hat and coat. No one will suspect. We don't have to go all the way into town. We'll pick up a signal on the outskirts."

Nathan donned his jacket and hat. His fingers fumbled on the zipper. "You'd better drive."

As much as Nathan hated being in the passenger seat, ceding control of the vehicle to his assistant was the best choice.

The thought of speaking to Mandy, of hearing her voice again, spurred his spirits and consumed his thoughts. So much so that he didn't notice the vehicle behind them until it was too late.

CHAPTER TWENTY-SEVEN

Conor circled the block, looking for a parking space. His POS sputtered. "Oh, come on, baby. I know I haven't treated you right, but please don't die on me now."

He gave her some gas. The engine revved back to life.

"That's my girl." He nosed into a spot around back and checked the time on his phone. The museum had just opened.

In the first room off the entryway, nasty little Lindsay was dusting exhibit cases. "Mr. Sullivan, what can I do for you?" Her tone made it clear she wasn't limiting his options to museum business.

"I'm looking for Dr. Hancock."

"Dr. Hancock isn't here." Lindsay flashed an evil smile. Something was up.

"I'll wait."

Lindsay shrugged him off. "Whatever." She dusted her way toward the hall and clomped up the stairs.

Conor began his museum tour with the doorway marked EMPLOYEES ONLY. Dr. Hancock's office was small and tidy, which would make searching it easy. An antique desk took center stage, but the rest of the furniture was bargain-basement. The desk drawers were full of office supplies. He opened a metal filing cabinet behind the desk and thumbed through the hanging files. *Ah-ha.* A neat label identified the file on the theft. He pulled the manila folder free and swiveled around.

"What are you doing here?" Dr. Hancock stood in the doorway.

My bad. "I was looking for a piece of paper to leave you a note." Conor whipped out an excuse faster than a grinch with a stolen Christmas tree.

"Look, Mr. Sullivan. I don't know what you think you're doing, but if you're not out of this museum in one minute, I'm calling the police."

Lindsay appeared in the doorway behind the doctor. "Here's a box for your personal things."

"Thank you." Dr. Hancock said through clenched teeth. She took the box and set it on a chair. She gave Lindsay a White Witch–worthy glare. Lindsay backed away. Not as dumb as she looked.

Dr. Hancock frosted Conor next. "I would appreciate you vacating my chair and my office so I can pack up."

Conor tried to shove the file under his arm, but she snagged it on her way past. "They canned you?"

Her lips compressed into a white, paper-thin line. "At this point, I'll be lucky if I'm not arrested."

"Why would you be arrested?"

"The thieves entered through a first-floor window. There was no sign of a forced break-in. I'm being investigated."

"That sucks." Conor lingered. "Since you're already fired, why not show me that file?"

"Why on earth would I do that?"

"Because if I find your stuff, it'll clear your name."

She hesitated for all of two seconds. "Meet me at the diner across the street in thirty minutes."

———

With equally heavy feet and heart, Mandy emerged from the trail. Danny was right on her heels. Four vehicles sat in the clearing: the girls' Ford Edge, Jed's truck, and two other SUVs.

"You look beat." Jed frowned at her.

Jed's description summed it up. She'd taken a beating, both physically and emotionally. Lack of sleep. Hiking through most of the night. Making love with Danny again despite her decision to put distance between them.

Not finding the girls.

"Two other teams went out after the storms passed over. They aren't back yet, but so far, no one has seen any sign of the girls."

"Where's Doug?" Mandy pulled the camera from her pocket. "We found this. But we don't know if it belonged to one of them. It isn't working."

"He got a call. Said he'd be back." Jed opened the truck door for her. "Doesn't matter. He already called the state for help when you reached the lake this morning without finding anything. We'll have a full-scale search-and-rescue operation up by this afternoon."

Mandy swayed. Danny and Jed each grabbed an arm. With no energy left for protecting male egos, she ignored the look that passed between them.

"Let's get her back," Danny said.

In the truck, she leaned back on the seat and closed her eyes.

"We're here." Someone tapped her on the shoulder.

She jerked awake. They were parked behind the inn. She must have dozed off. Grabbing her pack, she got out and trooped across the grass. On the back porch, her fingers fumbled with the wet laces of her hiking boots. The dog barked inside.

"Honey doesn't usually bark much." Jed clumped up the porch steps.

"Mandy?" Danny stopped behind her. She turned. He was pointing few feet to her left. She followed his finger. Next to the back door sat the pot of drooping pansies.

Mandy's empty stomach cramped. She lunged for the door.

Three retirees in fly-fishing vests were in the kitchen helping themselves to juice and muffins.

"Good morning." Mandy slowed her steps. "Is my mother around?"

"We haven't seen her," one fisherman said. "We're getting a late start today, though. She could've been up earlier. "

Honey ran to the door to the family quarters and scratched. Mandy pushed past the dog. The living room was empty and quiet. Too quiet for a house with Bill in it. Mandy went down the hall that led to the bedrooms. She knocked lightly—"Mom?"—then opened the door. Her mother lay facedown on the braided area rug. One hand clutched her chest. The other extended toward the nightstand, where the cordless phone charged.

"Call 911," Mandy barked over her shoulder. Jed and Danny appeared in the doorway. Jed grabbed the phone. He moved to the corner of the room and dialed.

Mandy gently rolled her mother over. "Mom."

Her mother's eyes fluttered. "Find," she wheezed, "Bill."

Danny jogged down the hall, opening doors and calling for her brother.

Mandy's heart kicked again, pressure and panic constricting her throat. "Mom, where's Bill?"

Her mother's eyes drifted shut. Danny dropped onto his knees beside her. "He isn't in the apartment." He pressed his fingers to her mother's neck. "She's hanging on."

Barely. Her skin was gray, her breaths shallow.

Jed's boots clumped in from the kitchen. "Ambulance is on the way. Called Doug, too, but nobody can find him."

She looked up at Jed. "Bill's gone."

Numbness spread through Mandy's body; her mind overloaded as every fear she'd harbored for the past four months came to fruition. Her mother lay dying, and Mandy had failed to protect her brother. Bill, who would never hurt anyone, was now at Nathan's mercy.

CHAPTER TWENTY-EIGHT

Conor dug into a slice of blueberry pie. Across from him, Dr. Hancock sipped black coffee. Voices and utensils echoed in the tile-floored diner.

The doctor's French-manicured fingers flipped open the file. "The objects stolen are: a box of Celtic coins; a bronze cauldron; a few chips of the bluestones from Stonehenge; a bronze shield; three small bronze figures of horses; and some jewelry, including a ring."

"May I look at that?"

She handed him the file.

Conor sifted through a pile of photos. "What's the value of all of this?"

She quoted him a modest figure. "That's it?" He picked up a photo of a big metal pot and turned it over. *Belenos Cauldron, bronze, 4th Century BC, Scotland, 1987.*

She stiffened. "The true worth of these pieces is in their historical significance."

"I apologize, Dr. Hancock. I only meant that the pieces seem undervalued to me."

She sniffed, seemingly mollified. "Frankly, I don't know why anyone would take the risk to steal our artifacts. They're hardly things that could easily be converted into drug money."

Yeah. Fencing a mammoth tusk would take some work.

"If the pieces weren't that valuable, why were you fired?"

She rubbed the bridge of her nose. "The Celtic collection was actually on loan from a museum in Edinburgh. The loss isn't so much financial as an embarrassment."

"What would you use a cauldron for?" Conor asked.

"Cauldrons were used in daily life for cooking and such, but this was a more ornamental piece. Given the weight and complexity of design, it's more likely the cauldron was either a gift or an offering of some sort."

The hairs on Conor's neck wiggled. "Offering?"

"The Celts believed all forces of nature were controlled by the gods. Offerings were necessary for all aspects of life: good crops, success in battle, health, the weather. Usually these were conducted on one of the Celtic holidays."

"They celebrated the solstices, right?" Maybe nothing was going to happen until June. They'd have more than a month to figure out what was going on.

"There are eight major holidays. The solstices and equinoxes, plus there were four sacred days in between. The next holiday is Beltane, or May Day."

Uh-oh. So much for being safe until June. "When is May Day?"

"Tomorrow."

"Shit." Conor's phone vibrated in his pocket. Danny's number lit the display.

"What's up, little brother?"

"Bad shit. That's what."

Conor's gut tightened as Danny brought him up to speed on his disaster of a night.

"I'm leaving now. I'll be there in a couple of hours." Conor ended the call.

"What happened?" Concern furrowed Dr. Hancock's brow.

"Some people have gone missing."

"Does it have anything to do with my stolen exhibits?"

"Maybe."

She tossed back the rest of her coffee. "Give me twenty minutes. I'll pack a bag."

"Why?"

"I'm going with you."

"No, you aren't," Conor said. "If I find your artifacts, they're going to be with a killer."

Dr. Hancock snatched her folder out of his hands. "You lied to me and broke into my office. I don't trust you. For all I know, you could want the artifacts for your own purposes."

"It's too dangerous. You could get hurt. I'll take the pictures with me and let you know if I find them."

"Not good enough, Mr. Sullivan." Dr. Hancock grabbed her purse. "Finding those artifacts is the only way to clear my name. I'm going, with or without you." She left, forcing Conor to hop to it to keep up.

He followed her silver BMW to a garage under a swank condominium complex. Her penthouse was all glass and wood and gorgeous views. Either her job at the museum paid a lot more than Conor thought or the doctor came from the kind of money that was understated and very, very old. True to her word, she had an overnight bag packed in no time. She also changed her clothes to jeans, boots, and a blue sweater. Casual dress looked good on her. Her uptight do and attitude, however, remained.

Back in the garage, she cast a glance at his car. "We can take my SUV."

"My car runs."

"I'm sure it does, but it doesn't look like it can handle off-road. Rural Maine isn't Philadelphia, or Bangor, for that matter. You can do what you like. I'm taking my car."

She had a point.

"OK," he grumbled.

She fished in her purse. Not the skinny one she'd had earlier, but a larger, sack-like bag in brown leather. Lord, she matched them to each outfit.

At the chirp of her fob, the lights of a Porsche Cayenne blinked. *Oooh.*

She climbed behind the wheel. If he weren't so worried about his brother, he would have seriously enjoyed the sweet ride.

Conor resisted sniffing the leather seat. "Tell me about May Day."

She slipped into lecture mode the way Conor wore a broken-in pair of running shoes. "Beltane is one of the four great fire festivals that occur quarterly during the Celtic year. On the eve of Beltane, the Celts built bonfires, called Bel-fires, to honor Belenos, to celebrate the end of winter's cold and the beginning of spring warmth. People jumped over the fires to ensure good health or luck."

"Belenos. Isn't that the god of fire who's on your stolen cauldron?"

"Yes. He was a major Celtic god. Beltane Eve was also a celebration of fertility. One of the well-known symbols associated with Beltane is the maypole. Maidens would decorate it with flowers and ribbons and dance around it. Then couples would go off into the woods and, um, consummate a relationship in greenwood marriages."

"Basically, it was a giant phallic symbol?" Conor glanced over.

Blushing, she changed lanes. Cute. "Another May Day tradition is the May Queen, who represents the maiden aspect of the Celtic triple goddess. The goddess is maiden, mother, and crone, or past, present, and future, all wrapped up into one. Beltane is all about sexuality, passion, joy, and new life. Rebirth, if you will."

All things a dying man trying to save his only son would want. "So, this happens tomorrow, May first?"

"Actually, Beltane Eve is what is really celebrated. The festivities are usually conducted on the night of April thirtieth."

Conor's heart skipped. "That's tonight."

The ambulance pulled away. Mandy hugged Mrs. Stone. "Thank you for going with her."

"You find Bill. I'll take care of your mother. It's what she would want." The woman got into a battered sedan and followed the flashing lights down the street.

Mandy ran for the house. A few guests were milling around the foyer and parlor. She passed them without slowing. Danny followed her into the kitchen. She grabbed her knapsack from the night before and dumped it out. Jed was spreading a map on the kitchen island. Had they communicated telepathically?

"What are you doing?" he asked.

Mandy didn't look up. She pulled another pack from the closet and started stuffing water bottles and trail mix into both. "We have to get moving."

"What about the police?" Getting up to speed, Danny dumped his own pack and started refilling it.

"Can't find Doug," Jed said. "State police are on the way."

Danny had a floodlight moment. "Maybe Lang's the one who's been helping Nathan."

"That's my guess." Mandy tossed the emergency tent and sleeping bags aside in favor of a small rolled blanket and extra ammunition.

"We need to be gone before the police get here or we'll be tied up for hours." Mandy shoved a straggling piece of hair behind her ear. Wrinkled, damp, and dirty from the night in the woods, she looked a little crazy. He probably did, too.

"But won't they be able to coordinate a better search?"

Jed added a ziplock bag of dog kibble and a plastic bowl to his pack. "Search and rescue is already gathering at the river trailhead. They'll work from there toward the lake because that's the hikers' last known location."

"If there's anything to find on that trail, they'll find it. No point in our repeating efforts." Mandy tossed her pack by the door. "I'm grabbing fresh socks. Then we're out of here."

Danny followed suit. "Where are we going?"

Jed tapped a blue splotch on his map. "You found the camera near Lake Walker. We'll start there. But first we'll drop a radio at the search and rescue base in case we find something."

"Or they do." Mandy stuck her head through the doorway to the dining room. "Hello? Is anyone out there?" The three fishermen appeared.

"When the police get here, would you show them these?" Mandy circled the Lake's location on the map. She took the silver camera out of her pocket and laid it on the map.

They all nodded. "Sure."

"Thank you." Mandy turned back.

"You've been fighting me all week about Nathan," Danny said. "Why are you so sure it's him now?"

She whirled and raced into the apartment. She returned with a rifle slung over her shoulder, pair of socks in one hand, and three envelopes in the other. The ferocity in her eyes alarmed Danny. "Go ahead. Take a look. I've been lying all along. You can hate me, but don't get in my way."

Danny slid papers out of the envelopes.

Holy shit. Pictures of Bill with threats scrawled across them—and a photo of Mandy and Nathan locked in a passionate kiss.

"When did you get these?" Betrayal sliced through him like the sharpest of blades. Not much pain yet, but the knowledge that when it came, it would be devastating.

Jed gaped. In his eyes Danny saw his own shock and betrayal reflected back at him.

Her voice went monotone. "One came the day after Nathan disappeared. The other note came the day you arrived. I got the third after you moved into the inn."

His head whipped up. Mandy wouldn't look at him or Jed. Her jaw jutted forward. Her lack of expression warned him that she'd mentally gone somewhere without emotion. A place where a person functioned on autopilot to get the job done. A place where there was no room for feelings or the reactions they induced. He knew because he'd been there.

And with the evidence that she'd been lying to him right in his face, he was thinking about paying that special place a visit.

Mandy snatched the photos from him, stuffed them back into the envelopes, and stomped back to the kitchen. She tossed them on the map and weighed them down with the camera.

Guess she had no reason to lie anymore. Nathan had taken Bill. She had no one to protect. In fact, she was probably blaming herself right now. Hindsight was a relentless bitch.

Mandy picked up her pack. Rifle in hand, she went out the back door. Jed shook himself like one of his retrievers and started after her. Guess he could fake it as well. The dog trotted after them.

Danny grabbed his pack and joined Mandy and Jed in the truck. He and the dog shared the backseat. How could she have lied to him all this time? Her deception burned through his gut. No woman had ever sparked such a deep response from him. Was she lying about anything else? Had everything between them been an act? How could he ever trust her again? Danny squeezed his eyes shut and banged a fist on his thigh. Now wasn't the time. Even though Mandy had betrayed him, people were missing. Poor Bill was out there somewhere, alone and scared. The betrayal that hung between him and Mandy would have to wait. Iraq had taught him to compartmentalize with the best of them.

His phone buzzed.

Conor. "I'm on my way there. What's going on?"

Danny filled him in. There was no one he'd rather have his back than Conor. "We're headed to Lake Walker."

"Don't waste any time, Danny. Whatever is going down is happening tonight."

"What did you find out? And say it fast. I only have one bar of cell reception, and we're headed out of town."

"Have you ever heard of Beltane?"

The duck boat slid into the glassy water of Lake Walker. Mandy held the bow line as Jed drove the truck and trailer away from the lake and parked. They piled into the bobbing craft. The dog claimed the bow, sticking her nose in the air and sniffing the air. Mandy sat up front with Honey.

"We'll start where you found the camera." Jed started the motor and followed the shoreline. "We're about a half hour from the end of the trail the girls were hiking."

Mandy hadn't spoken in the hour since they'd left the inn. Danny and Jed had conferred on the search, but no one had mentioned her big revelation. Waves of anger and hurt wafted from both men, but Mandy shut them down. Every ounce of energy inside her was reserved for keeping her head on straight so she could find her brother.

Keeping panic at bay was her full-time occupation. She had nothing left to give.

She checked her watch. According to Danny's brother, whatever Nathan was planning would happen tonight.

Bill was afraid of the dark.

It took another thirty precious minutes to motor over to the North River Trail exit. Jed tilted the motor, and they dragged the bow onto the shore and tied it to a tree. Honey leaped out. Whining, she ran up and down the weedy shoreline.

"She smells something she doesn't like," Jed said.

The dog darted up the slope toward the trees.

"So do I." With a worried frown, Danny started after the retriever. Mandy and Jed fanned out twenty yards on each side of him.

Over the organic smells of soil and pine, a cloying scent lingered. Mandy stepped into the forest and walked past the little yellow ribbon that indicated the camera's original position. The buzz of insects drew her deeper into the woods. Her steps were quiet on the bed of wet pine needles underfoot. Both the smell and the buzzing intensified.

Flies. There were too many flies.

CHAPTER TWENTY-NINE

Something scuffled outside the barn. Kevin startled from a doze. The double doors across from his cage slid open. He squinted against the bright light until his eyes adjusted. A dry, clean breeze swept through the barn. Kevin got his first good look outside in days. The barnyard was a large cleared square the size of an infield, made up of mostly dirt and weeds. Beyond it, a meadow rolled out for about a hundred yards before the forest took over.

Kevin focused on the barnyard. A thick pole about six feet high had been erected in the far end of the clearing. Were those ropes encircling it? Goose flesh rippled up Kevin's arms.

He glanced at Hunter. His son was sitting next to him, cross-legged, watching the blond man with the sunken, glazed-over eyes of a wild animal in a cage. Kevin reached for his son's shoulders, drawing him closer to lean against Kevin's chest. He wrapped his arms around him. A shudder passed through Hunter's frail frame. Malnourished, sedated, overwhelmed by shock and fear, the boy was shutting down.

There wasn't a damned thing Kevin could do about it. Impotence and rage flooded him, almost but not quite obliterating the terror hammered into his bones. He was also helpless to save his son from whatever their crazed captor was planning.

Fuzziness invaded him again. He closed his eyes. Visions stampeded into his head. No! He wrenched his eyelids up. The nightmares that came during his drugged sleep were of the *Saw* and *Silence of the Lambs* variety.

He reached for the wooden post behind him and fingered the notches he'd gouged in the wood with a fingernail, one for each night he was aware they'd passed in the barn. Four. They'd been imprisoned for at least four days and nights. Movement above him reminded him they were no longer alone. A slim hand reached down through the bars next to his shoulder. Kevin grabbed it and squeezed in silent support.

The blond man walked into the barn. He glanced at Kevin with eyes that were glassy, nearly opaque, blinking away without change in expression, as if he didn't recognize him as human. Nobody was home. Kevin's empty stomach heaved. His captor was beyond crazy.

He approached an old black steamer trunk. He lifted the lid and removed a shiny metal object, oval in shape and discolored with age. A shield? What on earth...? Their captor carried it outside, where it gleamed dull bronze. He set it in the center of the barnyard, then returned and repeated the process with several wooden boxes. He opened one. It was full of small pieces of metal, coins perhaps, like a pirate's treasure chest.

What did he do, rob a museum?

The truth dawned brighter than the sun outside.

My God. He was building a shrine.

A sliver of bright yellow nestled amid the brown and green weeds a few yards ahead. Mandy turned toward it, but her strides slowed. A hand stuck out from under a pile of leaves and debris.

"Oh, no." She couldn't stop her body from moving closer, from squatting down, from lifting the branch and revealing Ashley's dead face. A fly landed on a milky white eye. Mandy flew backward, crashing into a tree trunk. Pain shot through her back. Oddly, its sharp bite steadied her.

Danny reached her first. He leaned over the body.

"Any idea how she died?" Jed held the agitated dog at a distance.

"Nothing obvious." Danny shook his head. "I don't see any blood or rips in her clothing. Her throat doesn't look bruised. Could be a wound on her other side, but I'm not touching her."

Mandy knew evidence, not lack of compassion, prompted Danny's declaration.

"I'll radio it in." Jed reached for the walkie-talkie in his pocket. He didn't need to say that they'd be moving on. There was nothing they could do for Ashley. "We'll mark the location."

Mandy straightened her wobbly knees and pressed on. They combed the surrounding area but found no sign of the other two girls. Every time Ashley's gray, mottled face popped into Mandy's head, she superimposed an image of her brother in its place. She'd mourn the poor girl after she found Bill.

Riding on a wave of numbness, Mandy climbed back into the boat. Danny settled in the middle. They didn't talk or make eye contact. An almost tangible wall of deceit had risen between them. His anger at her couldn't be greater than her own humiliation. She deserved every ounce of disgust. Being lonely was no excuse for letting Nathan manipulate her.

Jed started the engine. "Should we head north or south?"

Mandy glanced at her watch and scanned the shoreline. Four hours till dark. This decision could mean life or death for Bill and the others. It weighed on her soul like a lead mantle. *Where are you, Bill?*

She closed her eyes for a second and sent out a silent prayer that she wasn't condemning her brother to death. "North. He'll want seclusion. There are too many rental cabins at the south end. The northern terrain isn't as friendly."

The boat chugged through the smooth water. Mandy scanned the shoreline, looking for disturbances in the marshy reeds and thick green vegetation that edged the lake. Shadows lengthened as the sun moved across the sky.

She spotted an area of crushed reeds. "There."

Jed nosed the boat closer. "Shallow water. We'll have to switch to oars."

The engine cut off. Jed tilted the propeller out of the water. Danny started rowing.

The cloying odor of decomposition hit Mandy's nose like a blow. "No." The word slipped out as a whispered plea.

She covered her mouth with a hand. Her eyes watered, and her gaze searched the water for the source with frantic fervor. The boat slid into the reeds. Tall stalks surrounded the boat, the hull cleaving and crushing the plants in its path the way panic trod on Mandy's heart.

Thud.

The boat struck something.

Mandy froze. Whatever they'd hit was right below her. She leaned forward, her next breath locked deep in her lungs. She forced her eyes down.

The partially rotted carcass of a deer lay in the shallow water. Not Bill. Not another young girl. Just a deer.

Lights speckled her vision. A hand pushed her head between her knees.

"Breathe," Danny said.

She did. Air flooded her lungs. The rush of blood faded from her ears. She lifted her head.

"Let's keep going." Jed nodded toward the oars.

Danny took his seat. His eyes focused on Mandy for a second, then moved away.

She resumed her seat in the bow. Danny rowed them out of the reeds. Jed lowered the motor and started it up. The boat resumed its cruise up the shoreline.

Mandy fixed her attention back on the water's edge. The sun dropped toward the treetops. She checked her watch. Two hours till twilight.

Honey licked her face, and Mandy wrapped an arm around the dog's neck.

Find Bill.

"We're too late." Conor gripped the armrest, and they drove past three state police cruisers and turned in to the lot behind the Black Bear Inn. His belly tensed. "Wait. That's Danny's car."

Dr. Hancock parked next to the Challenger.

Relief budded in his chest. "But if he was here, why didn't he answer his fucking phone the twelve times I called?"

He bolted from the car to the inn. The doctor's long legs kept up just fine. He jogged up the porch steps and banged on the back door.

"Conor." The gravity in her voice stopped him. He turned.

Her porcelain complexion had faded to bleached concrete. She pointed to a pot of flowers. "That's my cauldron."

"Shit." A tall, thin man stood at the door. "I'm Detective Rossi." He shook their hands.

Conor introduced himself and Louisa. "I'm looking for my brother. Dr. Hancock is the curator for the Winston Museum of Art and Archeology."

Dr. Hancock explained the theft to the cop.

"That's a Celtic artifact from your museum?" Rossi asked.

"Yes," she said.

Rossi frowned. "Let's discuss this inside."

Guests gathered in the parlor. The police had set up camp in the dining room.

"Where's my brother?" The sick feeling inside Conor's gut answered before the cop.

"We have no idea where they are. They took off before we got here." Rossi swept a hand over a salt-and-pepper buzz cut. "It looks like your brother might have been right all along. Nathan Hall could be planning another ritual."

———

Nathan rearranged his offering, moving the shield to the center of the pile. Perfect. He glanced at the sky. The sun hovered low in the horizon. It would be dark soon. Time to prepare for the Bel-fire.

He would build it as carefully as a fire in his hearth. Paper on the bottom, then kindling, then the larger pieces of wood on top.

He went into the cool dim of the barn. His woodpile was to the right. Next to it he'd filled several plastic trash cans with dried leaves and twigs. Using a wheelbarrow, he spread the dead leaves in a circle. Twigs were next. Then branches. He saved some of the larger pieces to pile around the base of his effigy when it was in position. He set three cans of gasoline next to the pile.

He glanced to the maypole. His assistant should be here soon with Mandy. Excitement rushed in his veins, temporarily wiping away his mental sluggishness. He couldn't wait to see her, to hold her again. The maiden's love would consummate his rebirth.

Everything must be ready for his May Queen. Nathan ran for the tractor in the barn. He disengaged the boat trailer and drove it toward his effigy.

———

"I see something."

Danny turned as Mandy pointed to another trail through the reeds. Jed turned the boat into the natural corridor. Without the gray of twilight, darkness pressed in on the boat, and Danny's pulse upshifted. The hairs on his neck were waving in the breeze. This was it. He knew it.

Honey tensed, and her fur bristled. She'd spent most of the day standing in the bow, tail wagging, enjoying the wind in her face. Now her tail dropped, and she let out a high whine, half excitement, half distress.

Like the last three times, Jed and Danny went through the shift from motor to oars as they neared the shallows. Jed switched on a powerful flashlight. The beam illuminated a deep furrow in the muddy shore. Something had been dragged onto the bank. Something big. Like a boat.

Jed moved the light onto the mud just beyond. "Look."

Tire tracks. Not a car, though. The tracks were too deep, too knobby.

They beached the boat. Jed leashed his dog. She lunged into her collar. "Whoa, girl. Easy now."

Danny took the flashlight to free both Jed's hands for dog control. They each grabbed a pack and a rifle as they followed the tracks. The darkness and rough footing slowed their progress. Mandy forged ahead.

Next to him, Jed wheezed.

Danny reached a hand out. "Drop your pack and give me the dog."

Jed tossed his backpack on the side of the trail. Danny handed Mandy the flashlight and took Honey's leash. Eighty pounds of dog pulled him forward.

They resumed walking. As they moved deeper into the forest, insect chatter picked up. Gnats hovered in his face. Something bit him on the chin, but Danny didn't risk taking a hand off the leash. Honey plowed forward with determination. She knew where she was going.

Jed stumbled. "I'm sorry, Mandy."

"Take a rest, Jed," she said without slowing. "I'm going to keep going."

Breathless, Jed waved Danny on. "Go with her."

They left Jed leaning on a tree. Mandy and Honey pushed forward. Danny brought up the rear. Deep in the forest, under the thick canopy, full night set down with the finality of a coffin lid. Mandy kept the light low and focused on the tracks. Ahead, the trees opened up into a meadow.

"I'm switching off the light," she said in a low voice.

"Should we call for backup?"

"What if we're wrong, and that's not him? What if we call everyone here and Nathan is somewhere else?"

The dog pulled harder and whined louder. They reached the end of the trail. Tiny lights glowed on the other side of the field, and Mandy broke into a run.

"Shit." So much for sneaking up on them. Danny and the dog sprinted after her.

The blond man put the tractor in gear. The cage lurched forward. Kevin rammed his feet against the wooden bars. Nothing gave. There was no way out.

"Daddy?"

Kevin reached for his son and gathered him close.

Above him, a feminine sob was barely audible beneath the roar of the tractor engine. A woman's scream sliced right through the rumble. Hunter trembled in Kevin's arms.

The cage was dragged into the open. When it was centered over the carefully layered pile of wood, the tractor stopped. Shiny red gas cans lined up like soldiers waiting for orders.

Realization dawned on Kevin. They were sitting in a wooden structure parked on top of a pile of kindling.

The blond man was going to set them on fire.

The shaking started in his hands and spread until his entire body quaked. Tears soaked Hunter's hair as Kevin contemplated whether he'd have the strength to strangle his son before the flames burned them alive.

CHAPTER THIRTY

Nathan fastened the handcuff around Evan's wrist to the rope secured around the maypole. From here his son could safely witness his own salvation. Soon, Mandy would join him.

"You can't go through with it," Evan begged. "Please."

"When you're older, you'll realize I did the only thing possible. I saved you." His son didn't understand, and Nathan didn't have time to change that. It was his own fault. Nathan's uncle had taught him everything when he was a child. But Nathan had elected to bring his son up in the modern world. Evan lacked the training of a true Druid. Such a mistake couldn't be rectified in the span of one winter. He touched his son's head lovingly.

"I don't want you to do this." Evan jerked his head away and strained at his binds. Fresh blood welled around his wrist.

"Please don't strain, Evan. You'll only injure yourself."

"Let me go!" His son pulled harder, but there was no chance he'd escape. The drugs and imprisonment over the winter had weakened him.

"I'm sorry it has to be this way." Nathan rose. "I pray that tonight goes well so that you might live long enough to hate me well into your old age."

Druid tradition was passed down orally, through rote memorization. To protect its secrets, rituals were never put to paper. As Nathan had elected to forgo his son's rightful education, Nathan would be the last Druid in their family. So be it. If he freed his son from the family curse, he could live with the rest.

He retreated to the barn for the final touches. Using a long pole, Nathan positioned the wicker head on the center of the uppermost cage. He hung the branch arms from the wooden pegs. The structure now roughly resembled a human.

The wicker man, complete with a belly full of sacrifices for the gods. Such offerings successfully kept the Romans out of Scotland. Surely, it would be sufficient to keep a single disease at bay in one family.

He stiffened at the sound of an engine. His assistant's car approached on the long driveway. It came to a stop fifteen or twenty yards from the barn. His assistant got out of the car and walked toward him.

Alone.

He turned away from his masterpiece. "Where is Mandy?"

"She wasn't at the inn."

Nathan's insides heated. "What do you mean she wasn't there?"

His assistant's hands clenched together. Unclenched. Clenched again. "I assume she's at the hospital or looking for her brother. Her mother had a heart attack. Guess she couldn't deal with her son going missing."

This could not be. He had it all planned. How could he be reborn without the maiden, his May Queen?

"I need my May Queen!"

"Why can't I take her place?"

Anger boiled in his belly and swirled red in his vision.

His assistant's eyes bugged. "I didn't mean permanently, but I could stand in, just for the ceremony."

"This isn't a Broadway production." His right hand found the knife at his left hip. He swept it clear of the sheath and across his assistant's throat in one smooth movement. Blood fountained from the wound and splattered across Nathan's pants, Jackson Pollock style. He walked away before the body hit the dirt.

Nathan's heart splintered. All he'd worked for. Gone because his assistant had failed.

No. He could still save his son. It was Nathan's salvation that was in jeopardy. As always, Evan came first. As long as his son lived on, without fear of the disease that ravaged Nathan's brain, he was prepared to die. Willingly and without regret.

He looked up and saw a miracle.

A woman running across the meadow toward him. Even in the dark, he recognized her shape, her gait. The gods were with him. They'd sent her to him as a reward for his loyalty.

It was time.

Ignoring the screams of the offerings inside the wicker man, he opened the gasoline and poured it around the structure. He pulled a box of matches from his pocket.

Life had come full circle.

⸻

Mandy stopped where the meadow ended and looked up at the abandoned farm. A sagging barn sat next to a crumbling ruin of a house. In the barnyard, a few camp lanterns cast shadowy light over the yard. A figure moved around a tall structure erected in the center. A tractor was parked behind it.

Was that Nathan?

She swung her rifle into her arms. Whoever it was tipped a container toward the ground. Damn. She couldn't see well enough to identify the figure, let alone get off a clear shot.

She moved forward. Details clarified as she approached. Her spine buzzed with alarm. The structure was a giant cage filled with people. A crude head and arms gave it a primitive human appearance. Inside, people screamed. Mandy's gaze riveted upon her brother, locked in the third level. Caged, trapped, like a steer waiting for the slaughterhouse. Terror widened his eyes.

She slid to a halt.

Nathan stepped into a circle of light, but she barely recognized him. His formerly Hollywood-perfect blond hair was long and scraggly. He wore khakis and a polo shirt so filthy the original colors weren't discernible. Dark streaks across his clothing looked fresh and wet. His jacket was torn. Something lay behind him. No, not something. Someone. A woman in a skirt and heels. Her face was turned away, but dark splotches stained the dirt around her head.

Oh, my God. It was Carolyn.

What was she doing here?

Panic whirled in Mandy's chest; her breaths shortened.

The smell of gasoline burned her nostrils.

Glancing back at the structure, she took in the carefully layered brush, the gas cans, the cages built entirely of wood. Nathan was going to set them on fire. Human sacrifice by immolation.

The horror of his intention skidded through her belly.

Nathan stood next to the statue. He held a gas can in front of his chest. Thank God she hadn't shot at him. The whole thing might have blown up.

"I knew you'd come." A maniacal smile lit his face. "It was meant to be."

"What was meant to be, Nathan?" she asked, in as calm a voice as she could manage. *Stall. Give Danny time to figure out what to do.*

"Us. Forever."

"I'm here for you." She'd say anything to keep him from lighting that fire. Hell, she'd *do* anything to save those people.

"After this is over, we can be together. I'll be cured."

"I want you to hold me." Mandy forced a smile on her face. "Why don't you come over here? I've missed you."

"First we have to burn the wicker man. The gods will accept my offering and cure me. Evan will be saved." Nathan nodded toward a post on the other side of the clearing. Oh, God. Evan was straining at the ropes that bound him to a post on the other side of the barnyard. Nathan took a match from the box. "Once the gods have rid my son of this curse, then we go off into the forest for the night. Just you and me."

Mandy moved forward. "Wait."

Nathan dropped the gas can and struck a match.

———

Danny crouched behind the barn. While Mandy ran headlong into the situation, he'd found cover and circled around. The dog lunged and whined.

"Sit." He tugged on the leash. Honey sat, but her body quivered from nose to tail.

Danny peered around the corner. Nathan was standing next to the giant wooden man. Inside the structure, people in cages screamed. Nathan's eyes had gone from crazy to don't-drink-the-Kool-Aid. Gas cans littered the ground at his feet. He held a book of matches in his hand.

The scene shifted. The barnyard faded into a dusty Iraqi street. Danny's nose filled with diesel fumes. Men screamed, and fire engulfed an overturned Humvee.

Danny blinked and shook the image from his head. *Nathan. Focus on Nathan.* He brought the rifle around. Sweat dripped into his eye. He wiped his brow with his forearm and sighted down the barrel.

Mandy walked right between Danny and Nathan.

Shit.

Nathan dropped the match. The kindling caught fire with a *whoosh*. Flames burst at the bottom of the wooden cage structure. Danny let go of the leash and ran forward. The dog sprinted ahead. To his left, Jed limped into the barnyard, one hand pressed against his belly. Mandy was moving toward the fire. Toward Nathan.

No!

Danny paused, ready to veer his course to intercept her.

"Help!" The man in the bottom cage huddled around his son in the center, trying to stay out of the reach of the flames. The girls in the next level screamed. On top, Doug Lang lay limp and still. In the cage with the cop, Bill pressed on the bars. Oh, God. Bill! Danny could not let six people burn to death. He had to get them out.

Honey raced around the fire, barking.

Praying that Jed and Mandy would be OK, he ducked into the barn. Scanning the wall of rusted tools, he grabbed a saw and a hatchet. Halfway across the yard he realized the fire was growing faster than he could possibly chop through the thick timber. The flames were reaching for the fisherman and his boy.

The tractor. It was hitched to the structure. Danny dropped the tools and climbed onto the seat. The engine sputtered then turned over. He shoved it into gear, dragging the cages away from the burning debris. He looked over his shoulder. A few of the thick timber bars smoldered, but the fire hadn't fully caught on the thicker, newer wood. The dog stood on her hind legs and put her paws on the wood. Bill stretched his hand toward her.

"Get us out of here, please." The fisherman clutched his son to his chest and waved the smoke away from the coughing boy.

The girls wrapped their arms around each other and wept. Tears shone on sooty faces. "Hurry."

"I'm coming." Danny ran toward them. Where was Nathan? There. He was in front of Mandy. Firelight gleamed on something metal in his hand.

A knife!

Mandy breathed. Danny saved them. The rush of smoky air into her lungs made her lightheaded.

"You ruined everything!"

Nathan was less than ten feet away. The blade in his hand reflected the orange glow of the fire.

"I never thought you'd betray me. If I can't have you, no one will." In a swirl of déjà vu, Nathan lunged. "You'll have to take their place as the sacrifice tonight."

Jed jumped in front of Mandy. The knife slipped into his torso with a sick, wet sound. Clutching his belly, Jed fell to his knees. Nathan raised the knife level with Jed's neck.

CHAPTER THIRTY-ONE

Mandy's gun was in her hand. She aimed at the center of Nathan's chest and pulled the trigger. The bullet struck him dead center with a quiet *smack*, the impact jerking his body. He focused on Mandy and lurched toward her, the knife still clenched in his bloody fist. Mandy fired again and again, until the gun clicked on an empty chamber. Nathan fell backward into the fire. A high-pitched, inhuman shriek sliced through the smoky air. Embers shot into the sky. His head struck a piece of wood, cutting off his screams. The flames embraced him.

Ignoring the burning body, Mandy rushed forward.

"Jed!" She dropped to her knees beside him. She ripped his shirt open. Under his rib cage and above his scar, blood seeped from a wound much smaller than the last one. She balled her sweatshirt up and pressed it to the cut.

"Danny!" She frantically looked around. He was climbing off the tractor. The wind shifted. Glowing embers blew toward Evan, still tied to the pole.

Grabbing the saw and hatchet from the ground, Danny freed Evan, then ran to the wicker man and handed the saw to the man in the bottom cage and the hatchet to the girls. "Here."

The man started sawing. Samantha worked the hatchet.

"I'll get another tool." Evan stumbled toward the barn.

Jed's body convulsed.

Danny was at her side. He moved her hands and lifted the sweatshirt. The wound was barely bleeding.

"He's not bleeding as badly as last time." Mandy reached down to clutch Jed's hand, cold despite the heat thrown by the fire.

Danny didn't respond. He didn't have to. Mandy knew this time the knife had found a more vital target. Jed was bleeding all right, just not on the outside.

In the flickering glow, Jed's face was bleaching out, the color in his skin fading to black and white.

Mandy cupped his face in her hand. "Don't die on me!"

Danny reached into her discarded backpack. He pulled out the radio. "Do you read me?"

Static burst over the handset. "Loud and clear."

"We need a medevac." Danny gave them the details and their approximate location. "A vacant farm about a mile east of Lake Walker. Just look for the fire."

Jed's eyes lost focus. He blinked hard and looked up at Danny. "You can't fix this."

Danny spread the sweatshirt over Jed's shivering torso.

Jed locked eyes with Mandy. The pain in his eyes wasn't only physical. "I don't care about Nathan. Not your fault. He fooled me, too, and then betrayed us all. Just wanted you to know."

A tear dripped from Mandy face onto Jed's. "I should've told you."

"It's OK." Jed swallowed. His legs twitched. He glanced at Danny. "Just promise you'll take care of her."

Danny nodded. "I will."

A sigh wheezed through Jed's chest like an inner tube with a pinhole. He coughed. Frothy blood dotted his lips.

"Stop it." Tears poured from Mandy's eyes and blurred her vision. "You are not going to die, Jed Garrett. You can't leave me. You promised, remember? Through thick and thin."

"Sorry," he whispered. His mouth moved but nothing came out except a hiss of air.

Mandy leaned over and put her ear to his lips.

He squeezed her fingers. "Love you. Always have." His fingers around her hand went limp and slid to the dry earth.

"No!" She fell forward and sobbed on his shoulder.

"Mandy, he's gone. I'm sorry. I tried." Next to her, Danny wiped his hands on his legs, then pulled gently at her arms.

She resisted, burrowing her face into the wet flannel of Jed's shirt. She didn't want to let him go. He'd been at her side all her life. Her best friend. "No. No. No."

A hot, dry wind blew over her skin. Something crackled.

Whoosh.

"Mandy, the fire's spreading to the barn." Over the roar of the fire, Danny's voice sounded far away. "Get up."

An ember landed on her arm. She could smell the burning of her skin but was numb to the pain. Danny brushed it away.

She lifted her head. Jed's face was slack, his eyes open and glazed. No gruffness or impatience or annoyance would ever fill them again. Danny reached over and closed Jed's eyes.

"Don't!" Pressure built in Mandy's chest until she couldn't draw a breath. Her vision tunneled and dimmed.

"We need to get him away from the fire." Danny hauled her to her feet and gave her a push. She stumbled backward.

Through misty eyes, she saw Danny lifting Jed under the armpits and dragging him away from the spreading inferno to a safe spot toward the house and drive. "I'm going back to help them get the others out."

She watched the rest play out like a movie, her emotions brought to their knees by grief. One by one, Danny and Evan sawed the wood cages open. The two young women clutched each other and stumbled out. Bill jumped down, then half lifted Doug Lang to the ground. The man carried a young boy toward Mandy. He laid him on the ground next to her. They were both streaked with soot.

Mandy watched the firelight play over Jed's features. Disbelief hollowed out her chest until there was nothing left but empty space. How could Jed be gone?

A hand touched her arm. Mandy turned.

"Do you have some water?" The man coughed. He cradled his son's head in his lap. The boy's eyes were closed. His thin chest rose with a breath. He exhaled with a hacking cough. Staring at the child, Mandy's instinct took over. "Yes." She stood. "I'll find it."

She found Danny's pack on the ground and pulled out bottles of water. She slipped out of her jacket and wrapped it around the little boy's shoulders. Samantha and Victoria dropped onto the ground next to them. Both girls were shivering and crying. They flung their arms around Mandy's shoulders. Bill half carried Doug Lang. Drugged or hurt, the cop couldn't stand upright.

Mandy peeled the girls off her and got them the emergency blanket from the pack. Bill enveloped her in a tight embrace. She pressed her face against his chest. A shudder passed through her. Honey sat at their feet, leaning on Bill's legs.

Evan stood a few feet away. His slight body was thinner than she remembered, and his eyes were the bleakest of all the victims. Months of imprisonment at his father's hands, watching his father disintegrate and commit terrible deeds, had no doubt left a permanent stain on the young man's soul. How would he recover?

Danny was on the radio again, but he didn't look at her as he talked into the handset.

She tried to move toward Jed's body, but Bill's arms held her fast. "I'm sorry about Jed, Mandy."

God, how would she recover? Her next breath rattled through her chest. She was choking on loneliness.

She gave up on leaving Bill's embrace. The *whump* of helicopter blades approached. But it was too late. There wasn't anyone left to save.

Danny dug into the pile of scrambled eggs Conor dished onto his plate. The smell of bacon overwhelmed the sooty stench stuck in his nostrils even after a shower and fresh clothes.

While his brother worked the stove, Detective Rossi sat at the inn's kitchen island. A notebook was open next to a full plate of steaming food. At the other end of the counter, the museum curator, Louisa May Hancock, PhD, sipped coffee and watched Conor with the focus of an archeologist studying a new species. When he slid a plate of bacon and eggs in front of her, her brows crunched together in confusion. Honey stretched out on the floor at Danny's feet.

Rossi added cream and sugar to his coffee and stirred. "Evan Hall said his father was keeping him locked up and partially sedated." The cop forked eggs into his mouth with the zeal of a man who'd been up all night.

"He was tied to a post when we got there." Danny drank his coffee black and scalding, but the hot liquid did little to dispel the aching cold lodged in his gut. He glanced at the door to the apartment. Mandy was at the hospital with her brother and mother, who was in ICU after a second heart attack. Even after being Tased and drugged, Bill had appeared to be in better shape than Mandy. The inn had an empty feel without Mandy and her family in it. Even with the guests sleeping upstairs and the four people crowded into the kitchen, loneliness burrowed inside Danny and nested.

Too much death and despair had that effect on him.

It wasn't because Mandy wasn't here.

The cop set down his fork. "So, Dr. Hancock, what was Nathan trying to do tonight?"

"The Celts believed human sacrifices would gains the gods' favor. Offerings were made to ensure good crops and change the weather. To ensure victory in battle. The Celts drowned victims, slit throats, bashed them over the head, and burned them alive. Nathan built a wicker man." Louisa's face smoothed out. "During the Roman invasion of Britain, Julius Caesar wrote accounts of the Druids burning wicker man statues full of prisoners to keep Britain from being conquered."

"Did it?"

Louisa picked at her eggs. "The Romans quit at Scotland. They didn't think the highlands were worth the effort. The weather and the terrain were factors, but perhaps the ferocity of the Celtic warriors was also considered."

Danny gave up on eating and put the dish on the floor for Honey.

"The thing I can't figure out is how Carolyn Fitzgerald played in all this. She was helping Nathan?"

"According to Evan, Carolyn helped them from the beginning. She left the threats for Mandy, including a picture of Nathan and Mandy she'd taken in a fit of jealousy when she ran across them by accident. Carolyn and Nathan had an affair years ago, when her husband first became ill. She broke it off but still had a thing for him."

"Who broke into the museum?"

"That was Carolyn, too. Her son told us she'd been accidentally locked out of properties many times. As long as there wasn't an alarm, she could usually find a way in. She started leaving one downstairs window unlocked in the vacant houses she listed. That way, if there was a problem with the lock box, she could always get in. We think she visited the museum before closing and unlocked a first-floor window. After dark, she let herself in."

Danny remembered the unlocked window in Reed's house the night he arrived.

Rossi continued, "Carolyn had the majority of real estate listings in town. People were so used to seeing her everywhere. She was the one who brought supplies. She helped Nathan ditch his vehicle and gave him her son's ATV. The vacant farm was listed with her realty company. It's been for sale for years."

"Why would she do all this for him if they weren't together anymore?" Danny asked.

"Nathan promised her the ritual would cure her husband. His Alzheimer's disease was progressing rapidly. Carolyn was losing it from lack of sleep and desperation. Her son said his dad was becoming more violent every day." The cop downed the rest of his coffee. "On another note, I received the arson investigator's preliminary report on the fire at Reed Kimball's house. The bedroom windows had been nailed shut. Not sure we can prove Nathan set the fire, but that wasn't an accident."

A fresh case of the creeps crawled around in Danny's gut.

"Also, I talked to Ray about your suspicions that he'd been in Nathan's house. Turns out, Ray is strapped for cash. The last few months of extra business haven't been enough to compensate for several years of losses. He's been sneaking into Nathan's house and the diner and stealing anything of value. He's been selling it on eBay." Rossi stood. "If you think of anything else, call me. Otherwise, I'll be in touch later today or tomorrow."

Danny walked the cop to the door. "Thanks for everything. I should have called you earlier."

"Yes. You should have."

"But we didn't have anything solid."

"Still, would it have done any harm? What's the worst that I could've said? No?"

Danny sighed. "You're right."

"Of course, we would have taken over the search and maybe not found Nathan at all. Who knows?"

"You're OK, Rossi." Danny shook the cop's hand.

After the cop left. Louisa excused herself for the night. Danny had given her the key to the inn's only empty room.

"You should get some sleep." Conor dried the frying pan and hung it on the overhead rack. He draped the dish towel over his shoulder.

"You sure you don't want the bed? I doubt I'll sleep."

"Nah. The couch'll be fine." Conor slapped Danny's shoulder, then pulled him in for a full hug. "I'm glad you're not dead, baby brother."

"Me, too." Danny hugged him back. He trudged up the narrow staircase to his room. Stretching out on the bed, he stared at the ceiling. Jaynie was safe. She could live like a normal person now that Nathan was dead. He'd accomplished his goal.

But the business with Mandy had left a hole in him. He wasn't angry that she'd slept with Nathan. He'd manipulated the whole town. Mandy was lonely, overworked, and stressed. She was vulnerable to a predator like Nathan.

But her lie still stung.

Sunlight streamed through the dining room windows. Blinking, Danny walked in. Guests were tucking into a full breakfast. A rush of nervous energy prodded his blurry brain. Mandy must be back. He continued through to the kitchen.

Disappointment stopped him like a smack on the chest. Conor was at the stove. He had a griddle going and pancakes stacked everywhere. Louisa shuttled a platter of bacon to the dining room. A few strands of hair had escaped the cool blonde's super-tight bun and frizzed around her face.

"Your curator looks a little frazzled."

Conor gave him his up-to-no-good grin. "I know."

"Did Mandy come home?"

"I didn't hear anybody come in." Conor grabbed a pair of tongs and turned slices of bacon in the frying pan. "People were hungry, so…"

The hell with propriety. Danny opened the door to the apartment. The quiet was disturbing. "Shit."

"She's probably at the hospital with her mother and brother. Why don't you just go find her?" Conor turned off a burner. "This is hardly rocket science, Danny. You obviously have feelings for her."

"It's complicated." Danny told him about the blackmail. "She lied to my face. I'm having a hard time with that."

"Do you think if Jed had lived and you had died, that he'd be having this discussion?"

Danny looked out the window. The clear air and bright sunshine held the promise of a beautiful spring day. New beginnings. He had no doubt that if the situation had been reversed, Jed would be with Mandy now. Jed had loved Mandy with his whole heart, enough not just to forgive her, but to die for her. Did Danny have that kind of love in him?

"Two questions." Conor wiped his hands on the dish towel hanging over his shoulder. "Do you love her? And would you have done the same for Jaynie?"

"You know I'd do anything for Jayne." Not excluding die, cheat, lie, and kill.

"Then what about the first question? Do you love Mandy?"

"Probably." But the certainty of it bloomed in his chest like spring blossomed outside the window. No matter how cold and dark the winter, it didn't last forever. "Yeah. I think I do."

Conor leaned back on the counter. "Danny, I have no doubt you would give anything, including your life, without hesitation for the people you love. I know you. You would have taken that knife for Mandy if that's the way things worked out. Why is forgiveness so much harder to give?"

Suddenly, the desire to see Mandy nearly overwhelmed Danny. He grabbed his keys and reached for the doorknob.

"If you really love her, be there for her. Don't fuck this up. You'll regret it for the rest of your life." Conor turned to the piled-high sink. "How do you think Louisa feels about scrubbing pots and pans?"

Mandy got out of the car. Every movement of her body was slow and painful, as if she were riddled with arthritis. Looking up at Jed's cabin, grief hit her, a relentless wave of despondency that threatened to knock her to the ground. Every time she got up, it came back.

Barking echoed from the kennels. Mandy forced her legs to move forward. Though one of Jed's friends had already taken care of the dogs early that morning, she checked water bowls, patted heads, and cleaned cages. Anything to avoid facing Jed's house alone.

She stopped in front of the first cage. Bear cocked his chocolate-colored head. His tail thumped on the concrete. Mandy opened the cage door. "Come on, boy."

He fell into step beside her. Side by side, they walked toward the house, her hand trailing on the dog's head. The door wasn't locked. She opened it, but Bear hesitated at the threshold. The only dog Jed let inside the house was Honey. He'd been adamant the rest were hunting dogs, not pets.

"It's OK." She patted her thigh. "Come."

He trotted in. Mandy left the main door wide-open and closed the screen door. Pine-scented air filtered into the house.

The kitchen, dining area, and living room were one open space. Bear trailed through, sniffing the wood-paneled perimeter. Mandy stood in the center, lost in memories.

Just lost.

Her imagination could place Jed cleaning his guns at the oak table or pulling a beer from the fridge.

She went to his desk and sat down. Mail was stacked on the blotter. Next to it, a shipping box lay open. A black box with a large white button was nestled inside the Styrofoam packaging. She unfolded the packing slip and read the invoice. K-9 rescue phone.

She thumbed through the stacks of mail. A cream envelope had a logo of a dog next to the return address. Mandy slid the letter out. Across the top, SERVICE DOG CERTIFICATION REQUIREMENTS was typed in bold print. The application was half-completed in small block letters. She read through the form.

It was no accident Honey knew how to comfort Bill or that she stuck by his side and could find him on command. Jed had been training Honey to be Bill's service dog.

A fresh current of grief swamped her. She'd thought she was lonely before Jed's death. Sitting at his desk, with the evidence of his selfless love for her in her hand, sadness swelled until the pressure constricted her heart and lungs.

Someone knocked at the door. She looked at Danny through the screen. Her heart bumped. The door squeaked as he pushed it open and walked in.

He squatted in front of her. "I'm sorry. I shouldn't have left your side last night. You shouldn't have been at the hospital alone."

"Mrs. Stone was there. She still is." Mandy looked down at her clenched hands. "I should have told you. You saved my life in December. I should have trusted you. I was just so afraid."

"I wouldn't have taken any chances with Jayne's life either." Danny took her hands in his. She was careful not to squeeze the new bandage.

Her conscience sighed in relief, but her heart started crying all over again. She shut it down. Danny's forgiveness didn't change the fact that he'd be leaving soon. And she'd be alone again. In fact, letting herself think otherwise just left her open to additional pain when she couldn't handle one more ounce. She stared at the certification letter in her hand.

Danny put a finger under her chin. She closed her eyes and leaned her cheek against his palm. She was going to miss him.

"What's that?" He nodded toward the letter.

"Jed was getting Honey certified as Bill's service dog. That's what he was doing all winter. He knew how difficult Bill's anxiety was to manage. He was going to give me his most prized possession to make my life easier."

"He loved you."

"I loved him, too." Tears burned Mandy's swollen eyes. "Just not the way he needed me to love him."

Danny didn't respond with words. He pulled her to her feet and wrapped her in his arms. "Do you need to do anything else here?"

She shook her head.

"Then let's go back to the inn."

"God, the inn. I just let everything go. My guests—"

"Are fine," Danny assured her. "My brother is holding down the fort."

"Really?"

"Really." Danny steered her toward the door. "You won't have to run the place alone anymore."

Mandy stopped. "What do you mean?"

"I can run a tavern. An inn can't be that much different. I thought I'd stick around for a while."

"You're staying?"

Danny frowned. "Why wouldn't I? I don't know exactly what we have here, but it's something I'm not just going to walk away from. I have feelings for you I can't verbalize yet. We need some normal time to sort things out."

"But no one stays in Huntsville." She'd spent her whole life wishing she could leave. "Won't you miss Philadelphia?"

They stepped out onto the porch.

"Sure, but it's just a place. It's people who matter. It's only a day's drive if I want to see my family." Danny stopped and turned her to face him. "Unless you want me to go. I'm sorry. I didn't even ask. I assumed you felt the same—"

"I do." Huntsville didn't seem so bad. Philadelphia was only a day's drive. Maybe someday she could make that trip with Danny.

"Thank God." He pressed a kiss to her lips. The sun's heat soaked into her skin, and warmth encompassed her heart.

The dog squeezed his nose between them. Danny lifted his head and laughed. He gave Bear a pat.

Mandy scratched the lab's head. "Let's take Bear with us. I think he misses Jed."

The dog rode shotgun, bowing his head to avoid the ceiling in her little wagon. He would have fit better in Danny's car, but Mandy needed the company. If it worked for Bill, maybe a little canine therapy would help her work through her grief.

One week later

"Are you sure you're ready?"

"I am." Mandy leaned over the side of the boat. She dipped a hand in the rippled surface of the lake. The water was cool and refreshing in the humid summer afternoon.

Danny shut off the outboard motor. Peace descended over Lake Walker. At the water's edge, a heron stood in the shallows. The boat drifted into a patch of vegetation. A handful of ducks burst from the tall reeds nearby. Bear, standing in the bow, cocked his ears and wagged his tail as he watched them fly off.

"Stay," Danny commanded. Bear sat down, his butt bouncing in excitement.

She smiled. "Well, look at you, Mr. Dog Trainer."

"I wish I could take responsibility, but Bear was already trained."

"He was." On that note, Mandy reached for the urn at her feet. If she hesitated now, her courage would fly off like a spooked mallard. As Jed had instructed, she opened the top and slowly poured the ashes into the water. They swirled and floated, gradually sinking into the calm water. "Bye, Jed."

"Are you all right?" Danny asked with the same patient tone that wouldn't let her shut her emotions down over the past week.

"Yeah. I expected to be bowled over by sadness again, but I'm not." Mandy set the empty urn in the bottom of the boat. "I feel…lighter."

"I'll always be grateful to him for what he did." Danny reached for her hand and gave it a squeeze.

"I'll never forget him, but I'm going to try to focus on the good parts." She wasn't letting go of his memory, just the sadness and guilt. Jed would be in her heart forever.

"He would want you to be happy."

"I know." Mandy wiped a tear from her face. "I'm sorry. I wasn't going to cry." She'd thought she was out of tears. Danny and Mandy had attended Ashley's funeral in Boston. A structural defect and the Taser charge had combined to cause the young woman's heart to arrest. Her asthma hadn't been the only cause of her shortness of breath. Two days after returning home, the sadness weighed on Mandy's heart. No parent should have to bury a child. It was unnatural. So was suffering at a parent's hands, though. Evan was still in the hospital, his sanity and health precarious after four months of imprisonment, watching his father plan to murder people on his behalf. The fate of Carolyn's son was also uncertain, but a cousin had driven up from Boston to take the boy home with her. With no one to care for him and his disease turning him more violent by the day, Colonel Fitzgerald was being moved to a nursing facility.

"It's OK." Danny shifted a seat closer and took her hands in his. The scar on his left arm reminded her that he knew all about pain and loss and acceptance. "Better to let it out than let it fester."

"I still can't believe he left me everything. I have no idea what I'm going to do with all his stuff." Jed's will had been both recent and very detailed. Honey belonged to Bill. Everything else, from the cabin to the boat to the dogs, went to Mandy.

"So, you'll know when you know. No rush." Danny rowed them back to shore.

A small group of people stood on the bank. Victoria and Samantha hugged each other. Swollen, red eyes attested to their grief. Their parents hovered a few feet behind them. Next to them, Kevin gathered with his entire family. The still-gaunt Hunter was sandwiched between his parents.

But they were standing there, alive.

Mandy's throat tightened. Even if she could speak, she didn't have words to express the complicated emotions bottlenecked inside her.

Danny squeezed her shoulder. He got it. "Thank you all for coming. I know this is hard, but Jed would have appreciated you being here."

"We had to," Hunter said. "Didn't we, Dad?"

"You bet." Kevin choked out. "We owe him—and you both—everything."

His wife stepped forward and wrapped her arms around Mandy. Hot tears soaked Mandy's blouse. Hunter's mother didn't say anything. She didn't have to. She hugged Danny and stepped aside. Samantha, Victoria, and their parents lined up for tear-filled embraces. When she'd worked her way through the crowd, Mandy was exhausted but oddly grateful.

Jed's courage had allowed her to stop Nathan, and Danny to rescue everyone from the flames. All these people were alive because of Jed. His death had meant something.

Hunter tugged on her sleeve. "Dad says it'll take time to not be scared anymore. Are you going to be OK?"

Mandy put her hand on his shoulder. "Hunter, my best friend gave his life for me. The least I can do is live it."

CHAPTER THIRTY-TWO

August, three months later

Danny leaned back on the blanket. Bear snoozed in the grass next to him.

"We should get going." Mandy buttoned her blouse. "Your family will be here soon."

"We have time." Danny tugged her down onto his bare chest. "And it's *my* birthday. They can wait."

Mandy laughed. "But I want to give you your present."

"I thought you just did." Danny kissed her. Yup. He'd been right all along. Some green grass and a pretty girl was all he needed in life. "Anyway, I have something for you." He reached for his jeans and dug into the pocket. He pulled out a small velvet box. "Will you marry me, Mandy Brown?"

"Oh, Danny." She sat up and opened the box. A small diamond ring glittered in the sunlight, like tears glittered in Mandy's eyes when she put it on her finger. "Yes. Definitely, yes."

"Geez, don't cry." Danny sat up. "I wanted to make you happy."

"I can't help it." She sniffed. "I am happy."

"Could've fooled me, but I'll take your word for it." Danny kissed her again. One hand strayed to the top button on her blouse. "Wanna give me another present?"

Mandy batted his hand away playfully. "Put your clothes on. We have to go home."

"Oh, all right." Danny tugged on his jeans, T-shirt, and running shoes. "I was thinking. What if I convert the garage into a little house? I love your mom and Bill, and I know you need to stay close to them, but a little privacy would be nice."

Mandy wiped a fresh tear from her face. "I think that would be perfect."

"Great. Winter will be here soon. While I'm digging the whole outdoor sex thing, it's going to be less appealing as the temperature drops."

They packed up the picnic hamper and blanket and loaded the dog into the used SUV Danny had sold his convertible to buy. Well, that and the ring. Worth every penny. Now that he had Mandy, he had no trouble letting go of his old life and embracing the future.

The drive back to the inn was quiet. Danny held her hand and let her think. In the backseat, Bear pressed his nose to the window. They parked behind the inn. Jayne and Reed's mammoth SUV dwarfed Danny's new truck. On the other side of it, Conor's beat-to-shit Porsche looked a little less like roadkill than it had the last time Danny had seen it.

"Your family's early." Mandy flipped down the visor and checked her eyes in the mirror.

"You look beautiful." Danny opened the back door for the dog. Bear bounded up the back lawn.

"Danny." His tall, redheaded sister bolted out the back door and across the grass. She grabbed him in a fierce hug. "Happy birthday, baby brother."

Danny laughed and hugged her back. Jayne let go of him and moved on to Mandy with the same enthusiasm, then she wrapped an arm around Mandy's shoulders and steered her toward the house. Happiness vibrated through Danny's sister.

Reed stood on the back porch, his posture more relaxed now that Nathan's threat to Jayne was eliminated. "Jayne was dying to see the puppies."

They went into the kitchen. Bear nosed into the laundry room and trotted to Honey's box. Six chubby furballs, two yellow and four chocolate, wiggled and yawned. Under Honey's watchful eye, Bear sniffed his pups and wagged his tail.

"So, we're making wedding plans." Jayne peered around the doorframe. "Nothing huge, just a simple ceremony. Are you two going to be able to come or should we have it up here?"

"I don't know," Mandy said. "Bill's pretty good as long as Honey is with him, but we have another four to six weeks before the puppies are ready to leave."

"We can wait. God, they're so cute," Jayne said. *Can you squeal and whisper at the same time?* "Which one is ours?"

Mandy laughed. "Whichever one you want."

Jayne leaned over the box and held her iPhone out. She snapped a couple of pictures. "Now for some video."

"Where's Pat and the gang?" Danny asked.

"On the way. They have to stop every hour. Someone always needs a pit stop." The smallest pup, a yellow blob of fat and fur, climbed over her siblings, stood, and hooked her paws over the top of the box. Jayne lowered her phone. "Is the littlest one a boy or a girl?"

Mandy lifted the pup and cuddled her against her cheek for a minute. She set her behind her brothers and sisters. Undaunted, she beelined for the prison walls. "The escape artist is a girl."

Bill shouldered his way into the fray. "I wanted to keep them all, but Mandy said that was way too many dogs." He sat on the floor next to the box and stroked Honey's head. The dog's tail slapped on the floor. "We get to keep Bear and Honey and maybe one puppy."

Reed looked over Jayne's shoulder. "These dogs are pure-breds. Honey's a champ. Why don't you sell them?"

"'Cause we want to pick where they go to live." Bill's voice held a smidgen of *duh*.

Reed put a hand on Bill's shoulder. "Are you coming to my wedding?"

Bill hesitated. He looked at the dogs. "If Honey can come with me."

Lots of new possibilities for Bill.

"Oh my God! That's a diamond." Jayne grabbed Mandy's hand and held it up. "Danny, you didn't say a word."

"Well, no one in this family can keep a secret."

Jayne released Mandy's hand and hugged her again. "Have you set a date yet?"

"No. We're taking things slow."

"A date for what?" Bill asked.

"Danny and I are going to get married." Mandy tensed.

Danny pulled her backward until her back was against his chest. Warmth spread through his body as she leaned on him.

She needn't have worried.

Bill smiled. "Does that mean you're staying forever?"

"Yup. It sure does." Danny nodded.

"Yay!" Bill rubbed Honey's head. "Did you hear that, girl? Danny's staying."

Mandy turned. Sheesh. More tears. "I love you," she whispered.

"Back atcha." He kissed the top of her head. There were lots of new possibilities for everyone.

THE END

ACKNOWLEDGMENTS

First and foremost, thanks go to my fabulous agent Jill Marsal for her help on this manuscript, and for all the other countless things she does for me. Another great big thanks goes to my editor at Montlake Romance, Kelli Martin, and everyone else at Amazon Publishing who strives to make a writer feel valued. I consider myself very lucky to be included among their author ranks.

ABOUT THE AUTHOR

Melinda Leigh abandoned her career in banking to raise her kids and never looked back. She started writing as a hobby and became addicted to creating characters and stories. Since then, she has won numerous writing awards for her paranormal romance and romantic-suspense fiction. Her debut novel, *She Can Run*, was a number one bestseller in Kindle Romantic Suspense, a 2011 Best Book Finalist (The Romance Reviews), and a nominee for the 2012 International Thriller Award for Best First Book. When she isn't writing, Melinda is an avid martial artist: she holds a second-degree black belt in Kenpo karate and teaches women's self-defense. She lives in a messy house with her husband, two teenagers, a couple of dogs, and two rescue cats.

Made in the USA
San Bernardino, CA
09 March 2020